Avenged

A **VANISHED** NOVEL

Revenged

E. E. COOPER

A VANISHED NOVEL

KATHERINE TEGEN BOOKS
An Imprint of HarperCollins Publishers

Katherine Tegen Books is an imprint of HarperCollins Publishers.

Avenged
www.epicreads.com

Library of Congress Control Number: 2016935937
ISBN 978-0-06-229392-3

Typography by Carla Weise and Joel Tippie
16 17 18 19 20 PC/RRDH 10 9 8 7 6 5 4 3 2 1
❖
First Edition

TO ANICA,

who always supported this book and me

"We're all mad here. I'm mad. You're mad."

—Lewis Carroll, *Alice's Adventures in Wonderland*

CHAPTER ONE

Cemeteries are actually very cool places. Marble stat-
ues, open space, quiet. I think people would hang out in
them more often except for the fact that you realize you're
totally outnumbered by dead people. It's a disconcerting
feeling.

It's also very disorienting to stand over the grave of
your best friend. Someone who had been more alive than
anyone else you'd ever known. Someone who smelled like
cinnamon gum and suntan lotion, even in the middle of
winter. It's even more unsettling to realize you're standing
there with your other best friend, the person who murdered
her, and know that you have to keep your rage inside and

play the game so she doesn't realize you could be a threat. She doesn't cope well with threats.

Brit brushed some wilted flowers off of Beth's gravestone, but held on to the bouquet of white roses that she'd brought. "I feel like we should say something," she said.

How about, I'm sorry for killing you? Especially since you didn't actually mess around with my boyfriend. And then I'm sorry for dumping your body in the lake and letting everyone think it was mine, so I could have all the drama of watching how much everyone missed me. Oh, and I'm sorry I pretended to be you while I tried to figure out if I really wanted to come back.

I swallowed the thoughts. Whenever I was with Brit, I had to turn off my internal feelings. She'd only been back two weeks, and the sight of her still made my teeth clench together so tightly that I worried they would crack. I was afraid Britney might be able to read my mind like one of those TV psychics. Sense how when she was around my heart raced and the hair on the back of my neck stood at attention. If Brit had the slightest idea the kind of things that ran amok in my head, I would be in trouble. Serious trouble. The only plan I had was to stay close so I would be there when she finally screwed up and made a mistake I could use against her. And if I needed to be close, I needed to give her a reason; she needed to believe we were still best friends. I tucked my hair behind my ear. "I think Beth knows what is in your heart," I said.

Brit reached for my hand and squeezed it. "Thanks for

coming with me. I don't know how I'd get through all of this without you."

I grasped her hand back and for a fraction of a second enjoyed the feeling of connection before I felt a wave of disgust. It was like there were two Brits. The one I knew and had been friends with, and this monster who looked just like her. "You know I'm always here for you, Brit-bear," I said.

Brit brushed away a tear, her lower lip quivering just slightly. "She was the best friend I ever had." She took a step forward so she could kneel down and place the white roses on Beth's marker. I shifted the flowers slightly so I could see Beth's name carved into the granite headstone. I wanted to trace the letters, like I used to trace the outline of Beth's jaw with my fingers.

My throat tightened and I had to close my eyes to shut everything out so I could maintain control. I counted to six, six times, letting the familiarity of the numbers relax me. Thinking about how I felt about Beth wasn't going to help me now. I had to keep focused on my goal. Prove that Britney had done this. Make her pay. I inhaled the scent of fresh-cut grass and the faint smell of the hothouse flowers. A tear ran down my cheek.

Brit stood and pulled me close. "We're lucky we have each other."

I still couldn't push any words out of my throat, so I nodded. Brit's arm felt warm and solid around me. The only person who even came close to loving Beth as much as I did was Brit; it's all we had in common anymore. And despite everything that had happened I couldn't fathom that some part of her didn't miss Beth too, didn't regret what she'd done. And if she did feel guilt, if it was eating her up inside, then I would use that somehow.

"I know how hard this is for you, given, you know, what was going on between you two." Brit smiled at me, as if she found the idea of Beth and me being in a relationship adorable and just slightly ridiculous. Like when a puppy tries to do a trick but just can't quite pull it off. "I hope you know, Kalah, if there's anything I can do to help, all you have to do is ask." Brit's face was scrunched up in concern. It made me feel unbalanced because I suspected she actually did feel bad for me. Or at least she wanted to see herself as the kind of person capable of caring. She would do almost anything to make me feel better, even if she was the one who caused all the pain. She'd found some way to separate herself from what happened. Maybe she'd even convinced herself that it had nothing to do with her. Blocking out reality was one of her gifts.

"You can count on me too," I said softly.

"I know." After a moment of silence Brit squared her shoulders and looked around. "I thought the media might be here."

Now it was clear why she'd dressed up. The first week after Brit returned I couldn't turn on the TV without seeing her staring back at me. Reporters clustered around the school grounds hoping to get a shot of her, but they had moved on. There were new stories taking the nation's focus.

"It must be nice for you to have things getting back to normal," I said, knowing that she missed the attention. The universe was shifting, moving her away from the center, and she hated it.

She pressed her lips into a bloodless smile. "Of course." She took a deep breath. "Enough seriousness for today. What do you say we get out of here and get some fro-yo? We'll get a double cone in honor of Beth."

"Chocolate?" I asked.

Brit's eyes twinkled. "Would Beth have it any other way? And you have to get those disgusting chocolate cookie dough bits she liked."

"Why not you?" I asked.

"Because you two were the ones dating," Brit said. "I'll stick to M&M's, which everyone knows is the superior topping."

I laughed. I used to find the cookie dough hunks too sweet, but they had grown on me. "Deal."

I took a step toward the parking lot, but then Brit pulled me close again, one hand around my waist, her phone in her extended arm in front of us.

"Selfie shot of all of us!" Beth's grave was just behind us, the white roses making a perfect backdrop. Brit's blond all-American looks a perfect contrast to my dark coloring.

Yin and yang with a headstone. I yanked away from Brit, revolted.

It was only for a split second. An instant later I leaned back in. "Sorry, ticklish," I lied. I forced a smile onto my face.

Brit watched me, her eyes flat and appraising. I felt an icicle of fear slide into my heart. Did she guess how I really felt about her? I couldn't afford for her to distrust me. She needed to believe that I believed her if I stood any chance of her letting her guard down enough to make a mistake.

"Smile," she commanded. The phone clicked recording the picture, the two of us with wide grins, Beth's headstone centered just over Brit's shoulder. Both of our expressions fake.

"C'mon," I said, trying to make my voice sound light and cheerful. "I hear peanut M&M's calling your name." I tugged her forward and hoped she wouldn't notice my clammy palms.

She poked me lightly in the ribs. "I had no idea you're so ticklish."

I forced out a giggle. "A girl has to have some secrets."

Brit tapped me lightly on the nose. "Not from her bestie." She didn't wait for me to say anything else and didn't look to see if I was following her to the car. She knew I'd be there, trailing one step behind her, just like always.

Dr. Sherman leaned back her chair and stared at me. Her fingers came to a point just under her chin. She was a huge fan of these silences that were designed to make me want to spill my guts. I couldn't tell which of us was more annoyed, her because this tried-and-true method wasn't working, or me because she just kept trying. I'd hoped my parents would back off on their requirement that I still see her, but no dice. After what had happened at my last school, my parents weren't taking any chances with my mental health. They knew I cared for Beth and they wanted to make sure I was able to "process" everything that had happened. Despite the fact I'd told them I didn't need to go, I was stuck leaving school early and sitting here for an hour once a week. They thought there was "value in talking things over" and that I should think of it "like emotional fitness—you have to keep working out!" The only exercise I was getting was trying to keep two steps ahead of Dr. Sherman so I never told too much of the truth, but enough to make it seem like I was participating and making sure Brit never knew where I was going when I came here. I fidgeted in my seat. I was supposed to meet Brit after this. I couldn't be late.

Dr. Sherman sighed. "These sessions would be more beneficial if you'd open up to me."

"I don't know what else you want me to say," I said.

"Are you still having difficulty with Britney's popularity at school?" Her pen tapped lightly on the pad of paper in front of her. "And the attention she's gotten in the media?" I flashed to standing over Beth's grave yesterday afternoon. I ground my teeth down. I wasn't sure why Dr. Sherman had developed a new interest in Brit. Maybe she wanted to be touched by celebrity like everyone else. What Dr. Sherman didn't get, and I couldn't tell her, was that I didn't care that Brit was popular. What galled me was not only that Brit had murdered Beth and gotten away with it, but how she took every opportunity to tell everyone how much she missed her best friend, especially if there was a reporter around. I was sick of everyone at school rushing up to Brit, wanting to be close to her. She used Beth's tragedy, *the tragedy she caused*, as a way to get attention. I could tell that Dr. Sherman thought my problem was that I was the one dating Beth and no one wanted to talk to me and hear my story. It had been easier to agree with her than to try to tell her about the real reason.

"People are focused on Brit, but Beth is the one who's gone. I wish people would spend some time thinking about her." Even Brit's name in my mouth tasted polluted, like sour milk or swamp water.

"So you're angry with her," Dr. Sherman said.

I wanted to explode that I wasn't angry; I was livid. Brit killed Beth. Maybe it had been an accident, or maybe she planned it as revenge for thinking Beth was messing with her boyfriend Jason, but either way she'd done it and then covered up the whole thing. She'd been back for two weeks and not a single soul seemed to sense that anything about her story was off. To me her story seemed way too vague to be believed, but maybe it was the vagueness that made it seem plausible. That or the fact that Brit was a great actress. She looked too all-American and wholesome to be capable of real darkness. I kept waiting for her to break down or trip over her own lies, but she just kept going. I forced myself to take a long deep breath to the count of six.

Dr. Sherman cocked her head slightly to the side. "It's not uncommon to have feelings of anger after a death. We can feel left behind and upset that someone abandoned us, and since it feels wrong to be angry at the person we've lost, we sometimes direct that emotion at someone else."

"So you're saying I'm mad at Beth, not Britney." I crossed and then uncrossed my legs. "Maybe I am. Mad that we didn't have more time . . ." I had to stop and swallow hard to keep from crying. I hadn't meant to be so honest. The emotion came out of nowhere, like a jack-in-the-box that popped up when I least expected it. She was right. I was mad at Beth, but what I felt for Brit went way beyond that. What Dr. Sherman was picking up on wasn't sadness over Beth, it was rage that I couldn't tell anyone what I knew until I could prove it. I shoved down my feeling for Beth and refocused. "But it's not just her—I *am* angry at Brit. Beth was her best friend and she's moving on."

"People grieve in different ways, and it can feel as if others aren't experiencing the same level of pain, but that doesn't mean that Brit isn't hurting in her own way."

I stared out the window. Sometimes I wondered if Brit felt anything. How was it even possible for her to look at herself in the mirror when she knew what she'd done? She might have convinced everyone else that she had amnesia, that she couldn't remember, but I knew better. Brit had sent me emails and texts, all pretending to be Beth so she could figure out what was happening. She knew what she'd done. I was pretty sure that when she faked her suicide, her plan had been to never return, but the idea of running away from everything is way more exciting and romantic than reality. When I'd been playing along with her game, pretending I believed she was Beth and trying to convince her to come back, I'd been sure she'd be caught. I'd underestimated her charm. Everyone bought her lies, and the truth didn't seem to haunt her the way it did me.

Dr. Sherman was right. I *was* mad, not because Brit seemed to be better at "closure" but because she was the person who caused all of this and was acting like she was the victim. Her tales about how she would give anything to remember what had happened and her vows that she would never let anyone forget Beth made me want to pound her in the face, but instead I was cast as Brit's faithful support. It was my job to stand next to her and make sympathetic noises and pat her softly on the back.

"It's normal for you to be struggling to find your place with Brit in a post-Beth world. I know you were all friends, but now things have changed. The dynamic has shifted, and the two of you are likely trying to figure out what this friendship will look like. What's important to understand is that just as you find it difficult to see Brit get attention for her role in Beth's death, it must also be hard for her. Do you think the situation between you and Beth bothered Britney?"

Her question threw me. Even in my therapist's office I couldn't escape having to worry about how Brit felt. "Why would it bother her?"

"I imagine she sensed you and Beth were getting closer. If she knew you two were starting a relationship that must have been difficult for her, like she was losing the focus of her best friend. It would mean Beth and you had a relationship that she couldn't be a part of," Dr. Sherman said. "She likely felt left out."

I stared at her. "Are you saying I did something wrong?"

"No, this isn't a right-and-wrong situation. I'm asking you to reflect on the situation from a different perspective. How Britney's friendship with Beth had been changing, combined with her own amnesia, likely colors how she feels she can react about the loss now. In a group of three there is often a changing shift in roles and allegiances that can be difficult."

"Britney never knew Beth and I were in love. I only told her after she returned."

Dr. Sherman flipped through the pages on her desk. "I thought you said Britney indicated that she'd known about your relationship for some time."

My chest tightened in frustration. "That's what she

said, but I know she had no idea. It was a secret." I could hear the sharpness in my voice.

Dr. Sherman's tone stayed even. "That's possible. Maybe Britney felt that if you thought she knew and approved of you and Beth, it would bring the two of you closer."

"Maybe." I doubted Brit was motivated by wanting us to be closer unless she was going to gain something from it. She simply hated the idea that she'd missed something. And she needed to keep me close to make sure I didn't suspect her. Or at least that I couldn't prove it.

"Are you keeping a journal like we discussed?"

"I'm not really the kind of person who keeps a diary."

Dr. Sherman's lips pressed together. "I'd like you to try. Writing can help us open up and connect with what we're feeling. Sometimes emotions can get mixed up in our heads. Set the alarm on your phone for ten minutes and just let yourself write. You might surprise yourself." She pushed back from her desk, and I knew that was the cue our session was over.

Dr. Sherman meant well, but I wasn't confusing my emotions. I was mad, but I was scared too. Scared Brit would figure out that I didn't believe her lies and scared that she might not make a mistake.

CHAPTER TWO

Going to the mall was a sensory assault after the quiet of Dr. Sherman's office. The smells of buttered popcorn, fresh-from-the-oven cookies, baking bread from Subway, and spicy pizza all mixed noxiously with the clouds of perfume coming from the department stores. The clothing stores had signs screaming at people streaming past that they could *Save!* And that there were *Spring Deals!* And *Summer Dreaming!* The brightly colored clothes hung on racks, like parrots lined up for a review.

Music spilled out of the different stores and over the mall's sound system. There were kids yelling and screeching in the play area they had in the atrium. Sunshine was streaming through the glass roof and bouncing off the white tiles.

The combination was giving me a headache that I was trying to ignore as I trailed after Brit. All I wanted to do was go home and crawl under the covers, but I'd had to rush from my appointment with Dr. Sherman to meet Brit. God forbid I keep her waiting.

The search for the perfect prom dress was starting to take on Bataan Death March–like qualities. We'd been up and down the entire mall twice so far with no end in sight. What made it even more annoying was that Brit already had a dress for prom. It was fitted dark blue silk with ruffles of lace around the neckline. It had been fine before, but now that Britney was back from the dead she required something more. Something really special. Now all we had to do is find it, and I was stuck pretending to care. I glanced at her out of the corner of my eye. I didn't understand how a dress could matter when Beth was dead.

"I want to try on the one in here again," Brit said, pausing in front of a bridal store. "You don't mind, do you?"

"Are you kidding? This is what we came to do," I said, forcing an expression onto my face that I hoped would pass for excitement. If she was going to pretend to care, I was going to pretend right along with her.

"I wish we hadn't gotten a late start. I don't know why your parents are making you see a college recruiting consultant now. Why not wait until the summer?"

I shrugged and hoped Brit couldn't tell I'd lied. There was no way I was admitting to her that my weekly appointments were to see a psychologist. It was way better for her to believe my parents had suddenly become rabidly competitive about where I would apply next year.

I grabbed her arm and pulled her inside. "C'mon, this isn't a search for a dress—this is a quest."

"I knew you'd be back," the saleswoman trilled when she saw us. She pulled a pewter dress from a rack behind the register. "You look like a movie star in this."

Brit flushed. "Do you mind if I try it on again?"

We were ushered back into the changing room. I dropped onto the closest tufted bench in front of the three-way mirror, glad to rest even for a minute. Being around Brit made my muscles tense; my legs felt as tight as if I'd run a half marathon.

Brit slipped off her jeans and shirt and slithered into the dress. It was amazing. The fabric was covered in tiny silver beads; it looked like molten metal as it moved across her curves. Brit turned in the mirror, critically checking every angle. I could see myself reflected behind her. My eyes had giant dark circles under them.

"Do you think it's too much?" Brit asked. Her eyebrows were drawn together.

"How can anything on you be too much?"

"I don't want to look sleazy." Brit pulled lightly on the bottom of the dress. "Maybe I should try on the green one again," she said.

Mentally I flinched. I was never going to get out of this

mall. It was going to be like that myth about the guy who rolled the rock up the hill for all eternity, only for me it was going to be an endless loop of Macy's, the bridal store, and Forever 21.

"Sure, if you want, but I think this is the one," I said. "The saleswoman said it was a custom order that someone backed out of, which means there is zero chance anyone else is going to show up in the same thing." Of course, if anyone else foolishly arrived in the same dress as Brit they would immediately be banished from the prom or spontaneously combust from the shame and horror of it all.

Brit was staring at herself in the mirror, and that's when I noticed that she was about to cry. I leapt up and stood next to her. The idea that she was emotionally cracking up sent a jolt of excitement down my spine. "Brit-bear, what's wrong?"

She shrugged. Her lips were shaking, and a tear streaked down her cheek. "It's got to be perfect. Everyone is going to be staring at me. If there's anything wrong, *anything*, people will be all over it." Her breath hitched. "I know it doesn't matter in the big picture; if it weren't for Beth I wouldn't even be going to prom, let alone worrying about a dress." She wiped her nose. "And at the same time I feel like I owe it to her to have not just a good prom, but a *great* one. Almost like it's for her too."

I swallowed hard. "You don't have to be perfect."

She searched my face as if she wasn't sure I was telling

the truth and then hugged me hard. "I'm so glad I have you," she said, her breath warm on my neck. I wasn't even sure whether she'd been upset or simply testing to see how quickly I'd come to her side. It was always like this with her, a constant seesaw of emotions.

The saleswoman knocked lightly on the door. "How are you girls doing?" She slowly opened the door and then placed her hands over her heart as if she were overcome by the vision of Britney.

Britney turned back to the mirror and resumed her microscopic inspection of her image. "I can't decide."

"You need to see the whole picture. What size shoe do you wear?" the saleswoman asked.

"Eight and a half," Brit said.

"I'm going to dash down the hall and get a pair of shoes for you to try on with the dress."

"You don't have to do that," Brit said.

"Trust me. I'll be right back." The saleswoman hustled off before we could say anything.

Brit plopped down on the bench and I sat next to her. "Shoes might do the trick," I said.

"Maybe I'll click them together three times saying *there's no place like prom*," Brit said.

That's all Brit needed: a squadron of flying monkeys to do her bidding. She regarded her reflection and then reached inside the dress to hike her boobs up higher. "Jason's mouth will drop when he sees me in this."

"Why do you even care what he thinks?" Jason and Sara were still together, but the way Brit looked at him in the halls was almost predatory. I couldn't forget the party where Brit had sent Sara a box full of cockroach-stuffed teddy bears. I wanted to think she was done with him after he cheated on her, but unfortunately for Sara, she hated to lose. "Would you even take him back?"

"It's complicated." She checked out her manicure, frowning at a small chip in the shellac.

"He doesn't deserve you," I said. No one did. He should stick with Sara and count himself lucky.

"It's not that I think what he did was okay, but I understand it. Don't tell anyone, but we've gotten together a couple of times to talk." Brit rubbed her hands over the dress, smoothing it out. "I knew in my heart we wouldn't be together forever, but a part of me would still like to finish high school with him by my side, for old times' sake."

I nodded. Brit was lying again. I couldn't tell if she knew she was lying or if she'd convinced herself of this new revised history. Brit had a way of choosing the version of reality that best suited her. In this new version of what happened, Brit hadn't planned her and Jason's life out to its conclusion of college together, a ring just before graduation and then a huge house in the burbs with a couple of perfect children and a golden retriever. Now the story was that she'd always planned for them to go their separate ways.

Brit was delusional. She and Jason may have talked a

few times and I had no doubt he felt terrible about what happened, but Jason and Sara would be going to the dance together. No way was I going to remind her of that fact. If she wanted to believe Jason was lying awake at nights dreaming of taking her to prom, I wasn't going to burst that bubble.

I had a flash of when the three of us went dress shopping before everything happened. "It will be weird to have prom without Beth," I said.

There was a small twitch by Brit's eye. "Sometimes I forget that she's really gone. It's easier to imagine that she's still out there doing her thing. Taking the world by storm." Brit squeezed my hand. "You guys would have made an awesome couple at the dance."

I clenched my teeth together. "Thanks." Rage that Brit would talk about her so casually was all mixed up with a pang of longing for Beth. I could picture Beth spinning across the dance floor, the skirt of her dress whirling up to show her legs. She would look over her shoulder at me, and her eyes would have that glint, and I knew her mouth would taste like caramel from the rum and cola we would have drunk down on the beach before the dance. My chest hurt as if even my lungs missed her.

"It'll be okay. I've fixed the perfect surprise for you." Brit's eyes flashed with excitement.

My stomach felt like a load of cement had been dropped inside. "What's the surprise?"

Brit screwed her lips together. "I can't tell if you really want to know," she teased me.

"I really want to know," I said.

"Well . . . you can expect Ryan to ask you to prom this week." Brit pulled back as if she was waiting for me to applaud.

"Ryan?" My brain scrambled to think of who she was talking about. "Your cousin?"

Brit rolled her eyes, indicating I wasn't even close.

"Ryan Reyner? Senior? Killer blue eyes?" I said.

She shook her head like she was enjoying this.

"Why is Ryan going to ask me to prom?" I tried to remember if I'd ever said more than ten words to the guy in my entire life.

"I asked him to and he totally said yes right away. You'll love him; he's super fun." Brit took a tiny jump like she couldn't even contain her excitement.

"You set me up?" Disbelief dripped from each word, but Brit either didn't hear it or was ignoring it.

"You're welcome." Brit listed off Ryan's qualities on her fingers. "He's one of the hottest guys at our school, he's on the basketball team, he's going to Stanford, he's smart, and apart from Jason, he has the best ass I've ever seen."

"Do you have a date?" I asked her. If she had agreed to go with anyone who had asked her since she'd returned she hadn't told me about it.

She smirked. "Not yet, but I have options I'm considering."

Did she actually think Jason was going to go with her and we were all going to be some big happy party? "I don't want to go with Ryan," I said.

Brit's smile dropped. "You can't go by yourself. You're a junior. I'm going to have a date, so you need one too."

I had no idea what to say. "Look, I appreciate you trying to hook me up, but I don't even want to go to prom."

Brit waved me off. "Don't be absurd; of course we're going. It's *prom*. What else are we going to do, make popcorn and watch movies at your place? Trust me, you'll love Ryan. His family has a boat, could make for a great summer." Brit stood and turned so she could see her butt in the mirror.

Did she think it was that easy? That I would go with Ryan and then just magically be over Beth?

"What if I went with Zach?" I suggested.

Brit's nose wrinkled up. "You guys broke up."

"We're not dating, but we're still friends," I said.

Brit nibbled on her lower lip. "Kalah, don't take this the wrong way: you know I think Zach is adorable, but we're talking about Ryan Reyner! Ryan looks like he walked out of *InStyle* mag, and Zach looks more like . . ."

"Like he walked out of a *Star Trek* convention?" I finished for her.

"Exactly."

"The thing is, if I can't go with Beth, and if we're not going to go just us, I think I'd feel better if I was there with Zach," I explained. Brit didn't say anything, but I could see her mulling it over. Zach didn't fit with her picture-perfect idea of prom. "I'd make sure he wore a great tux," I added. "Please?" I hated myself for begging. I'd never asked her to fix me up, and now I had to plead to choose my own date.

Brit sighed. "Fine, if you want to go with Zach, then ask him, but do it Monday so if he says no Ryan still has time to ask you." She raised a finger. "And tell him no weird action figure corsages. Roses. White or maybe a light pink."

"Okay, here we go!" The changing room door flew open and the saleswoman hustled in with a couple of shoe boxes under her arms. She dropped to her knees as if she were about to propose to Britney, or perhaps as a show of fealty. She pulled a pair of slinky silver heels out of one of the boxes.

Britney giggled and turned to look at herself. The shoes were perfect. They made her legs look longer and more toned, and they matched the dress.

"What do you think?" She asked me over her shoulder. Brit fingered the tiny blue teacup pendant that I'd given Beth. Her story was that Beth gave it to her. We both knew this was a lie. My stomach turned sour.

"Perfect," I said.

CHAPTER THREE

After my last class on Monday I stopped short in the hall, letting people go around me as they rushed to leave. School would be over in a few weeks, and everyone was already more interested in summer plans than in being in classes. We were like prisoners with only a short amount of time left of our sentence. Even the school looked tired, the posters on the walls were torn and peeling, the white floors looked yellow, like old teeth, due to the buildup of floor wax, and teachers had stopped caring about updating the bulletin boards in their classrooms. We all wanted it to end. It was warm outside, but people were pretending it was the height of summer: shorts from Abercrombie, tank tops, and thin, sheer short-sleeve tops in bright ice cream colors.

Zach leaned against my locker. His eyes were closed, his head bopping and his foot tapping in beat with whatever was playing. He needed a haircut, and I was pretty sure he was totally unaware that his T-shirt was on inside out. I missed him. It was a dull ache in the center of my chest.

I took a deep breath and walked up, but he was so into his music that he didn't even notice. I tapped him on the shoulder and he jumped. Zach yanked out his earbuds. I could hear the sound track from *West Side Story*, the song "Tonight," until he clicked it off.

"Hey," I said.

"Hey."

We stood there looking at each other awkwardly. I chewed on the inside of my cheek.

"You texted me you wanted to talk?" Zach asked.

My stomach twisted. I had no idea how Zach was going to respond. Things between us had been weird since the party where he declared that he loved me and I confessed I *didn't*. We smiled at each other in the halls, but there was no doubt that things were a million miles away from fine between the two of us. "Yeah," I said. "I wanted to ask you about something. I've got the car. Do you want to get a burger or something?" I shook the keys.

Zach shook his head. "Nah, let's go over to Bryant Park. We can walk." I nodded and followed him out of the building.

We walked the couple of blocks along the road with

him in front. The cars going by made enough noise to make chatting difficult, and my shoes sank into drifts of old pine needles, the smell wafting up with every step. I inhaled deeply, hoping it would calm me down. When we got to the park, Zach motioned to the swings and we each took one. The chains were rusty from the winter rain and snow and squealed in protest when we sat down.

We'd barely talked in weeks. Officially we'd been on a "break" since just before Brit returned, but neither of us had made a move to either get back together or end things. In theory because I was giving him the space he wanted, but also because I had no idea how to talk to him. I'd behaved horribly, lying about Beth and keeping secrets. All I'd gotten was exactly what I'd deserved, but now I was going to ask for another favor. If I had to spend prom with Brit, I needed him by my side. Zach's feet made tracks in the wood chips below the swing as he went back and forth.

"I hate that things between us are so weird," he said.

I shrugged. "It's been kind of a weird year," I said stating the obvious.

Zach swung a bit higher. "How's Brit doing?"

"She's great." This was an understatement. At the rate she was going there would be a statue erected to her in the front lobby by the end of the year.

"I'm sorry about Beth," Zach said. "I know you guys were close."

I winced. He had no idea. I wanted to tell him, but it

would only hurt him further. Now that there was no chance that Beth and I would become a couple, there wasn't a point. "Yeah." I pointed my toes toward the sky and leaned back in the swing. We swung in silence for a while, the screech of the chains sounding like an exotic birdcall.

I glimpsed Zach out of the corner of my eye waiting for me to say whatever I'd texted him about. "I was wondering if you still wanted to go to prom together," I said finally.

I could tell he was surprised by my offer. His feet caught in the wood chips, and he almost lurched onto the ground. He didn't say anything and for a beat I wondered if I'd just imagined saying it out loud. I should have eased into asking him, but Brit wanted an answer today so she could decide what to do about Ryan.

"Does no answer mean no?" I asked.

Zach faced me. "Like as friends?" I nodded. "I bought the tickets ages ago," he admitted. "I couldn't really imagine going with anyone else."

"If we went together, we'd have a good time," I said. The tension in my shoulders loosened.

Zach acted like he was letting out this large, exaggerated breath. "Thank god. I was imagining I'd have to go with Karl and Nathan. Nathan wants to wear the Stormtrooper costume he got at Comic-Con."

I giggled, picturing Nathan with a carnation taped to the hard white plastic breastplate. And Nathan wondered why he had a hard time getting a girlfriend. "Tell me you're still planning to wear a tux," I asked in mock seriousness.

"I was considering wearing my *Doctor Who* outfit." Zach pointed at me. "Now, that's classy."

"Totally," I said. "A *Doctor Who* outfit says you're the kind of guy who's into time travel and isn't afraid of a bunch of weeping angels. A Stormtrooper is basically just a space army grunt."

Zach gave a humble shrug. "Not everyone is cut out to be a time lord."

"True." I could picture Brit's face if Zach showed up in anything less than the approved outfit. "Of course, you'd look brilliant in a black tux. Very Bond."

"I'm often confused with James Bond," Zach said. He smiled at me and started swinging again. "There's a bunch of people planning to eat at Zefferelli's. I can see if I can get us reservations."

I bit the corner of my lip. No way was Brit going to want to go there. "Can we decide later?" I asked.

"Sure. My mom will be glad to see you. She misses you. Not as much as Maddy does. I should warn you she might try and stow away for the dance. We'd be the only couple there with our own mini-assistant."

"And I should warn you, my parents will take a zillion pictures. And Maddy is always welcome to tag along; you know I love her."

Zach rolled his eyes. "Don't tell her that. I can barely get away from her as it is. She's half kid sister, half parasite."

I smiled and let the swinging motion calm me down. I no longer was counting, trying to get it to be a number divisible by six. He was willing to go with me. I pumped my legs, wanting to pick up speed. I suddenly felt lighter. I'd been dreading prom. I'd already shoved my dress to the back of my closet, where I wouldn't have to stare at it. I'd need to pull it out now and make sure it hadn't gotten wrinkled. I mentally started making a list of things I'd need to do. I should order some kind of flower for Zach, maybe get some new shoes too. "Thanks," I said softly. "I know you didn't have to do this."

"You were the one who got the guts up to talk about it. I'd been pretending prom wasn't going to happen."

I watched him go back and forth. "I am sorry, you know," I said. "About everything."

"I'm sorry too. I shouldn't have pushed some big talk at Tyler's party." Zach brushed the hair out of his face. "I don't know, I guess in some ways I wanted to get it over with."

"I know I'd been acting weird," I admitted.

"It wasn't just that. There was other stuff. I was crazy about you, but I was also pretending you were the perfect girlfriend and ignoring anything that didn't fit with that. Then I got ticked when you didn't act the way I wanted." He shrugged sheepishly. "I guess I was too used to having an imaginary love life. Real people are a whole different game."

I realized I was holding my breath and made myself inhale deeply. It never occurred to me that Zach wasn't a hundred percent happy with me. I'd been so consumed with Beth and how she made me feel, and finding that what I felt for Zach fell short, that I'd never considered that maybe I was less than his ideal partner.

"That's part of growing up, right? When you stop wanting people to fill some set idea you have in your mind and just like them for who they are." Zach jumped off the swing. "Man, that's deep. Who knew I'd be so good-looking *and* philosophical?"

I laughed, but I was still stuck on the fact that I hadn't been Zach's dream girl. It was stupid to be upset about it. I'd been cheating on him. I knew we weren't some love-struck perfect couple, but I'd liked the idea that I was exactly what he wanted. That he saw me as perfect. That someone did.

I stood and hugged Zach. "I'm lucky you're so wise. Not everyone gets their very own philosopher as a date for prom."

"You forgot good-looking," he pointed out.

I smacked my forehead. "Of course. Wise *and* good-looking."

Zach crooked his arm so I could take it. "You are indeed a lucky woman." We started walking back toward school, this time side by side. "Did you want to ask Brit to come with us?" Zach asked.

Hearing her name was like suddenly biting into something you expected to be sweet and having it being rotten and sour. I must have paused, because Zach stopped.

"I know you guys are best friends, and since we're not going as this hot romantic date, it might be fun to have a bit of a group," Zach said. He smiled, trying to look excited at the idea of doubling.

I blinked, trying to shove aside the image of Britney standing between Zach and me, smirking at the camera in all our photos.

"Brit *was* hoping we could double," I admitted.

I could see Zach's shoulders tighten. "Great. There's plenty of room in my dad's Prius." He started walking again. "Wise, good-looking, and driving an eco-friendly chariot. Damn, you really are lucky."

Lucky enough to have dodged spending prom with Brit's chosen match for me, but not so lucky as to get out of it altogether. I wanted to tell him that I knew spending prom with Brit was a nightmare, but that I needed to. I had to stay close to her. Sooner or later she would crack—she had to. How could anyone keep that kind of secret inside? When she broke, when she even wavered, I needed to be there. The very best of friends. Make her believe she could tell me. Tell me all of it. If I was going to stab her in the back, I needed her to trust me enough to be vulnerable. I just had to hang on.

CHAPTER FOUR

Entering the cafeteria with Britney on Tuesday was a bit like walking into a restaurant with a member of the royal family or a pop star. Everyone turned and watched her, noting what she was wearing, how she'd styled her hair, and what she'd picked to eat. They would store up the details so they could dissect them later, trying to figure out how they could copy everything. Brit would spend the entire time acting like she didn't notice every single eye was on her, all while making sure she looked perfect. She'd always been popular, but her recent celebrity and a hint of tragedy had only amplified her cachet. Plus, she no longer had to share the spotlight with Beth. She'd seen to that.

She plopped her tray down at our table. Britney pushed

her salad around with her fork and then glanced over at my tray. "I crave fries. I just look at them and my thighs expand," she said.

Fries were piled high on my plate, the grease giving them a shine. The smell rose up in fragrant clouds. "Are you kidding?" I asked. "You look amazing." As much as I hated to admit it, she did. Pounds withered under Brit's scorn. Apparently being evil is an aerobic activity.

Brit speared a tomato. "I wish. Cameras add something like ten pounds. I saw myself the other day—my mom was replaying the CNN interview—and it looked like I was some kind of bloated hamster with a stash of nuts in my face." Brit puffed out her cheeks.

"I think you look awesome. Then and now," I said. I felt my back teeth grind together. I stabbed a fry and jammed it my mouth to keep from saying what I really thought about the interview.

"With prom right around the corner I want to make sure I look killer in photos." Brit took a drink of water and then shot my tray another look. "I need to be in great shape, and that means losing a few pounds."

I dragged a fry through the puddle of ketchup on my plate. Was she really trying to imply that the mere sight of my fries was causing her weight gain? Either she was play- ing the pity card because she needed everyone around her to assure her yet again that she was the hottest girl on the planet, or she thought worrying about her weight made her seem like a normal person.

"It's just so hard to do. Looking good is practically a full-time job with the million temptations out there," Brit said.

Then I got it. I stood up with my plate, pushing away a wave of irritation. This was a loyalty test. "I'm going to dump these out. If you're eating salad, then I'm eating salad. Solidarity," I said.

Brit flushed. "You don't have to do that," she said. Her eyes pinned me in place, letting me know that I did have to do it if I wanted to keep my place as her second in command.

"Are you kidding? I want to do it," I lied. "If you can't count on your best friend to help you reach your goal, who can you count on?" I marched over to the garbage and slid the whole steaming mess into the can. I could feel her watching me, making sure I did exactly what she wanted. She needed to feel that she was still pulling the strings, and I needed her to believe that I was still in thrall of her every action and word. I spun around and gave her a cheery wave before getting in line for the salad bar. At least Northside had some decent options; I wasn't interested in existing on iceberg lettuce and beets.

When I sat back down Brit reached over and flicked the croutons off my salad with her fork. "Carbs are the worst." She watched approvingly as I ate the first few bites. "So I got your text last night. Things went well with Zach?"

I nodded. "I know my going with him isn't exactly what

you pictured for a prom double date. I really appreciate you being so great about it." I made myself laugh. "Of course, you're basically the best friend ever, so I don't know what else I would expect."

Brit rolled her eyes as if I was being a bit ridiculous, but I could see she was eating up the compliments. At least those were fat-free.

I touched her wrist. "I'm being serious; you're the best." I made myself stare into her eyes, trying to radiate that she could count on me. Tell me anything.

"If it means that much to you to go with him, of course I understand." She jerked her head over to the corner of the café where Ryan was sitting with a group of the basketball players. "Although I'm going on the record that you are missing out by not going with him; that guy is tasty."

I jumped in my seat when music blared out over the intercom. Everyone started looking around trying to figure out what was going on. It took me a beat, but then I recognized the music—an old song: "You've Lost That Lovin' Feelin'."

Two of the basketball players jumped up from their seats, faced our table, and sang out the opening line, although one of them couldn't stop laughing.

Another group one table over fell to their knees and continued the song.

Then guys who worked the dish line joined in and people cheered.

Now everyone was smiling and pulling out their phones. It was a flash mob. Heads swiveled around trying to figure out what would happen next, and that was when Jason appeared out of nowhere and leapt onto the table. He was wearing a powder-blue shirt I knew Brit had given him months ago for his birthday.

Brit stared at him her mouth falling open into a tiny O. She looked around and then put her hand over her heart like she was shocked by this outburst. Her cheeks were flushed. The rest of the basketball team was all on their feet doing what I was pretty sure was supposed to be a dance. For a bunch of athletes they weren't the most coordinated. Everyone in the cafeteria was laughing and clapping along.

Wait, not everyone. Sara was standing to the side of the room. I could see her swallowing over and over as if she were about to vomit. She grabbed her bag off the back of her chair and bolted out of the cafeteria. As she ran past me I saw tears in her eyes. Her band friends followed her out, but no one else seemed to notice her at all.

The song ended and people applauded. I could see Jason shaking as he stood on the table in front of us. "I made a huge mistake. I had the best girl in the entire world and I threw it away." He jumped down off the table and crouched down next to Brit's chair. "You've got no reason to forgive me, but I'm going to beg you to anyway."

I stared at him trying to see if I could figure out his motivation. Did he want Brit back because she'd become so popular and he wanted everyone's approval, or was he afraid of her? But maybe I only wanted him to be afraid because that meant someone else saw through her act.

Brit looked at him and then away. Apparently now she was some shy 1800s maiden overcome by the wooing of her ardent lover.

"What we had was awesome. Give me another chance and it'll be even better. Let me take you to prom," Jason pleaded.

A few girls made an "aww" sound, like this was the most romantic thing ever to happen at Northside. I sighed. He'd done it for approval. He needed to make things right with Northside's sweetheart. My stomach rolled uneasily. I wanted to reach over and slap him. When I'd heard he cheated on Brit I'd been angry with him for hurting my friend. He was dumping Sara to keep his image intact. Now I wasn't just angry with him, I was disgusted.

Britney waved her hand like she wanted Jason to stop, but she'd already turned her chair to face him.

"C'mon, baby. We belong together." Jason reached for her hand. "No one could rock prom better than the two of us." He swallowed hard. Everyone was watching. Brit could crush him right now if she wanted to. He'd had to risk everything to have a chance, but he didn't know how it would play out. My shoulders tensed, waiting to see what she would do.

Brit shook her head like she couldn't believe how absurd

Jason was being, but then she said something low and quiet.

Jason got closer. "What'd you say?" The entire cafeteria leaned forward, like Jason and Brit were a black hole, pulling us in.

"I said yes, I'll go to prom with you," Brit said loud enough for everyone to hear.

Jason pumped his fist in the air and let out a whoop. He bent and swooped Brit out of her chair, spinning her around. People clapped like this was some kind of theatre production, which I guessed in a way it was. Brit pounded lightly on Jason's back until he put her down, and then she let him kiss her. The basketball players high-fived one another for their part in the drama. Brit sat back down and patted her hair into place. She gestured to the chair, and Jason dropped into the seat next to her. Side by side again. Just the way she'd wanted it.

A few of our teammates rushed over to our table, squealing their excitement. I saw Kate give Amy a look. They also thought Jason's sudden return to Brit was less romantic and more pathetic, but Sara was a sophomore nobody and Brit was queen of the school. They knew who they were supposed to cheer for in this play. No white hat or black hat to tell the players apart required. I made sure to plaster a smile on my face. The "it" couple was back together again, and as their public servants it was our job to be happy for them. There was no room for doubt that Sara had lost. She might have momentarily stolen Jason from Brit, but it was nothing more than a temporary blip. An aberration. Things had been set to right once again. Jason had been too guilty to do anything else, and Brit would settle for nothing less.

There didn't seem to be any way to stop Brit. She was like some kind of force of nature, a hurricane or tidal wave. Anything that got in her way was mowed down, destroyed. I realized I was clenching my fists, and I focused on letting go. At first my fingers wouldn't obey, but they slowly uncurled as I counted to six in my head.

I wanted to put my head on the table and cry. It wasn't going to be enough to be close to her. She wasn't going to screw up, admit everything in a puddle of tears, and beg me to help her figure out what to do. She was going to go from one win to another. A gulf of hopelessness opened up in my chest, threatening to make me disappear.

Brit's face was flushed red. "I can't believe he did that."

The salad I'd eaten turned over in my stomach. I couldn't believe it either. "People are going to talk about this for years."

She gave a satisfied smile. "Yeah." She looked around the cafeteria, her smile fading. Everyone else was going back to their lunch, already talking about the next thing. She seemed to slowly deflate. "So . . . double date for prom?" she asked.

I blinked quickly and smiled. "Hell yeah."

Brit threw her arm around me. "We're going to have the best time ever."

CHAPTER FIVE

I picked at the oatmeal-colored tweed fabric that cov-
ered the chair in Dr. Sherman's office and wondered for the
thousandth time when I could leave. It would be a relief to
give in, to tell her everything—how Brit wasn't breaking
down the way I'd expected (if anything, things were going
even better for her) and how I didn't know what to do. Dr.
Sherman was trained to listen without judging. Everything
in the room, from the muted colors, to her forward posture,
to her long silences, was designed to make me feel comfortable enough to talk. To disclose.

Disclose in an interesting word. It almost sounds like
dis-clothed, to be stripped bare, naked, and that's what it
would be like. I could tell her the whole ugly thing, how I

was certain that Brit had murdered Beth and was getting away with it, and she wouldn't yell or scream. Dr. Sherman would be calm and promise that we'd "get to the bottom of things." However, I couldn't be sure she'd believe me. She might, but it was more likely that she wouldn't. My story was simply too bizarre. And if she didn't believe me, she would think *I* was the delusional one.

"Help me understand why you are so resistant to being back here for therapy." Dr. Sherman's pen hovered over her notepad, ready to write down my many problems. "I get the sense you feel this is some kind of failure."

"I know it's not a failure, but I feel like I can handle this by myself," I said. Then I figured I'd better throw her a bone, something so she wouldn't feel like I was disparaging what she did. "You taught me a lot of great coping strategies last time."

The corner of her mouth twitched, and I was pretty sure she knew what I was trying to do. "Glad to hear they're helpful. How has your anxiety been over the past few months, on a scale of one to ten?"

"Most of the time it's really low, maybe a two," I lied. Dr. Sherman made a murmuring sound. The truth was my mood was all over the map. The week had started off great, with things between Zach and me being settled and then crashing down on Tuesday, when I finally realized that Brit wasn't going to just fall apart. The rest of the week I felt like I was spinning in circles. I had to do something, but I had no idea what it would be. Now I just wanted the week to end so I could stop acting every minute of the day.

"I wondered if we might talk about something a bit different today," Dr. Sherman said.

A lump of dread squatted in my chest like a troll from one of Nadir's video games. Whatever she had in mind, I was willing to bet I didn't want to discuss it. "Sure."

"I thought it might be useful to go back and reflect on what happened at your last school."

My internal alarm went off. "I thought we exhausted that subject a year ago. Why are we going over this now?" I hoped my voice sounded more relaxed than I felt. I'd tried to forget about what happened at Windsor Prep. Madison had convinced me that she wanted me to be a part of her group, and I loved the idea of being chosen, of being special. What I hadn't realized was that it was just a game for Madison. She twisted everything to make it look like I was stalking her, that the idea that she wanted to be my friend was nothing more than a delusion in my head.

Dr. Sherman smiled. "Often things are connected in a way we don't always see at the time. It can be useful to look back, now that you've got more distance," Dr. Sherman said.

I made a noncommittal noise. Madison had gotten her group of friends to freeze me out. When I would go up to them they would act like they couldn't hear or see me. Instead of realizing they were a bunch of bitches, I let it get under my skin. Burrow into my brain. When they acted like

I didn't exist, it felt as if I was fading away. I kept upping the ante, determined to get a response. "I let Madison get to me," I admitted. I shifted in my seat—it felt like my skin was too small. Getting to me was an understatement; it came to a head in a gym class.

We were playing softball. I was running from third base to home and even though Madison had the ball she refused to tag me as out. That's when I snapped.

"Hit me," I screamed at her. "Don't act like you can't see me." I stopped between bases despite my teammates screaming at me to run home.

Madison looked away. Our gym teacher glanced between us and then made a decision. "Run home, Richards," she called out to me.

Madison dropped the ball and walked away. Linda was at her side in an instant, and I could hear them giggling.

"Richards, finish your run," our gym teacher called out, but when I didn't move she blew her whistle. "Okay, that's it. Hanson, pick up that ball and tag her out." Madison's teammate jogged over to the ball.

Instead of running I sank to the ground, closed my eyes, put my hands over my ears, and started screaming. I had a vague memory of my gym teacher leaning over and trying to get me to calm down, but I was beyond reasoning at that point.

"How did it make you feel when Madison said your version of events wasn't the truth?"

A headache started to build behind my eyes. Madison

insisted that she'd never ignored me. Or at least the few times that she did were because I wouldn't leave her alone. My guidance counselor didn't even pretend to believe me. Reality was twisted so I was the stalker and Madison the innocent victim. Next stop for me: therapy and eventually having to transfer schools. I was determined this wouldn't happen to me again. And yet here I was, back in my psychologist's office. "As far as I'm concerned, what happened in my last school was in another lifetime."

"Interesting," Dr. Sherman said, and I winced. Whatever she found interesting was usually not good for me. "Tell me how you feel you're different now."

I paused. Talking to Dr. Sherman was like having a chess game with a grand master. I had to be careful about not just what I said, but how those comments might be used several moves down the road. The problem was I usually had no idea where she going. "I guess I just meant that I've grown since all that happen."

She nodded. "How do you think Madison and Britney are alike?"

Where the hell was she going with this? I pictured each of them in my mind. "They're both manipulative," I said answering Dr. Sherman's question honestly. Maybe at some level Dr. Sherman also had some questions about Brit's story.

Dr. Sherman nodded encouragingly. "And?"

"I wanted to be their friend," I admitted. "I liked how

they were so confident. And fun. They're the kind of people that other people want to be around."

I sighed. I wondered how my life would be different if I'd become friends with someone like Sara instead. Hung out with the band geeks, or the girlfriends of Zach's friends in the improv troupe.

"I didn't realize what Madison was like. I don't think I ever really knew her, just the idea of her. Being her friend was about wanting to feel special. If someone like her liked me, then that made me better than I would be by myself."

"And it was different with Britney?"

"Madison was never my friend, but Brit was. Is," I amended. There were a mountain of lies between us and our friendship had twisted into something else, but there was no doubt we were still tied together.

There was never any confusion when it was the three of us that Brit was the one who wanted to call the shots. When she didn't get her way she would wheedle and cajole until it was easier to give in. Beth and I had joked about it because that's "just who Brit was." But Brit was way more manipulative than I ever could have imagined. I would never have conceived that she was sick enough to pretend to be Beth sending messages and use me.

"What can you learn from your experience with Madison that can help you in your interactions with Britney?" Dr. Sherman probed. I wanted to ask her why we had to talk about Brit and Madison at all when I was supposed to be here to get over Beth's death. However, I knew Dr. Sherman well enough to know if I acted like I didn't want to talk about something she would be even more focused on that area, certain that my emotional health hinged on what I wanted to avoid.

There was a burst of laughter outside the office window. A group of young kids were walking past. They were linked together, each holding on to a pink nylon rope, led by their day care teacher. I watched them go by as I tried to figure out if I had learned anything. Maybe I was one of those people who seemed doomed to keep repeating mistakes over and over. Everything was connected, like those kids. I could go back and see how each bad decision I'd made led me farther down this path, but I still couldn't see forward and figure out what I would do differently. "I don't know," I admitted.

Dr. Sherman leaned back, and I had the sense she was disappointed in me. Then I leaned forward. I *had* learned something. No one had believed me with Madison. And even though I was pretty sure Officer Siegel didn't buy Brit's full story, I didn't have any proof that she'd killed Beth. Beth's body was cremated as soon as it had been found. There wasn't going to be a *CSI* moment where a doctor declared that the true cause of death was homicide. I needed evidence or a confession or no one was going to believe me. It wasn't going to be enough for me to wait for Brit to break down. I was going to have to give her a push.

—45—

I sat on the edge of the seat. I was going to have to find proof.

"Okay. What I'd like you to do between now and our next appointment is to write a letter to Madison where you talk about what happened and what you have learned that you want to put into place moving forward."

I nodded while I turned over a few options to deal with Britney in my head.

"You won't send the letter; the experience is a part of therapy. It might seem like a waste of time, but if you want things to be better, you need to do things to make it better," she said.

I forced a smile onto my face. "Super," I said. "It should be fun." She was right about one thing, I needed to take action, and I had an idea of where to start.

CHAPTER SIX

I watched Brit apply another layer of mascara to her eyes as she sat in front of the mirror in her pink bedroom. The guys were supposed to pick us up in less than a half hour. Prom hadn't even started yet, and I was already wishing it were over. I dug deep trying to find a second wind. I had more to accomplish than just getting through a dance. I'd thought a lot since my appointment with Dr. Sherman and I planned to put some of my Operation Push Britney plans into action tonight.

I'd spent the entire day with Brit. It was a professional development day for the teachers, so with the day off we had hours to prepare. We went to the spa in the morning for facials and a massage. The massage therapist recognized

Brit from the TV and gave her an extra thirty minutes for free because Brit was "such an inspiration." Brit also got an airbrushed tan so that she was the perfect shade. Brit then insisted that we then go all the way across town for mani-pedis because she was certain she'd get some kind of killer nail fungus unless we went to the only place in town she trusted. She snapped at the technician for cutting her toe-nails too short. Just a flash of bitch before she covered it up again. She was contained, but if all went well by the end of this evening I'd push her closer to the edge.

Brit sprayed her hair one more time. The hair stylist had done an elaborate updo for her, with small tendrils of per-fectly Slinky-spiraled curls tumbling down. There was so much spray on her head that her hair wouldn't even quiver if a hurricane roared down on us.

I caught a glance at my own hair. I hadn't wanted to do anything too fancy. I wanted to look like myself. My mom had taken one of my grandmother's rhinestone brooches and had it attached to a barrette, giving me just a hint of bling. Brit kept insisting that it was too simple, so the hairdresser had given me "some volume," which seemed to consist of backcombing my hair until I looked like some kind of Texas preacher's wife. I had patted it down a thousand times since we left the salon.

Brit pulled me up so we could stand together in the mir-ror. I gasped when I inhaled—rosemary and mint. It was the same kind of shampoo that Beth had always used. The smell filled my head and rocked me back. For a fraction of a second it was as if Beth were standing there, and I forgot all about my plans. With my eyes closed I could almost imagine the whisper touch of a strand of Beth's dark hair brushing across my bare shoulder. When I blinked and saw Brit next to me in the mirror, the absence of Beth, the void where she should be, was like a punch in the gut. I almost bent over from the pain. I let out an involuntary gasp and had to tap my foot on the thick cream carpet in beats of six to regain control.

Brit's mouth was screwed into a tight knot as she pondered our reflection. "Your dress totally clashes with mine," she said.

"It's blue. Yours is silver. How is that clashing?" I said, pushing the words past the lump in my throat.

Brit rolled her eyes like she couldn't believe I was that much of a fashion idiot. "The fabrics are all wrong together. We should have coordinated better."

A hot stab of anger ran through my heart. Who gave a shit about fabric when Beth wasn't here and never would be? "Then you should have worn the dress you picked out to start with," I snapped. "I chose this dress to match the one you had originally."

Brit pulled back at my tone. "Excuse me for wanting things to look nice in pictures. Maybe you don't care, but this is my senior prom." She sniffed.

"It's just a stupid dance," I said. If anyone else were

around she wouldn't be acting like a dance mattered. I was the lucky one who got to see her selfish side. She'd been dreaming of a picture-perfect prom since she was a kid, and the murder of her best friend wasn't going to get in the way of it now.

Brit's eyes iced over and I felt my heart freeze. I'd gone too far. I wanted to push her, but not make her irritated at me.

Brit sniffed again. "I stand corrected. I didn't realize I was being so silly over a *stupid dance*," she said.

Oh, shit. She was pissed. I'd let hunger and irritation overwhelm me, and I'd dropped my mask as her personal ass kisser. "I'm sorry. I know how important prom is for you," I mumbled.

"There was a point when I didn't think I'd be here for this moment. I thought you'd understand that." Her finger trailed down the hand-painted custom wallpaper stripes. "This dance matters more than you think it does," she said.

"I do understand. I'm really sorry. I think I'm just nervous," I said. I had to remind myself I had my own plans for tonight.

Brit had already turned her back to me and was pulling on her shoes. "Why are you nervous? No one is looking at you, and you don't even like Zach romantically."

I scrambled to make things right. "It's not Zach, it's that I miss Beth. It's not the same without her."

"But she's not here and we are. I'm sorry she's gone, but

you can't let her death suck every moment of happiness out of the rest of our lives. You know what, she should be at graduation, but she won't be there either, or for her birthday, or next Christmas, or any other major life event." Brit's words were clipped and short. This was what she really thought, and it chilled me to the bone. I wished someone else had heard her, but when anyone else was around her act never slipped. This was why I needed to get her drunk tonight—let her façade crack a bit in front of other people.

Brit spun around to face me, and her mouth with its dark red lipstick was pressed into a thin line. I couldn't tell if she was really angry, or simply letting me know I wasn't playing the role she'd cast for me—endlessly supportive friend. I swallowed hard. I had to get the night back on track or I ran the risk of not being able to pull off part of my plan. "I'm really sorry, Britney. I didn't mean to ruin your night." I reached for her, but she yanked her arm back. She crossed her arms over her chest.

"I'm not saying this dance has to be important to you, but I thought if you were my friend you would understand why it's so important to me," she said. "Beth can't be there tonight, and we have a responsibility to make sure people remember her."

I felt the sinking weight of guilt and had to push it off. It was as if she were dancing me into a corner. "You're right, Brit. How can I make it up to you?"

In an instant she swapped her grimace for a grin. "Take

off that necklace and wear the one I picked out."

I was almost dizzy at her change in emotion. My hand went up instantly to the pocket watch pendant. "I thought it would be nice to have something of Beth's at the dance."

"It's totally wrong for the dress. Wear the one I got you."

Brit was still smiling, but her eyes were calculating, watching me closely. I reached for the pendant and pulled it over my head. I hadn't taken it off since I'd gotten it. I felt naked and exposed without it.

Brit pranced over to her vanity and pulled out the necklace she'd picked out. She was wearing one just like it. She motioned for me to lift my hair and the cold stones slid across my neck like a razor as she clipped it on.

"Now we match." Brit wrapped her arm around me, squeezing me close.

"I told you to check the batteries," Dr. Ryerson hissed to Brit's dad. He was fumbling with their digital camera, which had a lens large enough to take a close-up of the moon.

"Don't panic, I've got it." He motioned for Brit and me to stand together on the stairs. Brit instantly struck a pose, her shoulders cocked at an angle, chin down, and million-watt smile on full display. I most likely looked like a frumpy, frizzy-haired blue cow next to her.

I kept blinking, but all the flashes had made huge white spots in front of my eyes.

"Mom, do not start crying," Brit said.

I was shocked to see there were tears in Dr. Ryerson's eyes.

"I didn't think this was a moment I was going to get to see." She sniffed. Brit's dad wrapped his arm around his wife, and they both stared at us with these dopey expressions on their faces.

"Oh, Britney," her mom gushed, crossing quickly over to us. "Don't you go crying too! You'll mess up your makeup, and you look perfect."

Brit sniffed, but there weren't any tears in her eyes. "I was just thinking about Beth. I feel like this dance is really for her."

Brit's parents exchanged a pained glance. I wanted to pick up the Waterford crystal vase that was on the table next to me and hurl it at her lying face. So much for how we all had to move on.

Dr. Ryerson cupped Britney's face in her hands. "I know she's looking down from heaven at the two of you and busting her buttons with pride."

I wanted to gag. Beth would never even use the phrase "bust her buttons," let alone look down at Brit without spitting in her face.

The doorbell chimed. The guys were here. I took a step toward the door, but Brit caught my elbow.

"Let them come to us," she said.

Jason stopped short when he came in the room and then whistled. Brit giggled like she couldn't believe what a scamp he was.

My mouth fell open when I caught a look at Zach. He looked positively hot in his tux. He'd gotten his hair cut, and the suit fit him perfectly. He winked when he saw me. I could tell he felt out of place in the giant museum-like foyer of Brit's house.

"Get a picture with their corsages," Brit's mom said, elbowing her husband.

Jason was already pulling an orchid out of a plastic clamshell box.

"Is it a wrist corsage? I can't pin anything on this fabric," Brit said.

Jason smiled. "Of course. Would I let my girl ruin such a fine dress before everyone had a chance to see her?"

Zach stood next to me. "I didn't know about pins being bad for the fabric," he admitted, shuffling his feet on the floor. He held out a tiny spray of three pinkish-white tea roses. Then something caught my eye.

"Is that a My Little Pony ribbon?" I recognized the thin rainbow ribbon from Zach's sister's extensive plastic pony collection.

Zach shrugged. "Maddy insisted on tying it on. It came with a white one." He fished through his pocket. "I meant to change it in the limo, but I forgot."

I took the flowers from his hand. "I like it the way it is. It's perfect."

Zach flushed when he had to reach inside the neckline of my dress to pin on the corsage, and I managed to avoid flinching when he poked me. We then stood for what felt like a thousand more pictures. In every single one Brit managed to make sure she was at the center of the frame.

I caught a glance of myself in the mirror. The dress looked good. Almost as good as I remembered it looking at the store.

When I saw the price of the raw silk dress Brit had picked out for me for prom I flinched. My mom was going to have a cow.

"Count yourself as lucky that she doesn't insist you bleach your hair to match hers," Beth said. She was sitting on the bench in the changing room in only her bra and panties.

"I don't get why our dresses have to match," I said, pulling on the hem. The dress Brit had picked out for me was pretty, but even though it was the right size, it was more daring than something I would have picked out.

"What you'll discover is that it is far easier to give Brit what she wants than it is to argue with her."

"So you just give in?"

Beth laughed. "Don't look so disappointed. I can hold my own when I need to, but the truth is at least ninety percent of the shit that is life-and-death to Brit doesn't really matter. So why fight about it?" Brit looked at me. "You look good in that. It shows your figure."

I blushed and then struck a sultry pose against the door. Beth blew me a kiss. I stared at my reflection. I was going to get the dress. If my parents balked at the cost I would dip into my savings.

"If Brit insists on matching designer shoes, she's going to have to pay for them," I said.

"We're probably safe on shoes, but I'll warn you now Brit is going to have to decide where we all go for dinner. God help you if don't like seafood."

"Why is she like that?"

Beth leaned against the wall, her feet tucked up under her on the bench. "The thing about Brit is that she needs to be the center of attention. If she's not, for her it feels like things are spinning out of control. She's like one of those rare orchids that need just the right amount of sunshine and water or they fall apart. Despite how she looks like she has her shit together, she doesn't cope easily."

"That's sad," I said.

Beth nodded. "Something's missing in Brit. She'll figure it out someday. She's one of those people who will go to some weird spa/yoga camp in her forties and have a revelation while sharing kale smoothies with Oprah or something. But until she does she'll fill the hole by bossing the rest of us around."

"Is anything missing for you?" I asked.

Beth wriggled her eyebrows. "Now that I've got you? Hell no."

I was about to lean over and kiss her, but then I heard Brit coming with something for Beth to try on and I stepped back.

If I'd known how few chances I'd have left to kiss her, I would have done it anyway.

CHAPTER SEVEN

The theme for prom was Fifth Avenue Glam. The gym was supposed to give you the sense that you'd just wandered off the ritzy streets of New York City and into Central Park. That is assuming you could ignore the vague smell of the cleanser the janitor used, or the fact that Officer Siegel was dressed up at the door checking people's IDs. There were old-fashioned light posts covered in faux ivy from Michaels and white Christmas lights spaced around the room along with giant planters of bright tulips. The sophomores had painted a huge mural of a city skyline along the back wall. The whole thing felt shoddy and lame to me. The only thing that would have made the night right in my mind was Beth. She had the ability to make any situation fun; she was always cracking jokes, or making up challenges and games. Now that she was dead it was like the world had gone from Technicolor to being washed-out. Oz to Kansas. If she'd been alive, the gym would have felt magical. Now all I could see were the cheap paper decorations peeling away from the walls, and I hated myself for noticing.

"Do you want to dance?" Zach asked. He was bopping in his seat like an overeager toddler. I felt a rush of warmth for him.

"My feet hurt," I said. The straps from my heels had cut into my ankles. I'd started to take them off not long after we arrived, but Brit had asked if I was planning to go barefoot like some kind of farmer, so I'd kept them on.

Zach's face fell. "Okay, sure." He watched a few of his friends dancing wildly under the strobe light.

"Go dance with them," I said. Zach wavered. I knew he didn't want to leave me on my own at the table. I poked him in the ribs. "I'm serious. Go get your funky on."

"You positive?" Zach was already up and peeling off his jacket.

"Go," I commanded. I waved at him on the dance floor. I could see his friends yelling something in his ear over the thumping music, and his arms and legs were already jerking around as if he'd touched a live wire. The guy was basically pure joy trapped in a nerd body.

I searched the crowd for Brit and found her holding court by the drink table. When I was sure her attention was elsewhere I quickly poured some more rum from the flask that had been in my purse into her Diet Coke. My goal was to get her drunk. My last session with Dr. Sherman had convinced me that if I wanted things to be different I needed to *do* something different. I wanted her to lose the careful control that she always wore like armor. That would be the only way I could get proof. The only way people would believe me. I couldn't keep waiting for her to slip up—I needed to give her a push. I also needed to make sure she slept like the dead tonight, and if that meant making sure she basically passed out, that's what I would do.

Despite the fact that she was acting loopy and giggly with wide gestures and frequent hugging, I could tell she wasn't that far gone. It shouldn't take much; she'd hardly eaten anything in weeks. However, Brit was a master at holding her liquor; she must be made of sponge. As much as I was willing the alcohol to seep into her brain, she seemed to be able to shrug it off, but I was feeling the effects. I had tried to stick to pretending to drink along with her, but there were times I had to have some to keep up the act.

Jason worked his way back to our table and dropped a plate full of cheese and crackers in front of me. "You should eat something," he said.

"I'm fine," I said, but there was a touch of slur to my words.

Jason plopped down next to me and reached over to grab a cracker. "Your loss. The food is pretty good this year." He smiled at me. "The night is just getting started. You don't want to end up under the table before the party's over."

He was right. My head was swimming. I nibbled on a cracker. We both looked over at Brit, a group of people clustered around her. "People can't get enough of her," I said.

Jason nodded, but I could tell he wasn't really listening to me: he was focused on Britney. I was tempted to ask him how he lived with his decision to come groveling back. I knew in order for Brit's story to have the happy ending that everyone desired he needed to be by her side. People wanted the perfect couple to be together, and Jason was marching in step to give them, and Brit, exactly what they wanted. I hated him for being weak and because his leap to her side mirrored my own. I sighed. At least for me my loyalty was faked.

Jason turned to me, his eyes softening. "Look, I know it's hard to be Brit's friend. She's larger than life."

I looked at him in disbelief. "I am not *jealous* of her," I said. I pictured myself standing up and confronting Jason with the truth. Pushing him to admit that Brit's story reeked of bullshit.

Jason leaned back. "All I'm saying is that it would be easy to understand. Brit can't help who she is, but I know how much she values your friendship."

I pushed down a wave of nausea. I opened my mouth to argue with him, but an ice-cold hand landed on my neck. I spun around. Brit.

"What are you two canoodling about?" There was a smear of lipstick on her front tooth.

Jason inched his chair away from mine. "Just talking about how happy we are to have you back," he said.

Brit looked back and forth between us as if she was sniffing for lies.

"Attention, everyone." A squeal of feedback came from the stage, saving us from any more of her questions. "It's time to name the prom king and queen!" Matt Cheavers, the senior class president, pointed at the DJ, who turned on the sound effect of a drumroll.

Brit dropped into the seat next me and plastered a smile on her face. She pushed her hair out of her face and sat up a bit straighter.

"This year we had a couple of runaway winners," Matt declared. I couldn't tell if he wanted to drag out the suspense of who had won or wanted to justify the practice of having a king and queen all together. There had been a protest letter going around earlier in the spring that the tradition was outdated.

"This year's Northside's prom king is Jason Read." A cheer went up from the crowd. The basketball team stood and chanted his name. A light searched the room and before it hit our table Jason reached over and squeezed Brit's hand. When the light was on him Jason stood and then bounded over to the stage. The whole room cheered. Just weeks ago he'd been the public whipping boy for bad behavior, but now he'd bounced back to king. Matt balanced a crown on Jason's head and handed him a scepter.

Brit leaned over and quickly swiped a fresh coat of lipstick on her mouth. I tapped my tooth and she ran her finger over her front teeth. When she saw the smear of red I'd saved her from she shot me a look of gratitude.

"And our prom queen, heck, the queen of our school, is the divine Britney Matson!"

The spotlight whipped back around so it was shining on our table. Brit raised her hands to her face like she was shocked, as if we hadn't all known the outcome was destined. She squealed and jumped to her feet.

I leapt up too, and Brit threw herself into my arms for a hug. The smells of her perfume and the rum she'd had filled my head and made my nausea worse.

She was already moving toward the front, stopping along the way to embrace other friends. As soon as she was close, Jason leaned over and offered his hand to help her up onto the stage. Brit bowed her head slightly to receive the giant beauty-queen crown.

Someone stepped forward to give Brit a bouquet of roses. There was a silver ribbon tied around the stems. It matched her dress perfectly. Coincidence? I doubted it.

The crowd was cheering. I clenched my teeth hoping that I looked like I was smiling and not grimacing. I clapped in beats of six, willing myself to remain calm.

A small bunch of girls were standing near the door.

They weren't applauding. Sophomores. I was pretty sure they were in the band. Their faces watched the stage, disgusted. I didn't know them, but I'd seen them in the halls. They were friends of Sara's. It made me feel better that not everyone had decided to forgive and forget.

One of the girls realized I was looking over and she slowly mouthed the words *fuck you*. I jolted back, surprised, as if she had yelled it in my ear, spraying my face with spit. The girl next to her grabbed the other's elbow and they walked away.

The DJ had turned on Brit's favorite song, something by Adele. Jason and Brit started to sway together under the spotlight, and Brit made sure she was facing out so the cameras could get a good shot. Other people started to couple up for the dance. Zach was suddenly at my side.

I took his hand and let him lead me out onto the floor. There was a mirrored ball spinning above that sprinkled the dance floor with circles of light spinning around making me feel dizzy. Glittered confetti and balloons were drifting down from the ceiling. It was as if I were walking on the deck of a heaving boat, unsteady.

Brit looked positively glowing. I'd hoped her spay tan would make her look orange, but it didn't. Everything about her looked ideal. The way she'd planned it down to the smallest detail. She never seemed to take a single misstep. My gag reflex was cued, and for a second I thought I might vomit right in the middle of the dance floor.

Zach stopped dancing. "Are you okay?"

"Do you mind if we sit back down?" Zach placed his palm in the center of my back and wove me through the crowd back to our table. Once we were seated Zach dashed off and came back a second later with an ice-cold water bottle. I pressed the sweating plastic to my forehead for a beat and then opened it, taking a deep drink. "Sorry, I think I had too much to drink."

"Are you sure that's it?" I glanced up at him. "I know you must miss Beth," Zach said. "Sometimes when everyone around me is the happiest is when I'm most aware of what's not right in my life."

His words hit me. My lower lip shook. Zach didn't know the whole story and yet he still cut through everything to the truth. Being mad at Brit for getting her dream of being prom queen was easier than missing Beth. I took a deep, shuddering breath.

"You don't have to talk." Zach squeezed my hand. I leaned my head on his shoulder and let the music just wash over the two of us.

"Okay, everyone, let's raise a glass to our queen!" Melissa called out a few minutes later once the official royal dance was completed. Nearly the entire field hockey team was surrounding Britney. Brit was flushed as if she'd just scored the winning goal. Everyone let out a cheer and raised their cups.

"I love you guys," Brit said. She swayed slightly in her heels. The rum was finally catching up to her—that or she was drunk on attention.

"I bet the picture of you getting crowned goes viral," Kate gushed. "You look killer in that dress."

Brit cocked a hip and puckered her lips. The sight of her mugging for all the cameras made me want to shove her. I took a deep breath. Now was the time to push, but not physically.

"Let's raise a glass to Beth too," I said, making sure to avoid Brit's eyes. "Having her here would have made tonight perfect."

Everyone lifted their cups again. "To Beth!" they cried out.

People started sharing stories about Beth, and I kept shooting glances at Brit, seeing if the move of the spotlight would make her snap, make her perfect exterior slip as it did sometimes when we were alone, but she was watching me with an odd smile on her face.

Brit stepped forward, cutting Kate off midstory about how Beth used to help out new players on the team. "I'm glad Kalah mentioned Beth; it gives me a chance to make an announcement."

What was she up to? I'd wanted her to snap at someone that her getting the prom crown now was more important than something Beth did months ago, but she didn't seem fazed at all. Brit paused to build the tension.

"As you guys know, my parents had collected a bunch of money for a foundation in my name, and while I totally am in support of their goal of using most of that cash to set up some counseling programs, I've talked to them about setting up a scholarship to remember Beth. I've arranged for the news to be released to the media tonight." She motioned to the back of the room, and that was when I realized that many of the people who had been taking pictures of her were reporters.

Our group went totally silent. Amy's eyes went wide and she made an "aww" sound.

"I want to leave a legacy that recognizes Beth." Brit smiled. "I think she would like the idea of helping someone who was struggling to pay for college costs the way she was."

"That is the nicest thing ever," Melissa said. "It's like a monument to your friendship with her."

Brit waved away the compliment. "It's not about me; this should be about Beth." She wagged her finger at all of us. "Don't get me wrong. Beth was no saint, but I loved her even more for her flaws. Besides, I'm no saint either."

Our teammates insisted she *was* practically a saint. Brit covered her face.

"I miss her so much." Brit drew in a sobbing breath, but I could see there were no tears on her face. "Beth should have been prom queen," Brit said. The team rushed to tell her that no, she was the one who truly deserved the crown.

They oozed platitudes like how Beth would have wanted Brit to be queen and how even now she must be smiling down on her. As Melissa hugged her, Brit looked over at her shoulder, straight at me, and smiled.

I watched everyone fuss over Britney, and it struck me how unfair it was. The real Beth was slowly being forgotten, wiped away by selective memories. The truth was that Beth could be a bitch sometimes, but she was also the same person who would patiently spend hours with someone who needed her. She was a real person, a mix of flaws and wonderful things all spun together. Now that Beth was gone, she was flattening out, becoming a cardboard cutout of who she had been. Soon all that would be left would be photos in the yearbook and bland stories sucked dry of the energy that had made her so special. They say time heals all wounds, but the truth is it isn't time, it's that the memories dull so they can't cut you anymore.

I wanted to keep Beth with me, but with every day, every minute, she faded and there wasn't a single thing I could do about it.

CHAPTER EIGHT

The evening was finally starting to wind down. The guys had their jackets off and their bow ties hanging loose around their necks like they were crooners from 1950s Las Vegas. People were already starting to swap memories, as if things had happened years ago instead of just earlier in the evening.

I was ready for it to end. My feet hurt and my head was still spinning from all the rum. I didn't feel tipsy and drunk anymore; I'd skipped that giddy phase and instead felt off balance and exhausted, like I'd already moved into the hangover stage. My plan to get her drunk and have her real personality break through had been a bust. If anything

I had the sinking sensation she knew what I'd been trying to do.

The DJ demanded everyone get back out on the floor. Brit sighed dramatically and flopped back in her chair. "I don't know if I can dance anymore. My feet are going to fall off. I can't believe the photographers took so long." Brit's family had arranged for the media to show up and get a picture of her, crown on, of course, holding the sign for the foundation. Dedicating a few dollars in Beth's name had given her an excuse to be in front of the cameras yet again. No wonder she'd wanted to make sure her dress was perfect.

"We should decide where we want to go after this," Jason said.

"I thought Kalah might want to stop at the cemetery, at Beth's grave," Brit said. Zach reached for my hand under the table and gave it a squeeze. "If things had been different they'd be here together. The couple with the mostest."

Zach stiffened. "What?"

"God, they couldn't keep their hands off of each other," Brit said with a laugh.

Zach was glaring at me, wanting me to deny the whole thing, but I couldn't. It was as if my lips were stapled shut. He ripped his hand out of mind and he pulled back from the table so quickly that his chair made a loud screeching noise on the floor. Before he bolted he looked at me and the pain in his eyes tore through me.

Brit giggled. "Oopsy. I thought he knew about you two."

Jason was staring at me in shock. "You and Beth were hooking up?"

"Like all the time," Brit said with a leer.

I sat on the edge of my chair trying to figure out if I should go after Zach or not. I wanted to smack the expression off of Brit's face. She was making what Beth and I had had together sound dirty.

"Do you want me to talk to him?" Brit asked, her face turning serious. "I'll feel terrible if he's really upset. I swear I thought he knew or I wouldn't have said anything." She patted her forehead with a napkin. "It's all the rum. It's totally messed with my head." Her eyes slid over to me, calculating.

"Don't talk to him," I said, getting up. "It needs to be me." I thought about telling her that she'd done enough, but there was no need to say it aloud. She smiled up at me and I knew as clearly as if she whispered the words in my ear, each one trickling in like poison, that this was no casual slipup; this was a message, a threat.

I walked around the edge of the room trying to see if I could spot Zach, but he seemed to have disappeared. Even if I found him there wasn't anything I was going to say or do to make it better. We weren't dating now, but he'd believed I'd been faithful when were together. He'd never trust me again. Brit's little slip of the tongue had cost me the one person I could count on.

Couples swirled past. Some faces I recognized, Tyler and his boyfriend Tomas. Amy and Stephen. Melissa and Grant. People from my classes and the halls were almost unrecognizable in fancy dresses and tuxedos. A group of Sara's friends from band clustered near the stage. They turned away when they saw me.

There was a flash of dark hair as someone near the back twirled. Her dress, turquoise silk, had a full skirt that spun out. Her legs were long and lean, and you could see the line of muscles from her thighs, down her calves and then her small bare feet. My breath locked in my chest.

Beth.

I lurched toward the corner. The girl turned and instantly I realized it wasn't Beth. As much as I wanted to believe in ghosts and spirits visiting from the great beyond, I knew it wasn't really possible. Beth hadn't appeared from beyond the veil, and if she could somehow transcend death, she wouldn't waste her time coming to prom. I slid past people and stumbled out into the foyer.

I leaned with my head pressed against the window. The glass was cool against my hot skin. I felt clammy; my dress was a thick silk fabric, better suited to cooler weather. It was stuck to my skin with sweat.

A group of girls burst out of the bathroom, a cloud of perfume and laughter spilling out in front of them. I pressed against the wall and wished I were invisible. I stumbled and my ankle twisted to the side.

"Drunk, much?" I heard one girl whisper to the others, and they giggled again as they slipped back into the gym.

I heard the door open. "I thought I saw you go out here," a voice said.

I flipped my hair back, my fingers snagging in the tangles of sticky hairspray, and there stood Officer Siegel in a simple black dress.

"You look nice," I said.

Officer Siegel chuckled. "Try not to sound so surprised."

"I came out here because I needed a minute away from all the noise and heat," I explained.

She looked me up and down. "You've been drinking."

"No, I haven't," I said quickly. That was about the only thing that would make this night worse: having her call my parents and bust me.

Her left eyebrow cocked in disbelief. "Okay, sure." Office Siegel took me by the elbow and led me into the bathroom. I winced when I saw myself in the mirror. My hair looked matted and my eye makeup was smudged. The corsage Zach had given me drooped, pulling the fabric out of shape.

I repinned the flowers on my dress, looping them through my bra strap so they would stop flopping forward. I grabbed one of the rough brown paper towels, wet it, and then wiped the black smudges out from under my eyes. I ran water over my hands and then flipped my hair over my face, trying to scrunch some shape back into it.

Officer Siegel faced the mirror. She put on a fresh coat of lipstick. "Are you having fun?"

"It's okay," I said.

She wiped a tiny spot of lipstick off where it smudged below her lip. "I'm not interested in busting you. You've been through the wringer this year, but, kiddo, take this in the nicest way, you don't look good, and in my experience drinking rarely makes anything better."

I pretended a sudden interest in finding my lip balm buried in the bottom of my tiny clutch bag. I made a non-committal noise.

Officer Siegel touched my shoulder. "I want to help."

Her offer of kindness was like someone tearing off a scab over a wound, allowing the infection to spill out "It's Britney. She's . . ." I stumbled as I reached for her. "She's evil," I managed to get out. "She did it all. She's responsible for everything."

"Look, I agree there's something off with her story—"

I flashed to when I had talked to Siegel outside of Brit's hospital room. It was possible she would be my ally in this. "It's more than her so-called lost memory. I think she was responsible for Beth."

Her eyebrows shot up. "You think she pushed Beth into the water?"

"No, I don't think it happened at the Point. That's just her story, I'm almost sure of it. It's complicated." It was as if I were standing outside myself. A part of me knew I was doing this all wrong and was screaming for me to shut up. Officer Siegel was suspicious of Britney, but I needed to present my case carefully, logically. Instead I was slurring and talking about evil. As the words petered out, I looked at her face and knew I'd made a huge mistake.

Officer Siegel grabbed some more paper towels, wet them down, and passed them over to me. "Wash your face," she said.

"You don't believe me," I said.

"This is a serious accusation," she said, but she paused, considering it. "They teach us in the academy that the truth is usually the simplest answer. What you're talking about is complicated."

"But Brit *is* complicated," I said.

"If you don't like Britney, why did you come here with her?" Officer Siegel crossed her arms over her chest.

"You know what they say: keep your friends close and your enemies closer," I said bitterly.

"You need to be careful," she said.

A flicker of excitement lit up my chest. "You think she did something?" I said.

"What I think isn't the issue. Do I think something is off about her story? Sure. Do I think she's capable of what you're talking about? Unlikely."

She was about to say something when the door swooshed again. Britney stood there. My mouth shut with a click. Officer Siegel went back to freshening up her makeup as if nothing had happened. Brit paused for a second and then joined us at the sinks. She ran the cold water and pressed a wet paper towel to the back of her neck. She was still wearing her crown. It looked like it had always been there.

"You guys having a girl chat?" Britney giggled, but her laugh sounded forced.

"I got a bit dizzy," I said. "I needed some air."

"Looks like you're doing better now," Officer Siegel said. "Are you okay?" She didn't look at Britney, but kept eye contact with me.

I nodded enthusiastically and then made myself slow down. The movement brought back another wave of nausea. "I'm fine. Just overheated," I said.

Britney plopped a soaked paper towel on my forehead. The water dripped on my dress. It would probably leave a spot. "Not everyone gets a queen as her own personal nurse," she teased.

"If you're not feeling well, I can call your parents. I'm sure they'd pick you up," Officer Siegel offered.

"No thanks, I'm fine now."

She held my gaze for a beat and then snapped her clutch shut. "All right. I'd better get back out there."

"I sure appreciate you offering to give your evening to volunteer as a chaperone," Brit said. Her words were polite, but there was something about the way she said them that seemed to drip superiority. Condescension came naturally to Brit. "We really benefit from having mentors like you."

Officer Siegel smiled, but her eyes were flat. "No problem. Happy to help."

After Officer Siegel left, Britney held up her finger to her lips, motioning for me to be silent. She quickly crossed the room and flung the door open. I could tell she expected to see Officer Siegel with her ear pressed against it, but the foyer was empty.

My heart was fluttering in my chest like a trapped bird. Had she heard me talking to Siegel? My skin was tingling like every nerve in my system was on high alert, ready to shove Brit aside and run for safety.

"What did she want?" Brit asked.

"Um, nothing," I mumbled.

Brit raised one eyebrow in disbelief. "I heard you guys arguing."

My mind spun, trying to come up with a story, and then it clicked into place. "She accused me of drinking," I said.

Brit turned around as if she thought Siegel might be sneaking up on her. "Did you say where you got it? Do you know what they would do if they caught me with booze? I could lose my crown."

"I know," I said peevishly. Did she think I was stupid? "I told her she was wrong, that I didn't have anything."

"Stand by the door," Britney told me. Once I had it blocked, she pulled out her flask. She spun the top, took one more sip, and then poured the rest down the drain. "I knew we shouldn't have brought anything into the dance. We should have left it in the limo. Do you still have any?"

I nodded. "She didn't search my bag."

"Thank god. Stupid cow." Brit held out her hand and I passed her my flask. She dumped it and filled it with water from the tap to make sure there wasn't a drop left. Her crown tilted and she pushed it back. "Jesus, could they have made this thing any larger?"

She was trying to sound annoyed, but she loved it.

"Congrats again, by the way," I said, motioning to the giant tiara.

"My mom is going to lose it when she sees the picture. Did you know she was prom queen when she was in high school?"

I shook my head, but I wasn't surprised. Brit likely came from a long line of prom queens dating back to some distant period during the Renaissance when they actually were royalty.

"I think the news about Beth's scholarship will make some of the national papers," Brit said. She kept talking about how she would have told me about the announcement, but had wanted it to be a surprise. I knew the truth, she made the announcement now because it gave her a chance to grab the media attention yet again, this time while dressed to the nines.

"Earth to Kalah."

I snapped back to the bathroom. Brit was waiting for a response. "Sorry," I mumbled.

"It's a good thing I cut you off from the rum; you're out of it," Brit said. "I was saying that we should get the limo driver to take us down to the beach."

The idea that there were still hours and hours to go made me exhausted. All this time spent with Brit was building up, burying me under layers of brittle glass. Every second I spent with her smiling in her face, pretending to buy her lies, and holding myself back from launching at her face, nails pointed at her eyes, was pushing me toward the breaking point.

"Kah-bear!" Brit snapped her fingers millimeters from my face. "Seriously, focus. Are you about ready to go?"

"I don't feel too great. Maybe I should just go home." I'd been stupid to think my lame plan was going to accomplish anything other than ticking her off.

"Don't be absurd. No one goes home this early on prom night."

"I don't know—" I hedged.

"I *do* know. I refuse to let you ruin prom. If you go home, I might as well call your parents and announce you had too much to drink," Brit smiled.

Was she joking or threatening me? I paused, but she didn't say anything else. "Okay, let's go," I said.

Brit looked down at my feet. "Gross." The back of my ankle was bleeding where a blister had burst and then chafed the flesh raw. The fact I'd told her hours ago that I wanted to take my shoes off seemed to not even register. She pulled a strip of Band-Aids out of her bag and passed them over to me. "Lucky for you, you're with me."

CHAPTER NINE

I was lying in Brit's trundle bed, exhausted but fighting to stay awake. Sunlight was peeking around the edges of Britney's thick curtains. After prom we'd gone to the beach until the just before dawn. Jason and his teammates had made a giant bonfire and brought stuff to make s'mores, along with more booze.

Zach hadn't come with us. He must have left right after Brit told him the news. I tried sending him a text, but he didn't respond. I wanted to go over to his house and explain, but there was no excuse. I shook off the fact that Zach was now pulled into my scandal. There wasn't time for me to be distracted by him. All I had wanted to do was pass out, but I had to wait for Brit to fall asleep.

"So what do you think was the best part?" Brit asked, her voice floating down to me in the dim light.

The last thing I wanted to do was have a blow-by-blow replay of the evening. It had been bad enough living through it the first time. "I don't know," I mumbled.

"I was shocked when they called my name for queen," Brit said.

"Really?" Did she expect me to believe that? She must have known the crown was hers. Who else was going to beat out the girl who'd returned from the dead?

"I guess it wasn't really a shock," Brit admitted. "I was pretty sure I'd win, but I thought it would be this amazing thing, but at the end of the day the crown is still just some cheap beauty-contest tiara. I guess I imagined it better—I don't know, *more*," she added. "It was exciting for a minute or two, but then it was almost a letdown." Her voice was flat.

"I think the older I get, the harder it gets to impress me," I said.

Brit leaned over the side of the bed, her smooth blond hair hanging on either side of her face, and looked down on me. "Exactly! Like there was all this stuff that I was always sure would be amazing, and it's good, but it's not really anything special."

"I guess that's life," I said.

"I don't accept that. I think life should be amazing. You only get to do it once, right?" Brit's voice swelled with intensity. "It seems like you should spend the time you have doing what makes you happy. I'm going to have a life that matters. . . ."

Brit was still talking about her theory on the purpose of life, but I stopped listening closely and instead I slid my foot out from under the covers and put it on the floor, trying to stop the bed spins that came on every time I closed my eyes. I was never going to drink rum again.

"The thing is I feel like I'm supposed to do something amazing. Why would I have the desire to be great if my destiny was to be just another nobody?"

The sound of Britney's voice was oddly soothing. If she was sure her destiny was to be great, then what was mine? I'd been sure it was to find justice for Beth, but every time I tried it my life seemed to slide further down. Maybe the universe was trying to tell me something. Could I do that? Could I just let go of what happened? Chalk it up to a horrible thing, but something that was in the past? I knew what I was planning to do was risky and there was no guarantee that it would even work.

I was pretty sure Brit knew I had some suspicions about her story but was also sure I couldn't prove anything. It wasn't just that she didn't want the truth dragged up; she wanted me as her friend. As long as I never stabbed her in the back or questioned her story, she would be there for me. Brit was loyal like that, until you crossed her.

I turned my pillow over to find a cool side and made a

noncommittal noise to Brit, who was still talking about her life. I wished she would just shut up.

"Are you asleep?" Brit whispered.

I jolted. I must have started to drift off. "No," I said. I pinched a thin sliver of skin on my thigh between my nails and focused on the pain to wake myself up.

"I'm sorry about Zach," Brit said softly. "I hope he didn't ruin prom for you."

I noted that she didn't apologize for being the one who'd told Zach. I suspected she felt that was something she had to do to teach me a lesson, but at the same time she felt bad that it happened. Sort of like a parent who regrets having to spank a kid. "It'll be okay," I said, although I wasn't sure that was true. Zach would forgive a lot, but this betrayal may have been too much.

"Zach was never good enough for you. I tried to tell you that."

"You'd think I'd know to listen."

Brit laughed softly. "Did you see Sara's friends storm off after Jason and I were crowned?" Brit snorted. "They shouldn't allow sophomores at prom. They're like children."

"I didn't see Sara at all," I said.

"She didn't have the guts to show her face. Most likely she was sitting at home crying into a giant bowl of ice cream."

"She'll probably gain ten pounds before the summer

starts," I added. I felt bad mocking Sara, but I knew it was expected of me.

"I need you to help me with something," Brit said. She swung her head over the side of the bed again. Her eyes were bright even in the dim light.

"Sure, whatever," I said.

"I'm going to get Sara. Make her pay for what she did."

The muscles across my shoulders and up into my neck tensed. "You've got Jason back; what else do you need?"

Brit's nostrils flared. "She screwed with me. That was a huge mistake. I mean, the fucking arrogance of her."

"I don't think she's worth your energy," I said.

"It's worth it to me. So can I count on you?"

"Always."

Brit sighed and lay back down. "Sleep tight, Kah-bear."

"You too, Brit-bear."

Within seconds, Brit's breath evened out and she was asleep. The room was still spinning as fast as my mind. I propped myself up. What was Brit planning for Sara? Whatever it was, it wasn't going to be good.

I looked at Brit. As she let out her breath her nose gave a tiny whistle. She looked like someone's idea of Sleeping Beauty, complete with the prom crown resting on the pillow next to her. She may look innocent and sweet, but I knew what the brain behind those closed eyes was capable of doing.

I realized I was clutching one of her throw pillows in my

hands. It would be so easy to reach over and cover her face. I let the fantasy unwind. She would fight back as I pushed the pillow into her features, her hands would claw at my arms, but as long as I was kneeling on top of her she wouldn't be able to unlodge me. I was stronger, at least physically. The idea of smothering her, of pressing the life out of her lungs, was almost orgasmic. I blinked, realizing that I was breathing heavier and both hands were clutching the pillow.

I'd go to jail. There was no way I would get away with it. It was the most primal kind of justice, an eye for an eye. She killed Beth and I'd kill her. It was almost poetic.

Brit grunted in her sleep and rolled over onto her side. How would she respond if she knew what I was thinking? I smiled. Knowing Brit she would almost be proud of me. She didn't think I was capable of that kind of passion and commitment. A sudden rush of tears filled my eyes. She was right. I liked the idea of doing it, but I never would. I lacked whatever it was in her that made it possible for her to go from thought to deed. I was always the one who sat back, but she was going to find out things were changing.

I made myself wait, the digital clock on her dresser slowly clicking off each minute. A half hour slid past. She had to be really out by now. "Brit," I whispered. She didn't stir. "Britney," I said a bit louder. Her breath continued in measured waves. I slipped out from under the covers and stood. I was locked in place. My brain was telling my legs to move, but the connection seemed to be broken.

I wasn't even sure what I was looking for, but this was my chance. Brit was a minihoarder. She saved everything—matchbooks to remember restaurants, old birthday cards, magazines, paper drink coasters, notes, tags from expensive clothes, seashells from a summer vacation, and even a tiny bottle of sand from a Hawaiian vacation. She collected links to her past—it was a compulsion. She *had* to have something from when she was gone—something that would prove that she hadn't been wandering around in an amnesic fog. Something that would give me a hint of what to do next.

Her closet door squeaked as I pushed it open, and I flinched. I looked over my shoulder, but Brit hadn't moved. I had my phone with me and I turned on the flashlight app. My hands slid over her clothing, quickly checking pockets. Other than a few crumpled tissues and a tube of Burt's Bees, there wasn't anything. She had rows of shoes and boots, but I didn't see anything that was out of place. Brit had an entire shelf of handbags—Coach, Kate Spade, Louis Vuitton. I could go through each of them, but she hadn't taken any of them with her. For her suicide story to work, she'd had to leave almost everything behind. She wouldn't have taken anything that might have been noticed.

I slipped back out of the closet and crossed the room to her bathroom. I quietly shut the door behind him. My heart slowed down: if Brit woke up she wouldn't find it strange that I was in here. The black-and-white tiles were cool under my bare feet. There was a motion sensor in a night-light that clicked on, casting a dim light around the room. The marble counter was covered with pots of eye shadow, lipstick, and a spilled puddle of congealing hair goo from when we'd been getting ready. One of Brit's false eyelashes was stuck to the marble like a spider cut in half.

I slid open each drawer and quickly rummaged through. Picking up each item, hoping for something to be off. Maybe a price sticker on a box of tampons that would show it came from a store out of town, but nothing.

I sat back on my heels. I knew it wasn't going to be easy; I just had to think. I stepped back into the bedroom. It took my eyes a moment to adjust to the dim light. I watched Brit's chest rise and fall. I tiptoed over to her desk and sat in the chair. If she woke I could say I was looking for a pen so I could write something down. I pulled each drawer open flipping through stacks of paper, notes, papers from school. Nothing useful. A sharp pain. I yanked my hand from the drawer. A paper cut. I stuck my finger in my mouth and sucked the drip of blood off.

Brit grunted and rolled over. I froze in place, but she slipped back to sleep. There was one more place to check. At the foot of Brit's bed she had a carved cedar chest. It had been her mom's; Brit called it a hope chest. I knew Brit kept her most precious stuff in there. It was the most likely place she would keep something special and the one place that I had zero excuse to be poking around in.

"Brit?" I whispered, checking one more time. She didn't

move. The lid seemed to stick, but with a push it creaked open. The corsage Justin had given her for fall's homecoming dance was mummified in a clear plastic container on top. No doubt her prom crown would go in here eventually. There was something lacy, a bunch of Valentine's Day cards, and her old yearbooks. There was a small jewelry box, and I opened it. A pair of diamond earrings, her class ring, a bunch of badges from Girl Scouts, and what looked like an antique ring. I slid the jewelry box back into the chest and noted something folded along the side. Cheap, like worn cotton. Not something that looked precious. I pulled it out. It was a strip of black fabric, folded over to make pockets with strips sewn to the ends. There was a faint smell. I held it up to my nose—spicy. Then I saw the tiny words in the corner. *El Az*. I'd seen these before.

My heart picked up speed, beating a drum against my ribs. El Az was a Mexican restaurant in East Lansing, hugely popular with MSU students. My brother, Nadir, took me there almost every time I visited for their cheese dip and mole enchiladas. Why would Brit have a waitress apron from there? There was no reason. Unless that's where she'd been after the murder. I'd suspected she'd hidden out in a college town where a teen girl on her own could easily blend in, and a rush of victory ran down my spine. I quickly folded the apron up and closed the lid to the chest. I shoved the apron into the bottom of my duffel bag.

I slipped back into my bed. I wasn't sure what it proved,

but it was something. At least I was *doing* something. Now I had a place to start.

"Can't sleep?"

I nearly jumped out of bed. Brit's face was leaning over the side looking at me. I held my breath, had she seen what I'd been doing? I pictured her watching me through half-slit eyes as I rummaged around her room.

"No," I said softly.

Brit smiled in the dim light. "Try counting sheep." She rolled back over, out of sight. "Works for me every time."

CHAPTER TEN

I'd been sure I wouldn't sleep at all, but I woke up around noon on Saturday when I heard Brit in the shower. My eyes darted over to my duffel bag. Had it been moved? I shouldn't have taken the apron—it was a mistake. I had no idea if she ever checked on the things in her chest, but if she found it missing she would know something was up. It wasn't like a robber was going to break into her parents' giant house and bypass all the electronics and jewelry to steal a used waitress apron. I wanted to kick myself. I'd been so excited to find something it had never occurred to me that the apron didn't prove anything—all it did was raise questions. If Brit really did have posttraumatic amnesia and couldn't remember a thing about while she'd been gone, why was she saving this? Knowing Brit she'd find a way to explain it. It did give me something to chase down—at least it was a place to start—but keeping it would be a mistake.

I slid out of bed and unzipped the duffel so I could put it back. The shower turned off and I stood in the middle of the bedroom. Wavering. I took a step toward the chest and then back again. My hands were shaking. I yanked the lid of the chest open and shoved it inside.

As the lid dropped down, the bathroom door flew open and Brit came out, a thick plush white towel wrapped around her.

"God, that felt good. My hair was gross." Brit paused and looked at me. "Going somewhere?" I realized I was still holding my duffel bag clutched to my chest.

"I thought I should head home. My parents are going to want all the details from the dance," I said.

Brit's eyebrows crunched together, and I was gripped with the irrational fear that she had X-ray vision and could see the apron lying on top of her chest instead of folded and tucked along the side. "You sure? My mom will make us some lunch."

"I really should go." I stood there as if I were waiting for her permission, which in a way I was.

Brit ran a comb through her wet hair. "Your call. You sure you don't want a shower?"

"Nah, I'll clean up at home." I backed toward the door, yanking a sweatshirt over my tee. "I'll see you Monday," I said, fighting the urge to turn and run. Once I was out of her room I flew down the stairs. My mom would kill me for not finding Brit's parents and thanking them for letting me stay, but if I had to keep up appearances for one more second I was going to lose it.

"Let's go out."

I jumped. I'd been reading in my room, almost half-asleep, and now suddenly Brit was there. After prom I felt we'd had enough time together, and I'd been counting on not having to see her until tomorrow.

"Have you seen this?" Brit thrust a paper at my face.

I pulled back so I could actually make out the print. "What is it?"

"Were you sleeping? Your parents said they were making some big Sunday brunch, but I told them we made plans to go out."

"Out?" I felt like my thinking was on some kind of time delay. I couldn't make sense of what she was saying.

Brit was already rummaging through my closet. "You need to get dressed. We have to talk. We'll go get something to eat."

"I'm not hungry," I complained.

"Are you going to help me or not?" Brit's jaw was set.

"Help you with what?" I asked.

Brit's finger jabbed the paper, almost jamming straight through it. I glanced down.

WHERE WAS BRITNEY?

There was a picture of Brit underneath. It had been taken at prom. She was standing on the stage, balancing her crown. She was smiling, but it wasn't a flattering photo. Her mouth was twisted slightly, so it looked more like a sneer, and the way her head was tucked gave her a slight double chin.

"What is this?" I was trying to take all of it in at the same time, but my eyes kept skipping around the page. Then I caught the byline. Derek Iriven. Holy shit. He was the reporter who hadn't liked Brit right from the start. I skimmed through the article. The article questioned why the police hadn't bothered to investigate where Britney had been while she had been "amnesic" and implied that the fact that her family had money meant no questions had been asked. It mentioned the donation to the foundation, but it definitely came across as an afterthought.

I got up and went across the hall to the bathroom. I splashed cold water on my face and yanked my hair back in a ponytail. I made sure the smile, or even the hint of a smile, was wiped off my face.

When I got back to my room Brit was pacing back and forth. "This guy is going to try and make a name for himself by dragging mine through the mud."

"That's what he's known for. He's always writing those op-ed pieces that are designed to tick people off," I said.

"If he thinks he's going to get away with this, he's going

to be sorry." She stared at me as if I were the one who had written the article, and I shifted uneasily.

I picked the paper back up. "What exactly does he say?"

Brit snatched the paper out of my hand, nearly ripping it in two. "He basically wrote that there is something shifty about how my case was handled."

A ripple of excitement ran through my chest. "Shifty how?"

Brit's face was mottled red. "He says that the cops totally mishandled what happened to Beth because my parents have money. Some anonymous source told him that I was hiding out in Ann Arbor, but who cares where I was? I had amnesia."

"He said that?" I wanted to grab the paper and look for myself. I wondered who the source was. It meant I had an ally out there. I was sure the apron meant she'd been in East Lansing, but it's possible she'd been in both cities at some point. Both were college towns—easy for one more teen girl to blend into a crowd. Maybe Derek's story would result in some kind of action by the police.

"He's not stupid. He doesn't say it directly, but it's crystal clear if you read between the lines. One of things Derek the Dick makes a big deal about is that my parents were able to talk to me when I was found before the cops had a chance to question me."

"But why is it a big deal if you saw your parents?"

Brit threw her hands up in the air. "I know! I had a

freaking head injury. I'd been suicidal. I had this huge trauma, and he acts like it's weird I would want to see my family before anyone else." Brit tossed me the paper and crossed her arms.

"Unbelievable," I said. I mulled over what she'd told me so far.

My eyes scanned over the paper, trying not to look excited. My brain scrambled, trying to think of who might have told him where Brit was. "I can't believe this happened," I said.

"I hate that guy," Brit said. "I hate that anyone would talk about me behind my back. Imply that I'm some kind of horrible person."

She hated it because she knew it was true. Brit didn't want to face the fact that she was nothing more than a filthy liar. Then I remembered what I should be doing. I threw my arms around her and hugged her. "It's going to be okay," I said.

"I waited so long to be queen, and he's ruined all of it. He hardly even mentioned Beth's scholarship. If he thinks he, or anyone else who would try to betray me, can take me down, he's got a lot to learn." Brit took a deep breath to calm herself.

I hoped Derek had crossed every *t* and dotted every *i*, and that his source was well hidden, because Brit was going to go after them full speed ahead.

"Why aren't you dressed yet?" Brit said, her mood

seeming to spin again. "I'm starving."

I looked down. I was still in the ratty yoga pants I always wore when I planned to hang around the house. "Give me ten minutes."

"Five. You don't need to look good."

I pulled open a drawer and pulled out a shirt. "What are we going to do?"

"First we're going to get some food and then we're going to figure out how to make Derek the Dick sorry he ever wrote about me."

I paused. The hairs on the back of my neck stood up. "We're not going to do anything *to him*, are we?" I hoped all she had in mind was something like egging his car, but I was uneasy. Brit had solved one problem in a very permanent way. I was almost a hundred percent certain that what happened with Beth had been a spur-of-the-moment thing, but what if it wasn't? Or what if she decided that since she'd already killed one person, a second would be no big deal?

"I also need to figure out how to handle tomorrow morning. Everyone at school is going to have seen this." She sucked in her cheeks. "Oh, you just know that Sara creamed her pants when she read it."

"What she thinks doesn't matter." I managed to avoid pointing out that Sara didn't need to see it in black and white to know that Brit didn't have to play by the rules. How Brit talked about Sara was making me uneasy.

"I hate the idea that he thinks he has something on me."

Britney picked at a piece of red, swollen skin on her index finger.

"It's just his opinion. Everyone will know he's making it as wild as possible for attention," I said. Of course I was counting on the fact it would make people start to wonder just what the hell she *had* been up to all that time. If there was some real scrutiny, Brit's story would start to crack. "Things are going to work out the way they're supposed to," I said, and then I crossed my fingers that I was right.

CHAPTER ELEVEN

On Monday I practically floated into school. After Brit dropped me off yesterday afternoon I'd gone back out and gotten my own copy of Derek's op-ed piece. I smuggled it into the house like it was weed instead of a newspaper. I'd read it so many times I could quote it verbatim. He wanted to know why hadn't the police spent any real time trying to figure out where Brit had spent those weeks. What made me the happiest was that I wasn't alone. Someone else was checking into her story, and that doubled the chances of finding someplace where she'd slipped up and made a mistake.

Brit's story was full of holes. No one had really investigated what she'd said when she returned. She had a story, her parents backed up her trauma amnesia theory, and everyone around her swallowed it without a single question, like a dog being tricked into eating a pill hidden in cheese. Once real questions started to pepper the walls of lies she was hiding behind, they would crumble. Things wouldn't add up, and the inconsistencies would be so glaring that no one could ignore them. And if I could check out her story in East Lansing and this source could get the police to check out Ann Arbor, then Brit would feel the noose start to tighten. I'd have a front-row seat for the whole thing, right up to when they clicked the handcuffs on her and arrested her for the murder of Beth. The thought of that moment floated up in my chest like champagne bubbles.

Once they had Britney behind bars I would visit her. Years of watching *Law & Order* meant I could picture it perfectly. She'd be in one of those cheap polyester orange jumpsuits, slightly faded and worn from being used and washed over and over. Her hair would be frizzy because she wouldn't have access anymore to high-priced hair products or a good stylist. Her skin would look sallow both because she wouldn't be sitting out in the sun and because the high-carb diet would make her puffy. She'd pick up the phone on the other side of the glass, pathetically grateful to see me as she sank onto the rickety metal folding chair.

"I'm so glad you came," I'd hear her say through the receiver. Her other hand would touch the glass between us as if she needed to make a connection.

I'd look great, my hair blown out, nails done, and makeup perfect enough for a photo shoot. As if the lighting and air around me were somehow better. I'd be just a bit brighter, shinier, superior.

I would smile first, so that my words would be even more unexpected. "I know you did it. I knew the whole time," I'd whisper softly into the clunky phone receiver. She'd watch my red lips as if she could read something different on them. Her mouth would open and close in shock.

"Kalah?" Her voice would crack.

"Beth was a million times better than you. I hope you rot in here." Then I would hang up the phone before she could say anything else. I would waggle my fingers at her and slide my chair back. Brit would pound on the glass, screaming at me. There would be those tiny clots of spit in the corners of her mouth, like wads of Elmer's Glue. Because of the thick reinforced glass with wire mesh I wouldn't be able to make out exactly what she said, but the truth is, I wouldn't care. There was nothing she could say that would matter anymore. The guards would grab her and begin to drag her back to her cell, or maybe a brief stint in solitary confinement. I'd wave my fingers at her again, letting her watch me walk away before the cell door clanged shut on her.

"Watch out."

Almost shocked to find myself still in the halls of Northside instead of jail, I stopped inches from slamming into one of the junior football players.

"Look where you're going," he said.

"Sorry," I mumbled, but he was already walking away. I blinked a few times to ground myself in the here and now. Brit wasn't in an orange jumpsuit.

Yet.

I felt the smile spread across my face like warm honey. One step at a time. Then I saw Zach. He was fishing through his locker and he was alone. An opening to talk to him and explain myself. Before I could second-guess the plan, I went up to him.

"Hey," I said. Zach looked surprised to see me. "I tried to text you a couple of times over the weekend."

"I know." His face was blank giving, nothing else away.

I plunged on. "I cannot tell you how sorry I am."

Zach let out a bitter laugh. "I bet." He tossed his book, *World History: Journey from the Past to the Present*, into the locker hard enough that I could hear it bang against the back wall.

I bit my lip. This was going even worse than I'd expected. I'd known he'd be hurt, but he was also mad. "I want to explain," I tried.

Zach held out a hand to stop me from talking. "I don't want an explanation. The truth is I don't want a thing from you."

"I wanted to tell you about Beth, but I didn't know how.

You have to know that I really did care for you, *do* care for you. My feelings were all mixed up, but I do know you are one of my best friends. It was all just so complicated and then after Beth was gone I didn't see the point in hurting you."

Zach shook his head. "You didn't see the point?" He slammed the locker shut with a clang that echoed down the hall. People near us turned around, sensing a drama in the making. "Spare me the *I care for you*s. It doesn't make it better; it makes it worse because what's clear is that you don't have a clue about what it means to actually care about someone." He spun away.

I grabbed his elbow. "Zach, wait." He jerked his arm from my grasp.

"Leave me the hell alone." His voice was sharp and harsh. I stepped back as if he'd slapped me.

"Okay," I said softly. He stalked off.

I could hear whispers from people who'd seen the whole thing. I forced myself to put my chin in the air and look around. No one would meet my eyes, but they did shut up.

The news from Derek's article and finding the waitress apron had made me cocky. I should have given Zach more time. Let him come to me when he was ready. I took a deep breath and tried to erase the feeling that I'd just managed to make things worse.

I looked up to see Officer Siegel watching me from the doorway to her office.

I dodged down the hall and slid into the bathroom to splash water on my face. I'd see Brit soon, and I needed a second alone to prepare myself. I didn't know how she would be coping with the pressure, the snide whispers, and the sense that you've heard your name being spoken, but when you turn around no one is looking at you. I would need to be there for her. She was used to being on top; it would shake her to be on this end of things. I was just about to leave when the door swung open and a bunch of my teammates walked in.

"I swear if she wasn't going to Cornell she could be someone's personal shopper. That dress was beyond," Melissa said. "Oh, hey," she said when she spotted me at the sink.

I rummaged through my bag and pulled out my lip gloss. I nodded at her in the mirror.

"Did you see the prom pictures I put up? I tagged you in a couple," Amy said to me.

"Um. No," I admitted.

"Hands down, best prom ever," Melissa said. "The pressure is going to be on our class next year to even come close to beating it. Jason and Brit looked perfect."

As everyone primped their hair, they detailed the highlights of the dance. I found myself staring at their various faces waiting for one of them, any of them, to mention the article about Brit.

Then it hit me. They were sure I was Brit's bestie; they must be worried about bringing it up in front of me. I tapped open the one stall door that had drifted shut to make sure we were alone and then lowered my voice. "So did you guys see that thing in the paper yesterday?" I asked. I shook my head like I couldn't believe it. "Brit is super upset."

Amy shrugged. "I saw her this morning at the coffee shop and she seemed fine." She added another layer of sticky-looking pink goo to her lips, giving her reflection a smack.

"She's putting a good face on things," I said. "You know how Britney is, but the truth is she was crushed."

"I got the feeling her family knew he was going to write something about the police not doing anything for a while, that's why they wanted to make the announcement about the foundation last night," Kate said.

"That's cold," Melissa said. "They wouldn't do that."

Kate rolled her eyes. Her opinion of Brit's family was as high as my own. But if Brit had known about the article, why had she been so upset? Granted, seeing something in black and white is different.

"That reporter guy's a douche bag—Brit and her family knew that," Melissa said and then launched into how she wanted to go back to the place where she bought her prom shoes and demand a refund because the heel was coming loose already. I wanted to grab her by the shirt and shake her until she shut up.

"I think we should all try to make sure we give Brit some extra support today," I said, interrupting Melissa's lecture on declining retail quality.

"For what?" Kate asked.

I let out an annoyed breath. "Because of the article," I said tightly. "I know we don't believe anything is weird about how Brit came back, but some people might."

"Why?" Melissa said. "Who cares where she was when she was gone? The point is that she came back."

The girls around me nodded. My heart sank. They honestly didn't care. I'd thought the rumors would stir things up, make people curious, but instead they seemed to feel sorry for Brit. They thought she was the victim.

"You're sweet to worry about her," Amy said, giving me a jostle with her shoulder. "But you know Britney better than anyone; she'll be fine."

I pressed my lips into a smile. "She sure will."

The bell rang and everyone grabbed their stuff, splitting up in different directions down the hall, calling out that we'd all have to meet up later. I jogged toward my French class and then, when I was out of sight, stopped and leaned up against the closest locker.

The article hadn't made any difference. I'd been so sure people would suddenly see the truth, but everyone was far too invested in the story they'd already told themselves. I'd made a mistake this morning when I'd tried to talk to

Zach, and I'd made an even bigger one when I'd been foolish enough to think people would be swayed by some newspaper article. People believe the truth they want to believe. I was going to have to keep pushing.

CHAPTER TWELVE

"I'd like to talk about Beth today," Dr. Sherman said.

The sound of her name was an electric jolt to my heart. After the ups and downs yesterday, I wasn't sure I was up for this emotional roller coaster. I'd tried to beg out of today's appointment, but my mom had just kept smiling, and now I was stuck here again. The plain furniture, cream-on-cream color design, and lack of personal details made me feel like I was stuck in hell's waiting room. "What about Beth? She's gone."

"I think exploring your emotions surrounding Beth, and how that relationship worked, would be helpful." Dr. Sherman looked down at her notes. "How did you meet her?"

I shifted in the chair, casting my mind back to the

beginning. I didn't want Dr. Sherman digging around in my feelings for Beth in some kind of mental archaeological project, and at the same time I relished the idea of talking about her. Beth was a subject most people avoided; their faces would break into a tragic expression and they'd change the subject as soon as possible. The only person who didn't seem to mind talking about her was Britney, but for obvious reasons that was complicated in an entirely different kind of way.

"Beth and I were on the same team. We knew each other for a while before we hung out, mostly just to say hi in the halls, that kind of thing. It was really Brit who asked me to be a part of their group." Brit told me that she recognized something in me—something that was like her, but now I think she'd recognized something else. She'd somehow guessed that I would let her push me around.

Dr. Sherman's eyebrows went up slightly. "So Beth initially wasn't interested in spending time with you. That must have been difficult if you liked her."

"It was only after I got to know her that we got close," I explained.

"And eventually it turned sexual." Dr. Sherman's words seemed to land with a thud in the room.

I swallowed but willed my voice to stay calm. "Yes."

"But you were dating someone else, is that correct?" She looked down at the papers on her desk. "Zachary."

I flushed. I was ashamed of the situation with Zach.

There was no way to explain how I felt for him and Beth at the same time. It didn't make sense to me, so I had no way to explain it to anyone else. Now he wasn't even talking to me. "I never set out to cheat on Zach. It just happened."

"I hear some defensiveness on this subject in your voice. Did it bother you to have feelings for another girl?"

I wanted to tell her that talking about my sex life with a random adult was enough to make anyone defensive. "What bothered me is that Zach deserved better. At the time I was still sorting out my relationship with Beth. I wasn't sure where things were going. I knew I should tell him, but I didn't know how." I shook my head. "That's not true. It wasn't the *how* that confused me; I was just scared. It was complicated." *Complicated* didn't begin to cover it. I felt ashamed of what I'd done. Disgusted with myself for being so weak that I hadn't the guts to tell him and now there was no way to fix it. I was a cheater. I didn't want to see myself that way, and now I couldn't avoid it.

Dr. Sherman nodded. "Where did you want things to go?"

There was a thick knot in my throat, like I'd swallowed Roogs, my stuffed dog, and he was wedged halfway down. "I cared a lot about Beth. She was different. Special. She made me feel special."

"And you'd never felt that before?"

"Not like that. Not so all-consuming," I admitted. It felt like another betrayal of Zach. Zach was warmth and comfort. Being with him had been like coming home. Things with Beth had been bright colors and electric heat. It made me feel like I was finally alive, as if I'd surfaced from being under the water and taken my first deep breath in forever.

"And how did Beth feel?" Dr. Sherman asked.

I chewed on my bottom lip. That was the real question, wasn't it? I'd put off asking her because I wasn't sure I wanted to hear the answer, and now I never would. "I think she felt the same."

Dr. Sherman had her hands folded together as if in prayer and rested her chin on the tips of her fingers. "How would you have felt if Beth didn't share your feelings? What if the relationship for her was just fun, a fling of sorts?"

I flinched. "I'm not a mind reader. I don't know what she thought."

"I know you don't know her feelings; I'm not asking you to guess. I want you to imagine *your* feelings if she told you she wasn't interested. I understand from your parents that she wasn't the type to settle into a longer-term relationship."

I felt my hackles rise. "Are you saying Beth was a slut?" Dr. Sherman's eyes widened slightly. If she wanted to toss emotional grenades out into the room, she'd better be prepared that I would throw some back.

"No. I don't believe that women, or men for that matter, who choose not to engage in committed relationships are somehow morally deficient," she said smoothing her gray skirt over her legs. "Sexuality is a good thing, healthy, and how people choose to express it is their choice. However, it's important that the people they interact with have the same expectations." Her voice was calm.

"So you think she was playing with me." I wanted to get up and pace the room.

Dr. Sherman paused, her finger tapping on the side of the pad of paper. "I find your response interesting. I never said that she was playing with you. My question is how you would have felt if you discovered that Beth's interest in a relationship wasn't the same as your own."

"It would have been shitty," I said. "Is that what you want me to admit?"

"Kalah, I'm not asking you to admit anything."

"Then what's the point of this?" I asked. My voice came out sharp and clipped. I hated giving her the satisfaction that she was getting to me.

"Is it possible that you read the cues from Beth incorrectly?"

I closed my eyes. She wasn't going to give up; she was going to keep hammering on it until my heart was pounded flat. I opened my eyes and stared at her. "Yes. It's possible, but I don't believe that's what happened. I'm not saying that Beth was going to want to be with me forever, but do I believe that she honestly cared for me? Yes, I do."

"How was this different from what you felt about Madison wanting to be your friend?" Dr. Sherman cocked her head to the side.

Her accusation was a punch to my gut. I wanted to fold up in the chair. I couldn't believe she'd said that. "They're nothing alike. Madison messed with my head. That's what she does. She likes to manipulate people. Beth wasn't cruel."

"You seem to still have a lot of anger over Madison."

Was she kidding? A wave of red rage washed over me. "Yeah, I do have some anger. She totally fucked up my life. I had to change schools, my head got all messed up, and I ended up here."

Dr. Sherman leaned forward. "Your problems with anxiety are a medical condition. It's no different from if you had diabetes or arthritis. I believe the situation with Madison flared your symptoms, in the same way that if you tried to run a mile with no training it would worsen a knee condition."

I crossed my arms. Dr. Sherman could say what she liked. It wasn't that I didn't understand that mental health was as real as a physical problem, but there was no way things would have turned out the way they had if Madison hadn't made me a target. And I wouldn't be here now if Britney hadn't done what she had to Beth, and then lied about it to me. It wasn't that I didn't understand I had some role to play in things. I was a participant in the whole ugly mess.

"The reason I'm bringing this up is to help you explore if it's possible that what you felt for Beth, and what you believe she might have felt for you, has been filtered through your illness. If it has, then that might explain why you are struggling so much now that she's gone."

It took me a beat to realize what she was saying. "You think I was obsessed with her," I said. "That what happened with Beth was just a different spin on what went down with Madison. That I manufactured all of it in my head." I couldn't believe she'd said that to me. That she would have the gall to try and rip away what I'd had with Beth and make me someone who would go too far. I shoved away the image of me creeping around Brit's dark room looking for evidence. That wasn't weird—that was required. And it had worked. I had found something.

Dr. Sherman's face was neutral, as if she hadn't just detonated an emotional nuclear bomb in the room. "I'm not saying that's what happened, but I think you need to be open to exploring it. That's the only way you're going to get better."

"There's nothing wrong with me," I said. "Look, I get that I have anxiety and a whole bunch of issues, but what I felt for Beth was real. What we had wasn't in my head. I don't need to get over that as if it were some kind of sickness." I was shocked she would say this stuff to me. My parents sent me here to get over the trauma of Beth's death, not make me feel worse about it.

"Do you see any patterns in your behavior?"

"What kind of patterns?"

Dr. Sherman leaned back. "Therapy isn't about finding a right answer or a wrong answer, but rather exploring the possibilities and, almost more important, your response to those options." She reached across the desk and touched my hand lightly. "What I'd like to discuss is why you choose to take actions that aren't moving you toward something positive."

I wanted to push the chair away from her desk so I could have more space. "I'm not doing things that are bad for me."

"How are your interactions with Britney good for you at this point?"

Now I felt like crying. My emotions were on a roller coaster, angry one second then diving into depression before jerking into a hard turn of confusion. I wanted to get off this ride. "It's not good or bad, it just is."

Dr. Sherman watched me. "Okay. I think that's enough for today. We'll tackle this again next week."

I nodded weakly and stood. My brain hurt as if Dr. Sherman had been punching me instead of lobbing questions. I knew she was right: I wasn't well and the longer all of this went on the worse I was getting.

Being near Britney was like exposure to some kind of caustic chemical or radiation. But not for the reasons Dr. Sherman thought. It was the constant lying that was making me ill. Eroding my soul. But if I gave up now, if I just walked away, Brit would win. Sometimes you had to risk yourself because what you were trying to do was worth that risk, that damage. It's like chemotherapy: sometimes you need to make yourself sicker to have chance of getting better.

"I'm going to have your doctor call in a new prescription," Dr. Sherman said as I reached the door.

The hair on the back of my neck rose up. "Why?" I asked.

"I'd hoped to see a bit more of an impact from the medication we've got you on," she said. She must have seen the stress in my face. "Don't worry, it's not unusual for it to take a while to find just the right dosage. It's a part of the process; we want to start you on the lowest dose and then go up slowly. This will be just a slight jump."

"Oh," I said. I could picture the tiny white pill, like a miniature egg, balanced on top of the container of strawberry Yoplait my mom would leave out for me each morning. The same pill I would mime popping in my mouth, while actually keeping it cupped in my hand and then shove into my pocket. I had a tidy collection of the untaken medication growing in my locker. At this rate I'd be able to open my own pharmacy soon.

Dr. Sherman glanced up and realized I was still standing in her office. "Any trouble with the medication? Fatigue, dizziness?" I noticed she didn't go into the long list of possible side effects that appeared in small print on the insert that came with the pills. That included everything from trouble with coordination, to nausea, to really fun things like trouble breathing, vomiting blood, or developing a desire to kill yourself. Better living through modern pharmaceuticals.

I shook my head. "It's just that I don't like being on medication."

"Our goal isn't to keep you on it; it's to get you through this period. Think of it like wearing a cast on a broken arm. The cast doesn't make the bone heal—the body does that. The cast just gives you the support you need." Dr. Sherman smiled at me, and I forced the corners of my mouth to lift. Medication also made things fuzzy and a tiny bit less focused, and I couldn't afford to be off my game by even a millimeter. No way was I taking that risk.

CHAPTER THIRTEEN

I turned off the car and let out the breath I'd been holding. It didn't matter how many times I visited, driving in East Lansing always made me nervous. People drove faster and students had a habit of darting out into traffic. Driving felt like playing one of Nadir's video games, only if I crashed and burned there was no do-over. I dug my phone out of my bag and texted Nadir that I'd arrived and would wait for him at the parking garage.

I pulled my duffel out of the trunk and the shoe box I'd lined with foil and filled with homemade cookies for this spur-of-the-moment weekend trip to see my brother. I'd told my parents that I wanted to go down and visit Nadir because he seemed down with exams looming ahead. I'd told Nadir I was coming because my parents were worried he was stressing out over his classes and wanted someone to check on him. My phone buzzed. Nadir was on his way. I felt like shit about lying to my family, but what really worried me was the lie to Brit. If she figured out I was poking around East Lansing she might realize I didn't believe her story. I'd told her I was going to my grandparents'. I was trailing around a bunch of lies like toilet paper stuck to my All-Stars.

"Hey, tell me those are Dad's chocolate cookies." Nadir loped toward me across the parking lot.

I held out the box with a small shake. Nadir took the box, lifted the lid, and took a deep breath.

"I miss these." He took one and ate it in one bite, his eyes closing in bliss.

"Well, Mom and Dad miss you."

Nadir swallowed. "So what's up with them?"

I shrugged as if understanding the mysteries of our parents was more than I could fathom. "I think Mom is going through another one of those *all my babies are all grown-up* phases. I knew she'd feel better if someone came down and made sure you were surviving." I smiled.

Nadir turned in a slow circle so I could check him out. "You can officially report back that I'm eating and sleeping."

I poked at a spot of something on his dark green hoodie. "Doesn't look like you're keeping up with laundry. Isn't it a sign of depression if you're living in your own filth?"

Nadir scraped at the mystery stain with his thumbnail and sniffed it in curiosity. "Among college-aged men, this kind of thing is part of our charm. Like a patina."

I rolled my eyes. "Sure, tell yourself that."

Nadir took my bag from me and slung it over his shoulder. "We can grab a quick lunch at the Union if you're hungry. I've got a study group this afternoon—I can't get out of it; we've got a group project—but then I thought we could go out for dinner, and there's a party in the dorm tonight."

"Sounds great," I said trying to make sure my voice had some enthusiasm in it. "I might do some shopping while you're busy," I lied. I'd known all about the group thanks to his Facebook page. That's why I'd picked today to visit.

"And *now* we discover the real reason you came to see me."

For a split second my heart lurched thinking Nadir had guessed something and then realized he was just giving me a hard time.

I linked arms with him. "A little retail therapy never hurt a girl."

I thought I saw a twitch in his eyelid when I said *therapy*. "How are things?" Nadir asked, trying to sound casual.

"You mean has Dr. Sherman managed to make me normal yet?"

Nadir snorted. "The woman isn't a miracle worker; *normal* is asking a lot."

I punched him lightly in the side. "I'm fine." I took a few steps before I realized he'd stopped. "What? I am."

"I worry about you," Nadir said. "You're the only sister I've got, and I'm pretty sure I can't talk Mom and Dad into getting me another. Mom says she doesn't think you're sleeping well and that your anxiety is worse."

My stomach pinched. I hadn't thought she'd noticed. Suddenly it occurred to me that while I'd thought I'd talked my parents into letting me come down to see Nadir, they may have *wanted* me to come. They had agreed to give me the Honda for the night pretty easily.

Nadir touched my arm. "I'll do anything I can do to help you, but you've got to help yourself too."

I bit my lip. "I know. Believe me, I'm doing everything I can." Nadir searched my face and then nodded and started walking again, talking about how I should be sure to avoid some guy on his floor at the party. He and my parents wouldn't agree with what I was doing, but even though I couldn't make them understand, I was at least doing something.

As soon as Nadir left for his study group I bolted out of his dorm and headed for Grand River Avenue, the main shopping district across from the university. It was crammed with students making the most of the warm day. I made a mental note of things in the windows in case Nadir asked me anything. I ducked up the side street and saw the sign for

El Az. The lunch rush was over, but there were still lots of full tables. A group of sorority sisters, all wearing matching sweatshirts with their Greek letters on the front, were dissecting a date one of them had been on. There was another table with a group playing cards and splitting a giant platter of nachos and pitchers of margaritas. There were also few solo people hunched over a textbook or laptop on one of the big wood tables trying to cram some facts into their heads even on a Saturday.

The hostess dropped the worn, laminated menu on the table and slid a red plastic tumbler of water over to me without a word. I rubbed my palms on my jeans and took a deep breath of the tortilla chip–scented air. I felt like bouncing on the wooden bench seat. I was close. I could tell.

A waitress came over to my table, pulling out a small pad of paper.

"I wonder if you can help me. I'm trying to find someone." I pulled out the picture of Britney that I'd brought. I'd Photoshopped it so she had the dark hair she'd come back from the dead with. "She worked here."

The waitress looked down. "I don't know, I just started. You want me to check with the manager?"

I nodded. I'd come up with a hundred different cover stories, that Brit was a runaway, that I was her long-lost adopted sister, that she'd won some kind of lottery, but then figured I was better off keeping it simple. Brit was a friend of mine and we'd lost track of each other.

The manager had dark circles under her eyes. She was wearing an apron that matched the one I had in my bag. "Yeah?"

"My friend Britney worked here," I said. "She might have gone by her middle name, Beth?" I slid the picture across the table. "I wanted to ask some questions about her."

"Nope, sorry." The manager started to turn, her sneaker squeaking on the painted cement floor.

I grabbed her elbow to keep her from leaving. "Wait, I'm sure she worked here."

The manager looked down at her elbow and then at me. I let go of her. "She didn't work here," the manager repeated slowly as if I had a hearing problem.

"I'm trying to find out some information on her."

"I don't know what to tell you. She didn't work here. Now did you want to order anything or were you leaving?"

I blinked. Brit *had* to have worked here. The manager's foot was tapping impatiently on the floor. "Um, I'll have some cheese dip and a Diet Coke," I mumbled. The manager bustled back to the kitchen. I wasn't hungry, but I didn't feel ready to leave—something was off.

"You said your friend's name was Beth?" a guy one table over called to me. He had one of those giant circle spacers in his ear and tattoos covering almost every inch of skin. A dragon on his left arm was wrapped around a desperate-looking Homer Simpson. "Dark hair, kinda bitchy?"

I passed him the photo. He looked at it and showed it to his friend, who nodded.

"Yeah, that looks like her. She worked here," he said. He turned around to make sure no one was listening. "The shift manager, Helen, hires some people under the table." He yanked his head toward the kitchen. "That's why she's not going to admit anything—she'd get in huge trouble with the owner."

"But why?"

"Tons of people are willing to work for just tips, and Helen gets a bonus if she keeps labor costs down."

"Are you sure it was her?" I asked, tapping the photo.

The guy screwed up his face as he looked at the picture. "Pretty sure. I wash dishes here. I know most the girls. Nothing against you, but your friend was a shit waitress. She spilled salsa on some guy and yelled at him like it was his fault. She got fired after that."

"But it was her," I insisted, wanting him to be sure.

The guy shrugged. "I couldn't swear to it, but I think so. She didn't work here that long, maybe a couple of weeks max. Her hair was different. I don't think I said three words to her. It gets pretty busy in the kitchen."

The excitement that had been building in my chest started to deflate. I would need someone to swear to it.

Brit had already proved rumors weren't enough to shake her standing. I needed someone she talked to a lot. Someone who might have heard her call herself Brit. "Would anyone else here know her?"

The guy chewed a giant mouthful of nachos while he thought about it and then snapped his fingers. "You know, I'm pretty sure she was crashing with Nicole. Nicole picks up shifts here too—that's probably how your friend heard about the job."

I leaned forward. "How I can find this Nicole?"

There was a smear of salsa on the guy's upper lip. "I haven't seen Nic for a few weeks. She lives a couple of blocks over on Charles, by Linden Street, huge white house, someone's got a giant Canadian flag in one of the windows. They throw killer parties."

I pulled some money out of bag and left it on the table to cover the food I hadn't wanted. I tapped the side of the table five times and then made myself stop. I was giving in to the compulsions too often. "Thanks." I was getting closer. The fact I hadn't tapped the table six times wouldn't make any difference. I was done relying on magical thinking to fix the problem. Nicole would have the answers I needed.

The house was easy to find. The Canadian maple leaf was in the upstairs window the way the guy had mentioned. The window in the front had a giant beer can pyramid, and there were four cars parked in the driveway like a used car graveyard and a group of bikes chained to the peeling porch railings.

The front steps sagged and creaked as I walked up. I could hear the sounds of explosions and gunfire, a video game, coming from inside. I knocked on the door. Nothing. I knocked harder.

"Hang on," a voice yelled.

I waited on the porch. I checked the time on my phone to make sure Nadir would still be with his group. The door opened. The guy inside looked like he hadn't yet worked himself up to the task of a shower today—possibly for a couple of days. He ran his hands over his face, his stubble giving a raspy, insect-like sound. "Yeah?"

"I'm looking for Nicole," I said.

"Sorry, she's not here." He started to close the door, but I jammed my foot inside.

"I really need to talk to her. Do you have a number for her, or know when she'll be back?"

"Do I look like the fucking concierge? She moved out."

My heart dropped. "Where did she go?"

"If I knew that, I'd make her pay for her part of the electric bill." He started to close the door again and I burst into tears. It wasn't that I was sad—it was sheer frustration, but it was if all the pressure I'd been building up inside exploded out.

"Jesus, don't cry." The guy stood there looking up and

down the street like he thought someone might yell at him for doing something to me.

"I have to find her," I insisted. I forced myself to stop crying and pulled myself together. I wanted to explain I wasn't sad, that was too easy for what I felt. There was rage, frustration, despair, and fear all rolled up together, but there was no way to explain that to someone I'd just met.

He opened the door wider. "Look, come in, let me get you a Coke or something." He held out his hand. "Everyone calls me Lizard."

"Kalah," I said with a hiccup. I followed him inside. The house smelled like stale pizza and dirty laundry. I sank down on the sofa. It was too soft, as if the wooden structure had decayed, leaving only the cushions.

Lizard came out of the kitchen and passed me a can of Coke and a bunch of wrinkled paper Subway napkins. "I don't have any Kleenex."

I blotted my face and blew my nose. "Sorry. It's just really important that I find Nicole."

"I wasn't lying. I don't know where she is exactly. Nicole went to Europe a few weeks ago. She'll be back when the cash runs out, by next fall at the latest. She's only got a couple of terms left."

Fall? No way could I wait until next September. "Do you know this girl?" I fumbled for the picture and passed it over. "Someone told me that she was staying here with Nicole."

Lizard looked at the picture. "Nicole put flyers up around town looking for people to share her room. It was part of her plan to raise some cash for her trip. This girl might have stayed here for a bit." He looked over at me. "We've got eight people on the lease, but people always have friends over or people they're hooking up with stay the night. There are a lot of people in and out of here. Sorry." He shifted in front of me. I could see that his toenails were way too long, like claws. "You wanna see Nic's room? She cleaned it out, but there were a few things left behind. I haven't been able to get anyone in there 'cause the term's almost over. Maybe there's something that belonged to your friend."

I nodded. Lizard motioned for me to follow him down the hall, and he opened a door. There was a small room with two twin mattresses on the floor. Someone had tacked a cheap Indian-print scarf done in blues and blacks to one wall and a print of Klimt's *The Kiss* on the other. The closet door was open, empty except for a bunch of wire hangers and a pair of cheap flip-flops on the floor. I wandered over and looked over the desktop. There were a couple of paperback books, a few loose sheets of notebook paper, a couple of pens, and an empty Diet Coke can. Then I saw it. I snatched it up. It was a half-full bag of Glitterati hard candy. Brit was addicted to the tiny Italian fruit candy. I was never sure if it was that she really liked them that much or if she liked being the kind of person who had imported candy—no Jolly

Ranchers for her. They weren't a common candy. It meant she *had* to have been here. I poured six pieces out of the bag and put them into my pocket like a sugary talisman. She'd been here, all right, and if she had amnesia she still at least remembered her favorite snack foods.

I looked around. No wonder Brit came back. She'd taken a bunch of cash with her when she left town, but she'd probably spent it quickly. She's a girl used to having unlimited access to her daddy's credit card. I was willing to bet she'd stayed in a hotel for a few nights when she first took off. I could picture her wrapped up in a fluffy bathrobe watching movies on cable, but it would have been clear that she couldn't afford to do that forever. That's when things would have gotten complicated. Britney couldn't use her own ID since she was supposed to be dead. She had Beth's, but she had to be careful because she couldn't have anyone looking at it too closely. It made getting a legit job difficult and her escape plan nearly impossible.

"Do you have *any* contact info on Nicole—maybe an email or something?" I asked.

Lizard got up and dug his phone out of a pile on the table. "Yeah, I can give you that." He read her address out to me. "Thing is, I'm not sure how much she's checking it. Do you know Nic at all?"

I shook my head. "No."

"Nic's cool, but she's weird." He seemed completely

unaware that since he went by the name Lizard and had homeless man–like toenails it was a bit ironic that he was calling anyone else odd. "She's an aspiring writer. She wanted to take this trip with no access to social media as some kind of statement."

"Statement of what?"

Lizard rolled his eyes. "She was always talking about how we were all turning into technology's whores and how we've lost the ability to be in the moment." He waved his hand to indicate that he'd blanked out whatever else Nicole had said on the topic. "She was going to write about the isolation of travel being freeing to find your true self, blah blah blah. Like that chick who walked that trail in California and then wrote a book."

"Well, thanks for this anyway." I held up the slip of paper I'd written the email address down on.

Lizard walked me to the door. "I hope you find your friend."

I smiled. I shoved Nicole's address in my pocket. She was my best hope of an answer. Sooner or later she'd have to check her email. Brit might have pretended she was Beth while she was here, but I didn't think she could keep up the act 24/7. Somewhere she would have slipped up. Called herself Brit. Talked about her real life. Mentioned her boyfriend, Jason, or the names of her parents. Made a mistake. Her roommate would be the best person to spot that something about her story was off. Once I had her to prove that

Brit hadn't been some confused amnesic, I could start tearing her story apart, eroding her lies, letting her fall.

I stood with Nadir in the center of the packed Student Union food court.

"Did you find anything?" he asked.

"Not as much as I hoped," I answered honestly, not thinking about retail shopping the way he was. "But it was still worth the trip."

"Of course it was—you got to see me," Nadir said. His nose twitched in the air as he surveyed the different counters.

"I thought we were going to Crunchy's for burgers later," I said.

"Yeah, but study group made me hungry. It's all the brainpower being used." Nadir tapped the side of his skull. "It's like I've got my own thermonuclear reactor up here."

I rolled my eyes. "Uh-huh."

"How about ice cream?" Nadir pointed. "Just to tide us over."

I hadn't actually eaten at El Az, and I was hungry. My stomach growled, and that settled things. We walked up to the case with the frozen tubs encrusted in frost and Nadir instantly ordered his usual, vanilla. Thirty-one flavors and the guy got vanilla every single time. I perused the case, considering my options. I needed to go with two scoops just to cover my bases.

"Hey, isn't that your friend Britney?"

I spun around and looked out over the concourse. Panic flooded my system. There was a girl with long blond hair moving away from us. I couldn't see her face. I pushed past Nadir and tried to get a better look. Had Brit followed me down here? There was a group of students passing through and I had to fight the urge to shove them out of the way. The girl was way in front of me now, mixing with the crowds. I was losing her. I broke through a pack of girls at the top of the stairs and my eyes scanned the giant lobby. There were clusters of students on the sofas talking, a few were watching a volleyball game on the big-screen TV, and even more were sprinkled around with books and laptops, trying to cram. I couldn't see the girl anymore.

Nadir walked up to my side. "Where are you going? I thought you wanted ice cream."

"Are you sure it was Brit?" I asked.

Nadir's eyebrow arched. "I don't know, she just sorta looked like her. What's the big deal?"

I wanted to grab his shirt and shake him. "I need to know if it was her." My phone buzzed.

It was a text from Brit.

Hope u r having fun with grandparents.

A clammy sweat broke out all over my body. I searched the room but didn't see her. I typed back.

Hope your weekend is good too.

Not same w/out u! Gotta run xo

I swallowed hard. It might just be a coincidence. Nadir hadn't been positive it was her. If it had been her she would have confronted me. But what if she had been awake the night of prom and seen me find the apron? She would have been waiting for me to ask her about it and when I didn't she would know I didn't believe her lies. And if she knew that, I had no idea what she might do.

CHAPTER FOURTEEN

I lurked around the halls Monday morning hoping to spot Brit. I was almost certain Nadir hadn't actually seen her in East Lansing, but I wasn't positive. If she thought I'd lied to her she was going to be pissed. I'd prepared a story to cover my ass if needed, but it was a pretty weak lie. I chewed my thumbnail and craned my head down the hall, looking for her.

"Kah-bear!" Brit tackled me from behind in a hug. I almost stumbled to the floor. "I missed you."

I turned around. "Hey." I searched her face to see if she was ticked, but she looked relaxed and happy. Really happy. "You're in a good mood," I said.

Brit winked. "I got a feeling today's going to be a good day."

"Why?"

Brit shrugged, but the corners of her mouth kept twitching up. The bell rang and people began to rush to class. Brit leaned forward and gave me a loud smacking kiss in the center of my forehead. "Catch ya later."

As she walked away I let out the breath I'd been holding. It hadn't been her. That was a relief, but the fact I was paranoid for nothing wasn't good. Things in my life were bad enough without me making them worse by picturing Brit popping up here and there.

By second period, I found out why Brit was in such a good mood.

There are few things that spread around a high school faster than really great gossip, unless of course it also includes nude photos.

"If I had her mismatched nipples, I wouldn't send anyone pictures," Melissa said over lunch, earning a bunch of giggles from the crowd around our lunch table. "Seriously, did you see them? One of them is huge compared to the other. Nipple freak."

I stared down at my tray. I realized I'd been chewing the same mouthful of sandwich forever; it had turned to a thick paste. I struggled to swallow it down. Someone had

posted an ad on Craigslist on the weekend, supposedly from Sara, advertising her talents as a sex expert. Someone else had grabbed a screenshot of the ad, which included a photo, and spread it all over online.

The photo broke my heart. It was undeniably Sara. She was looking straight into the camera, her hands cupped under her breasts, offering them up. It could be seen as sexy, but I could tell she was shy. It was supposed to be a private photo. Sara must have really trusted someone to have sent it to them. Now every single person at Northside had seen it.

"They called her down to the office last period— technically sending that kind of thing is a felony," Kate said. "I bet she's in huge trouble. Can you imagine having to sit across from Hamstead and know he's seen your tits?" Kate shuddered.

"It's not like Sara posted the photo," I said. While the ad was written as if it were from her, it was obvious someone else had done it. And by *someone*, it had to be Brit. I wasn't sure how she'd gotten the photo, but this had her name written all over it. I'd hoped to catch her at lunch and ask her about it, but she'd had a student council meeting.

I had the urge to check my email again to see if I'd heard yet from Nicole. I'd sent two emails already, but so far radio silence. I needed Nicole to give me another lead I could follow up on, and the sooner the better. Leaked photos were just child's play to Brit. If Sara pushed back, or if Brit didn't

get the reaction she wanted, she might up the ante.

"If Sara didn't want her photo spread all over, maybe she shouldn't have taken it," Kate said.

"Spreading wide is apparently her talent," Melissa said, her voice dragging out the word *spread*, and everyone laughed. The cafeteria held at least a few hundred kids, and when I glanced around I was willing to bet at least 90 percent of them were talking about Sara. The room was full of an eager buzz, like when an orchestra builds to a big crescendo.

I wanted to point out that Sara wasn't the only one who'd taken a topless photo—she probably wasn't even the only one at this table. Sure, adults were always moaning about how digital mistakes took only a fraction of a second to make and a lifetime to regret, but people did it. Now everyone was acting like Sara had been discovered doing porn, versus being a nice band geek who'd sent a boob shot to her boyfriend. They had no idea of what the real stakes were.

I saw Jason slinking out of the cafeteria. A group of Sara's friends glared at him from their table. I mumbled an excuse to my group, but everyone was still too busy chewing over the scandal to notice when I slipped out after him. Jason must have given Brit the picture, and I wanted to know why he'd done it.

I turned the corner and then stopped short, backing up

so I wouldn't be seen. Sara had Jason up against the water fountain. She'd been waiting for him, or maybe she'd texted him to meet her.

"This is all going to blow over," Jason said to her.

"Easy for you to say—you're not the one being humiliated." Sara's voice was shaking, but I couldn't tell if it was from anger or tears. I lurked in the alcove that held a display of band trophies so I could overhear what they said.

"What can I do to make it better?" Jason's voice was low and soothing.

"There's nothing that will make this better. Have you seen the stuff people have been saying about me?" Sara took a sobbing breath. "You need to tell Brit she's gone too far."

"Hey, there's no reason to think Brit was involved," Jason said. "I get that you don't like her, but she wouldn't do something like this."

Sara barked out a harsh laugh. "Are you kidding? I know she's responsible. She hates me; don't you get that? She's determined to ruin my life."

"Ease up. Brit's not like that."

"Are you blind?"

I peeked around the corner. Jason looked annoyed, and Sara's face was flushed red.

"Look, I know you're upset that we broke up, but don't take that out on Brit. If you want to blame anyone, blame me. The photo was on my phone. I should have deleted it, but I'd forgotten it was there. My phone is always in my bag in the gym. Someone must have seen the photo and done this as a joke." Jason held up both hands as if surrendering. "I'm not saying it's funny or should have been a joke, but I'm trying to point out that anyone could have done it."

Sara shook her head. "You're delusional. You've made Brit into something she's not. What happened to all your talk about how Brit was trying to run your life, decide your entire future?"

Jason ran his hand over his short-cropped hair. "Brit and I were having problems, but when I thought she was gone I realized that our problems were at least fifty percent my fault. I never told her how I felt."

"I don't even believe her whole *I lost my memory* bullshit. She's manipulating everyone now," Sara said.

I felt myself grow light-headed. Sara got it. She didn't know what I did, but she suspected. Was there any chance that she was the anonymous source to the reporter? I wanted to dash around the corner and hug her. I'd never been so grateful in my entire life to hear someone say something.

Jason grabbed Sara by the shoulders and shook her. "Stop it. It's one thing if you want to blame me, but if you start spreading lies about Brit over this photo, or about some paranoid theory you have about her, I will stop you. She's been through enough."

Sara looked at him as if she had no idea who he was. She pulled out of his grasp. "So you'll do whatever you have to so you can cover for her. No matter how it impacts me."

Jason drew himself up so he was even taller. "I'll do what I have to in order to protect her from false accusations. I'm serious, Sara, leave Brit out of this."

"She's the one who won't leave *me* alone." Sara shook her head. "Forget it. You can lie to yourself if you want. This is all about you feeling guilty that Brit supposedly was ready to kill herself over you."

"This is about you being pissed I got back together with her," Jason fired back.

"Don't be so arrogant as to think it's always about you."

"Whatever." Jason stepped around Sara and headed down the hall. "I came to tell you I was sorry about the photo, but if you're going to throw around blame then don't ask me to help you figure out who really did it."

"I don't need your help," Sara yelled after him. When she whirled around she saw me.

I stepped fully out of the alcove. We stood like gunslingers in an Old West movie, both of us waiting to see who might draw a gun first. I was bursting with everything I wanted to say. That I was sorry about the photos, that I was certain she was right and Brit was behind it, that Jason was an idiot and how I was so happy, thrilled, to discover there was someone else who saw the holes in Brit's story. If she was the source, maybe there would be a way we could work together. I opened my mouth, unsure what might actually come out, but Sara backed up quickly.

"You like sneaking around and spying?" Sara spit. "Go on, crawl back to her and tell her the whole thing. You're nothing but her lapdog." She stomped off down the hall, leaving me standing there.

Brit came up behind me and linked arms. "I'm starving. Let's get coffee and split one of those chocolate chunk cookies they have." Apparently her salad-only diet was a thing of the past. Being devious made a girl hungry.

I wriggled out of her embrace. Brit smiled and waved a hand at someone as crowds swarmed around and past us, everyone keen to get out of school and into the early summer sun.

"I told my mom I'd go home after school. She's got a bunch of chores I'm supposed to do," I said.

Brit waved off what I said as if it were the irritating buzz of an insect. "What are you, Cinderella? You can clean the kitchen later. Cookies call to us now. Besides, you were at your grandparents' all weekend. I miss you. I need me some Kah-bear time."

I trailed behind her. Our cars were parked next to each other in the front row of the student lot. Every morning the two places were left empty for us, no matter when we arrived, or how many other people were jockeying for the last few spots in the back row, which was studded with pot-holes and huge puddles. There was no official Reserved sign with our names on it, but there may as well have been.

Brit jumped into her SUV. "See you there."

She hadn't waited to see if I was going to insist that I had to do what my mom asked. There was a part of me that wanted to go straight home and blow her off, but another part had some questions.

Brit had snagged a table in the front, and she lifted her latte cup in greeting when I came in. I got some tea and dropped into the seat across from her.

"Cookies are in the oven," Brit said. My eyes glanced over at the half-full glass cookie jar by the register. "I asked them to make a couple fresh," Brit explained. "Is there anything better than when they're hot? Besides, after today, I need a cookie—hell, I deserve it. I made them make one for each of us so I don't have to share."

I slid my bag over so I could get my feet fully under the table. "What happened? I thought you were having a great day."

Brit shrugged. "I don't know, nothing really. It's just the last few days of my senior year are just slipping away, and it should be a big deal, but it feels . . . I don't know. Boring." She looked around and leaned forward. "Apparently my parents think my problem is that I need help to get past the trauma of what happened. They're making me see this stupid psychologist, Dr. Sherman."

My mouth went dry. That couldn't be a coincidence. "Why?" My voice came out as a squeak, and I had to clear my throat and start again. "Why don't your parents talk to you? Why make you see someone else?"

Brit smiled. "You don't have to look so serious. Seeing a counselor is no big deal—it's not like I've got cancer or something." She tucked her hair behind her ear. "My parents can't see me on a professional basis; it's not ethical. Like I'd talk to them about anything real anyway." She paused and I had the sense she wanted me to confess that I was seeing Dr. Sherman too, but there was no way for her to know. I couldn't believe with all the times that Dr. Sherman had mentioned Brit, she knew that Brit was a patient too.

"So . . . ," Brit said, her voice trailing off. My foot was tapping out beats of six under the table. If she asked me directly about Dr. Sherman, what would I say? Itchy hives broke out on my chest. "So . . . do you think I've been acting weird since I've been back?" Brit asked.

It took me a second to realize what she'd asked. Acting weird? She'd killed her best friend, faked her own death, and was now covering the whole thing up like nothing had happened. *Weird* wasn't a big enough word to cover it. I bit the inside of my lower lip. "I guess a few times you've seemed on edge."

Brit sighed. "Maybe they're right. Ever since . . . ever since I've been back, things have been hard. Some days I feel like I'll start screaming with how dull things are."

"What about what happened today with Sara?" I asked. "That's not dull."

"I did it, you know," Brit said. I almost dropped my cup in shock. I never expected her to admit anything—maybe hint at responsibility, but I'd been sure she'd deny it. She laughed at my openmouthed expression. "Did you see the photo? It was brilliant."

"You made it go viral?"

"I put the picture on Craigslist, but it took on a life of its own from there." Brit leaned back and turned on her thousand-watt smile for the coffee clerk who was delivering a plate with two steaming cookies to our table. "Thanks so much," she gushed. She waited until he went back to the counter. "It warms my heart to think of hordes of loser geeks and stoners whacking off to her photo." She broke off a corner of the cookie and popped it into her mouth.

"I heard Sara freaked out," I said.

"If she's going to act like a slut, I don't know why she cares if everyone knows. She didn't have any problem sending Jason the photo. She likes to show off her boobs; all I did was help her get some extra attention."

I bought myself a second by sipping my tea. "How did you get the photo?"

"I went through Jason's phone." Brit licked a smear of chocolate off her finger. "Clearly, I was far too trusting before. You'd better believe I'm checking his phone on a regular basis now. I forwarded the photo to myself and uploaded it to Craigslist on one of the computers at the Apple Store at the mall Friday after school."

"What if Jason finds out?"

Brit rolled her eyes. "It wouldn't even occur to him. Just in case, I made sure to delete the email to myself."

"Maybe you should just let all of this go," I said.

Brit put her cup down hard on the table. "She stole Jason from me."

I considered pointing out Jason hadn't exactly been kidnapped. "But you've won. You've got him back."

"That's not enough," Brit snapped. "Sara has to know she can't just do something like that, not to me."

I glanced down and realized that Brit's nails were still chewed down to the quick and she'd chewed a strip of flesh from the side of her thumb. The skin was an angry red and puffy. "Maybe you should talk about it with Dr. Sherman," I suggested.

She threw her head back and laughed. "You're right, I should." She winked. "But I might keep my plans for Sara just between us."

"What else are you going to do?" I asked her.

Brit rolled her head in a circle to loosen the tightness in her neck. "I don't know; that's my problem. I thought the photo thing would make more of a splash."

"Everyone's talking about it," I said. That was the truth, and it was disgusting.

Brit sighed. "Yeah, but I still think I can come up with something better. I hate her," she said.

"I guessed that," I said dryly.

Brit laughed again. She handed me the other cookie and then tapped hers against mine as if we were toasting. "You know me too well."

We each took a bite. She was right. I knew every dark corner of her soul. The question was, how far would she go?

CHAPTER FIFTEEN

I hesitated in the doorway. When I was called down to Ms. Harding's office, I knew it wasn't going to be good news. There was no chance I'd been made student of the month and they just wanted to get a quick photo of me for the school paper. Sara and Brit were sitting across from Ms. Harding, their chairs pulled as far apart as the small office would allow. I wanted to back out and maybe pretend I'd never gotten the note or perhaps had gotten lost coming from calculus. That's when Ms. Harding saw me and waved me in.

"Thanks for coming, Kalah," she said. I shifted my books to the other arm and tried to act like I wasn't suffocating from the tension in the room. "I'm hoping you can help us clear up something."

"Will you tell the truth?" Sara asked. She was searching my face as if she could peel the skin off and see the thoughts in my head.

"Of course she'll tell the truth. Do you think I hang out with liars?" Brit asked.

"Girls." Ms. Harding stopped their sniping with the one word and turned to me. "I'm sure you'll be honest, Kalah, but I want to start by making sure you know how serious Northside takes this situation."

I thought about asking what situation she was talking about, but I figured playing dumb wasn't going to help. "Sure," I said.

"These types of photos are technically considered child pornography. It's a felony. Our issue is less the legal standing—we'll leave that to the police—instead we want to focus on the amount of damage that the release of these can cause. However, you should know sending them is a crime," Ms. Harding said.

"The only person I sent it to was my boyfriend. It was private," Sara said.

"Nothing about digital photos is private," Brit said. She smiled at Ms. Harding sweetly. "I remember the assembly we had last year, and you talked about how all that online stuff is forever."

Sara's jaw tightened. "That assembly also covered cyber-bullying," she said. "Do you remember that part?"

Brit looked innocent. "Of course, but I keep telling you, I'm not the one who posted the picture."

"Then who did?"

Brit shrugged like the entire situation was a mystery to her. "I have no idea. How many people did you send it to?"

Sara's mouth pursed and Ms. Harding raised a finger to stop her from whatever she was about to say. "I think that's a bit unfair, Britney. Sara has been very clear that the only person she shared that photo with was Jason. Mr. Hamstead and I have both talked extensively with him and we're certain he wasn't the one who posted it, and he denies sharing it with anyone."

"Of course he didn't." Brit huffed as if she found it insulting that she would date someone capable of such cruel acts.

Ms. Harding continued as if she hadn't heard Britney. "The original Craigslist ad shows what time the ad was posted, and we know for a fact Jason was at his part-time job during that time. The police checked with his supervisor."

"See?" Brit said to Sara. "Are you happy now?"

"I never thought Jason posted it. I know you're responsible. I don't know how you got the picture, but I know you did." Sara's hands were clenched in her lap as if it was taking everything she had to keep from reaching across and slapping Brit.

"My hope is that we can clear this up," Ms. Harding said. "Kalah, Britney said she was with you last Friday around three."

"We were going over equipment for the field hockey team," Brit said. "I told you that we needed to do an audit so we can figure out if there's stuff we need to replace for next year."

"Stop feeding her your story," Sara said.

The three of them turned to face me. My tongue felt huge and heavy in my mouth. "Um," I managed to push out. Sara leaned forward as if she wanted to hear what I had to say first. Brit was leaning back in her chair, like she didn't have a single worry.

"Do you remember what time you and Britney were together?" Ms. Harding asked. I noticed that she assumed that Brit's story was at least partly true. She was wrong. I'd never known Brit to do any kind of equipment audit. That kind of thing was something she'd make the freshmen do. Friday I'd gone straight home since I was taking off for East Lansing the following morning.

"Right after school on Friday," I lied. The words tasted sour in my mouth, but I had no choice. "We were going to do it on the weekend, but I had to go see some family." I had to keep Brit on my side. Admitting that I wasn't with her wouldn't even be enough to prove she'd posted the picture of Sara. Brit would insist she must have just mistaken the time; she'd find another way to wiggle out of it. I would lose the advantage of keeping Brit close, and for nothing. It also put Sara at risk because she would keep pushing. If she lost here and now, maybe she would back down. Sara would never believe me, but I was doing her a favor. I had to back up Brit's story even if it meant lying.

Sara stared at me. "I should have known you'd lie for her." A wave of shame crashed over me.

Brit sat up straight. "That's slander. Say what you want about me, but if you start calling my best friend names, then we're going to have trouble. My family has a lawyer."

Ms. Harding's hand waved in the air like she was trying to clear it of smoke. "Okay, there's no reason to allow things to become heated."

Sara seemed to have shrunk since I'd lied, as if all the fight had gone out of her and she was deflating. "Fine. Whatever," she said.

"I didn't want to bring this up, but I think I have to," Brit said. She pressed her lips together as if there was a painful secret wanting to escape. "I hate to even say it, but given that Sara's now willing to attack my best friend I have no choice. . . ." Her voice trailed off.

Ms. Harding's eyebrows were scrunched together. "Go on, Britney."

Brit sighed. "I think it's possible Sara put her own pictures online." She looked down at her nails. "The picture is Photoshopped. It makes Sara look thinner." She shrugged. "Who else would do that except someone who wanted to make sure Sara looked good?"

"Are you crazy?" Sara looked back and forth between Ms. Harding and me, hoping we'd see that Brit had gone around the bend. "Why would I humiliate myself?"

Brit picked at her thumbnail. "I know you hate me because Jason chose me."

"How I feel about you has nothing to do with what happened to me," Sara said.

"I think you thought if you did this Jason would feel guilty and come back to you," Brit said. "Plus, you could blame me. Attention and a chance to strike out—I mean, it makes sense. You've already pointed out that you and I aren't friends. There would be no reason for me to make you look better in a picture. That's pure vanity."

Ms. Harding glanced over at Sara as if seeing her for the first time. I could practically see the idea turning over in her mind. Jesus, Brit was good. Not only was she going to get away with this, she was going to manage to convince everyone Sara was nothing but a vindictive attention whore.

"That's absurd," Sara said. "I didn't do this. I would never have posted that picture."

Ms. Harding laced her hands together and put them on her desk. "I think what we can all agree on is that Kalah has verified Britney's story. If the two of them were together in the equipment room, then she couldn't have been the one to post the fake advertisement."

Sara's eyes were filling with tears. She didn't point out

the million flaws with that explanation. Brit could have convinced someone else to post the pictures while she was with me as her alibi. The two of us could have posted them together from the equipment room. Or the truth: that Brit had made her entire story up and I was all too willing to lie right along with her. Guilt squatted heavy and dull in my stomach. I hated who I was becoming.

"Britney, you and Kalah are free to go. Sara, why don't you stay so we can talk further?" Ms. Harding had on her calm counseling face. I bet as soon as we were gone she was going to tell Sara it was okay for her to admit that she'd done it.

I glanced back at Sara as we left, but she wouldn't look at me. I'd let her down. She must have hoped when pushed I'd tell the truth, but she had no idea what we were up against. I wanted to tell her that I would make it up to her when I could, but proving what Brit had done to Beth was more important than what had happened to her. Sara could survive a few embarrassing pictures. Beth hadn't survived her conflict with Brit.

Unless . . .

I stared at Sara. Her mouth was set in a tight line. She was barely holding it together. What would she do if Brit kept this up?

As soon as we closed the office door behind us, Brit linked arms with me. She pulled me along down the hall, practically skipping. When we rounded the corner Brit stopped and leaned against the lockers.

"Oh my god, did you see her face when I suggested she did it?" Brit laughed. "That may have been the best moment *ever.* It made it worth it to make her a bit thinner. You could tell she never saw that coming."

"I'm sure she didn't," I said.

"I knew you'd back me up. I meant to tell you yesterday when we went out, but I forgot and then I couldn't find you at lunch today."

"I was in the library," I said. "Trying to cram for finals."

Brit made a gagging sound. "Ugh, finals. I'm so over school. What's the point? I've already been accepted to Cornell. Are they really going to rescind their offer if my spring grades aren't stellar?"

"Not studying isn't really an option for me," I said. "I haven't even started applying yet. It doesn't help that my grades took a hit with everything that happened."

Brit ignored my worries. My grades weren't her problem. "You should apply to Cornell in the fall. Wouldn't that be amazing if you went?" Brit's eyes were shining. "We could be roommates in a year, maybe get a cute apartment off campus somewhere."

The idea of being trapped with Britney forever was terrifying. "I thought you wanted to get an apartment with Jason. You used to talk about it all the time," I said.

Brit sighed. "I'm glad Jason and I were together for prom, but I don't know. . . ." Her voice trailed off as if she couldn't even be bothered to finish the thought.

What do you mean you don't know? I wanted to scream in her face. She'd turned me into a liar, and she didn't even want him.

"I'm not sure. I know it's horrible. I was in love with him forever, and when I thought I'd lost him it felt like my heart was being ripped out, but now that we're back together it feels like . . . I don't know, flat." Brit chewed absently on her thumbnail.

"Flat?" My voice rang with disbelief. She'd killed Beth over him, and now the relationship wasn't exciting enough for her.

"Given everything that's happened you'd think that it would take our love to the next level, but it's the same as before. It's like nothing happened. He still kisses the same. He still says he loves me to the moon and back, which, by the way, is a line he totally stole from a Hallmark card. He's still thrilled for us to spend a Saturday night seeing some lame superhero movie and then hanging out with his friends." Brit's expression broadcast what she thought of these social plans. She fidgeted as if she couldn't get comfortable. "What I went through changed me. I realize I'm the kind of person who will do anything for the people in my life and I think I deserve someone who will do anything for me too."

"What do you want him to do differently?" I asked her.

"That's the problem. I can't figure it out. It's like that feeling when something doesn't fit you—maybe the sleeves are too tight or the waist is high, or maybe the tag is scratchy, but you can't stop fidgeting with it. My life feels like that: not quite right."

I knew what she meant. My life hadn't been right since Beth had disappeared. I never felt settled or really at rest. "I get that," I said.

Brit smiled. "I knew you would. This is why we're best friends, because you get me."

My brain was spinning through this new information. Her words bounced around inside my head. It was like nothing made her happy. She hadn't been happy, so she'd taken off, but being dead hadn't met her expectations so she'd come back. But now that wasn't working out either. "But if you're over Jason, why do you care what happens to Sara? I mean, the way you twisted it so it looked like she was the one who posted the photo for attention was cold. Heartless." Once I asked the question I wanted to take it back. Brit was going to be pissed, but instead of the tight wrinkle forming between her eyes, she broke into a laugh and hugged me.

When I'd first become friends with Brit, I would have done anything for her to embrace me like this. To feel that I really belonged. She started back down the hall, linking arms again. "In order to really make someone pay, to get them like I got Sara, you have to be cold. You have to divorce yourself from feeling so you can focus."

Did she mean she didn't feel anything? I nodded like I agreed with her.

Brit clutched my arm even tighter. "It's like ever since I came back things are so much clearer. I used to spend all this time worrying about what other people thought, or about how to make my parents happy, but what I realized is that it doesn't matter. Who gives a shit? All those times I was upset it didn't make a difference. When I clear my head of that stuff, it is like I can see what I need to do, and it's so much easier. I think I was always like this. I tried to fit in, to be what people wanted, but I couldn't because I wasn't wired that way." She seemed relieved to have this out. As if she'd admitted a sin and could be forgiven. Except she didn't seem remotely sorry. "Now I don't worry about their feelings and instead focus on how they're like a puzzle I need to solve to get what I want."

I felt a shiver down my spine. Did she mean for me to know this about her? Was it a threat—a way of subtly letting me know she could cut me off as easily as she had anyone else—or was it mistake? "I suspect you can do anything you put your mind to," I said.

Brit stopped and spun me so we were facing. Her eyes were really bright and she looked almost ready to cry. "You really understand me," she said.

"Of course," I said. "We're best friends. You're my Brit-bear," I added, trying to lighten the mood.

"I'm so sick of having to hide who I really am. I tried forever to be this perfect Britney, the daughter my parents wanted, the girlfriend Jason wanted, the captain the team wanted, and even the friend that Beth wanted. I think if they knew how I really felt they would be disappointed."

"No one could be disappointed in you," I said.

"The thing is, I'm learning that I don't care if they are or not. I mean, it never really mattered, other than I felt somehow ashamed of how I was." She looked away.

"And you're not ashamed anymore?"

"Nope. People like my parents and Jason are so worried about doing the right thing, about making sure that everyone approves of every little thing they do, it's like they're afraid to go after what they really want. They'll always have these small little lives because they don't let themselves do what they need to."

I stopped at the intersection of the hall. "I have to get back to calculus."

Brit winked. "Are you sure you don't want to skip? Your teacher will think you're still down in Ms. Harding's office."

"I'd better not," I hedged. "If I get busted, my parents will kill me."

"C'mon, let's go. We'll have fun."

I knew she wanted me to join her, but I couldn't stand to be with her anymore. "If I'm going to get into Cornell so we can be roomies, I've got to go back so I can nail the exam."

Brit poked my upper arm with her bony finger. "Fine,

I'm letting you off this time, but you'd better get an A."

"Cross my heart," I said, trailing my finger in an X over my chest. I turned and walked back to class. I wanted to turn around and make sure Brit wasn't following me, sneaking up on me, but I suspected if I did she would know what I was thinking. She would see it as a win for her. I steeled my shoulders and walked slowly and deliberately back to class, not turning around once.

CHAPTER SIXTEEN

When I opened my front door, I was so shocked at who was there that I dropped the half-eaten apple that had been in my hand. It landed on the front stoop with a wet smack and rolled to rest against Zach's foot.

"Sorry about that," I said. I bent over and picked up the apple. There were pine needles stuck to it. "I wasn't expecting you." I felt flustered, almost how I felt around him when we first started dating. I'd trip over myself or knock things off tables with my elbows. Once I laughed at something he said while eating lunch and shot a clot of yogurt out of my nose. Eventually I relaxed, but now I was back to feeling awkward every second.

"I need to talk to you, just us." Zach had his hands

jammed deep in his pockets and was shifting from foot to foot.

I stepped back. "Okay, sure, come on in."

Zach looked surprised, like he'd expected us to have the discussion standing in front of my house. For a second I thought he might refuse, but then he wiped his feet on the mat and followed me in. I sat on one of the stools at the kitchen island and Zach took the seat opposite of me. It was stiff and formal.

"Do you want something to drink?" I asked. "My mom made homemade lemonade last night, and I'm pretty sure there's some left." I started to stand, but he waved me back down.

"No, I don't want anything." He wiped his hands on his pants. He glanced around. "Are your parents home?"

"No, they're both at work." I wished he'd asked for a drink just so I would have something to do with my hands. They seemed stuck on the ends of my arms with no purpose. He'd given me the cold shoulder at school for so long I'd forgotten how to talk to him. "You ready for exams?" I finally asked to break the silence.

"Did-you-have-anything-to-do-with-what-happened-to-Sara?" Zach said, the words spilling out all over each other. I sensed he'd been saving it up to ask me for the past two days.

"Why would you think that?" I tucked my hair behind my ears and tried to lean casually against the counter. His accusation put me off balance.

"I know how Brit feels about her, and I know she's your best friend." Zach kept eye contact with me, like he was some kind of CIA operative trying to interrogate a hostile witness, assuming government agencies wore *Firefly* T-shirts. I supposed it wasn't an outlandish guess. Everyone knew that Brit blamed Sara for what had happened with Jason.

"Sounds like you need to talk to Brit about all of this," I said.

"I'm not asking Brit, I'm asking you. Did you have anything to do with that photo?"

I swallowed hard. I had no idea why he thought I was involved. "Do you think I could do something like that?" I looked down and realized I was still holding on to the grimy apple. I stood up, glad to have a distraction, and put it in the trash. I ran to the giant farmhouse sink and washed my hands. It felt good to break eye contact with him.

"I'm not sure what you're capable of doing anymore." I think he wanted it to come across as cruel, but it sounded more lost and sad.

I grabbed a towel and sat back down. "I don't know how many times you want me to say I'm sorry, but I am."

"This isn't about you and me. This is about Sara. She's a good person. She didn't deserve this. Can you imagine? Every step she takes down the hall, she knows everyone has seen that picture. People are writing all sorts of nasty shit about her, leaving notes in her locker, whispering."

I shifted on the stool. I didn't like thinking about Sara. "It's horrible, but what do you want from me?"

Zach slapped his hand down on the marble countertop, making me jump. "I want you to stop answering every question with another question!" Zach rubbed his face. "Do you even realize you're doing it? You haven't denied it since I got here. You've danced around it, but you haven't answered me. So yes or no, did you have anything to do with what happened to Sara?"

I swallowed hard. Lying to him was hard, but I hoped I could parse out enough to satisfy him. "I didn't post the picture."

Zach watched my face closely then slowly deflated. "You did have something to do with it."

I sighed and turned to get something out of the huge industrial fridge. I needed time to think of something to say. It felt as if I'd wandered out onto paper-thin ice. "I just told you I didn't post the picture."

"But you didn't deny you were involved. Don't you see how you've changed?" Zach's voice was almost a wail. "It's bad enough, but if you can't even see it, that's worse."

I was leaning toward him. I could feel the truth rising in my throat, wanting out, straining.

"Her friends are worried that Sara is so upset she could hurt herself."

My mouth slammed shut. Nothing would make Brit happier than if she drove Sara to suicide, the ultimate revenge. A prickle of unease ran down my spine—was that her plan? And if she could do that Sara, what would she do if she thought Zach was out to get her? I couldn't tell him. She couldn't see him as a target.

I put my palms down on the counter and leaned across. "Do you want me to deny it? I will. I didn't have anything to do with what happened to Sara." I could hear my heart thumping in my chest sounding like *I'm lying, I'm lying, I'm lying* to me.

Zach searched my face.

"Do you believe me?" I asked.

Zach was silent for a beat, and then he shook his head. "You're not being truthful."

Relief that I wasn't a great liar was mixed up with anger that he didn't take my word, and the two emotions swirled together in my stomach.

"Why are you doing this? This isn't like you," Zach said. He reached over and touched my arm. "You never used to be someone who would hurt people."

"If you're not going to take me at my word, maybe you should leave." I fussed with my parents' giant stack of cookbooks on top of the counter until they were in a tidy pile. I picked at a crusty blob of something that had dried on the cover of the top book. "I think we both need some time." When this situation was all over, I'd explain it to Zach. That yes, I had been involved with what happened to Sara, but I had to be, at least until I had proof. As soon as I heard back from Nicole I could take action, but there was nothing I could do now other than stay close to Brit. I didn't have a choice. With any luck he'd understand. Sometimes the end does justify the means.

Zach stood. "I don't need time. I don't want anything to do with you."

A hot wave of anger poured through me. No one appreciated what I was doing—how I was keeping them safe, even though it cost me. "You can save your dramatic lines for the stage."

"I don't even know you," Zach said.

"Maybe you never did," I shot back. Even as the words left my mouth I wanted him to know I didn't mean it. Zach knew me almost better than anyone, and if he didn't see that core still in me, the good part, then I worried nothing was left. I was turning into Brit, having to shut down emotion so I could maintain my focus. If I didn't resolve things soon, I ran the risk that there would be nothing of the real me left, just a hollowed-out rock-hard shell.

"Guess not." Zach turned and walked out. I half expected him to slam the door, but it shut with a quiet click.

I picked up a water glass from the counter and hurled it onto the floor, shattering it against the tile. I stood over it, almost panting with anger when the back door opened. I spun around to scream at Zach, but it was my mom. Her hands were full of grocery bags.

"Hey, was that Zach I saw leaving?" She placed the bags

on the counter. "I hope you invited him to stay for dinner. Even if you two aren't going out he's still always welcome. Who else will listen to your dad blather on about his robots? Remember that time—"

"Careful," I said, cutting her off. She followed my gaze to the floor, where the broken glass sparkled in the late-afternoon sun. "It was an accident," I said. What was one more lie?

Mom leaned over and kissed my forehead. "It's good to know you got some lack of coordination from your dad and me. I'll clean that up if you get the last few bags from the trunk." She was already unrolling a wad of paper towels to pick up the shards.

"I can do it," I said. "You don't have to clean up my mess."

Mom looked over at me, and I realized how sharp my words had come out. "It's fine. I don't mind. Moms are masters at picking up messes." She bent down. "Did you and Zach have a fight?" Her voice was tinged with sympathy.

I closed my eyes and wished I could just disappear. I wanted her to be angry with me too. It was easier than when people were kind. "Sort of," I admitted. "He's never forgiven me for things with Beth."

The pieces of glass made a tinkling sound as she dropped them into the trash. "One of the hardest things to understand is that when we make a choice we have no control over how other people will feel about that decision."

"So what do you do?"

She smiled at me. "You make the best choice you can and take comfort in that." Mom motioned to the garage. "Bring in those bags. I bought ice cream and it's going to melt."

I left her to finish cleaning up. I'd made the only choice I could, but I didn't have any comfort in it. My only hope was to hear from Nicole while there was still enough of the real me left to salvage.

CHAPTER SEVENTEEN

I took a deep lungful of air and felt muscle memory clicking in. My arms and legs moved together, passing the ball up field and then racing to keep pace with Kate. At times like this I felt like a Swiss watch, gears and cogs clicking together, perfectly balanced, doing what I was designed to do. Flawless. The constant noise and buzz in my head quieted down when I ran. The barrage of what-ifs and thoughts of Beth and Britney stopped bouncing around and were finally silent. The voluntary off-season spring practices were the only thing holding me together some days.

I heard someone cheering for me and I reached deep, pushing myself to run faster, to get ahead of the play. My thighs burned with the effort, but I could see how it was going to unfold. I didn't even have to look; I could sense Kate winding up for a shot. My stick met the ball and without a pause to overthink the angle, I fired it off the goal. It went right high side and slammed into the back of the net. My squad cheered, and I raised my stick in the air like it was a bow and fired an imaginary arrow into the sky. This was something I could still do well. This was still a connection to who I had been before all of this started.

I felt closer to Beth when I was on the field. I used to love to watch her play: not only was she good, but you could see that she loved it. As much as I hated to admit it, she and Brit had worked well together on the field, and it was sports that had brought them together. Beth told me they became friends in elementary school when Brit slammed her in the face with one of those red rubber balls used for kickball. Beth had been so mad she'd punched Brit. Somehow that seemed to summarize their entire friendship. Competitive.

Brit blew her whistle. "Nice play," she called out.

I jogged off to let the next line go on, high-fiving people as I went.

One of the sophomore players passed me a water bottle when I got back to the bench. "Great goal," she said.

I lifted the bottle like a toast and took a deep drink then wiped my mouth with the back of my hand. "Did you see Kate's pass? It was awesome. She was the playmaker there. If we keep up with those kind of passes, we'll be hard to beat." I'd learned this from Beth—if someone gave you a compliment, turn it to praise someone else. It made for a stronger team.

She nodded. "No other team is putting in this extra time. It's going to pay off. We're going to be a force next fall," she added. She bounced on her feet like she couldn't wait for the next season.

"We sure are." I couldn't even begin to imagine next year. Brit would be gone. She might be queen of the school now, but her reign came with a time limit: she was graduating soon. When I tried to picture my senior year it was a blank. There would still be the team, our chance to make state finals, college applications, and art class. It was as if I could see the individual puzzle pieces, but I couldn't put them together to make a picture. I shook my head and concentrated on the game.

A whistle blew on the play. I'd missed what happened, but my line was up again. As I jogged onto the field, Brit held up two fingers indicating she wanted to do a double back pass. I gave a curt nod so she knew I'd seen it.

Brit got the ball in the face-off, and once I knew she had control I put on the speed. Amy cut me off as I ran toward the goal and my foot slipped on the grass, sliding off to the side. I didn't fall, but it slowed me down. Brit was under pressure too, and she stopped short, hitting the ball over to me. I stretched my stick out, trying to make it work, but I missed the pass.

Melissa stole the ball and took off to the other end of

the field. I spun so I could go on defense, but before I could catch her one of my line mates got her offsides before she could get close enough to take a shot. I stood with my hands on my hips and sucked in air, trying to get my breath.

Brit's stick tapped mine. Some of her hair had pulled free of her ponytail and was stuck to the side of neck with sweat. "You gotta pick up your game if you want me to trust you to take these guys to State next year!"

I nodded, still catching my breath. I didn't bother pointing out that her pass had been wide.

"No way Kalah was going to get that," Kate said, smiling. "The only one who could pull in those wild shots in was Beth. Hell, she was always making those impossible plays."

"Are you saying I'm not as a good a player as Beth?" Brit asked. Her eyebrows drew together.

"You can't be the best at everything," Kate shot back, laughing.

"Well, since you're so great at evaluating how the team is doing, maybe you should be captain." Brit held out her whistle to Kate.

The easy smiles that had been on everyone's faces dropped. The entire team was silent; the grumble of buses pulling out of the loop in front of the school was the only sound. A flicker of excitement rose in my chest. Brit was showing her true self.

"I was just joking," Kate said. "I didn't mean anything by it."

Brit looked around the circle and forced her face into what I think she hoped would pass as a smile. There it was: that slip of control, that flash of anger. This must be why her parents wanted her to see Dr. Sherman. "I was just joking too. Gawd." Brit pushed out a laugh. "What's with all the serious faces?"

"You know we all think you're the best for helping us prep for next year, right?" Melissa asked. A few of the sophomore girls were shifting back and forth like they were antsy ponies ready to bolt. This side of Britney made them uneasy. They were remembering that she wasn't always Miracle Brit, back from the dead. She had a nasty side.

Brit tossed her head. "I'm fine. It was just a joke. You guys used to have a sense of humor." She blew the whistle, but no one moved.

"Let's finish this game," I called out, clapping my hands together, and Brit shot me a look of gratitude.

Everyone jogged into place, but they moved slower than before, as if the fun had gone out of the game. A few people were exchanging glances. Amy mimicked Brit's head toss and Kate snickered. I kept my expression neutral as if I didn't notice. Brit was ahead of me and I could see her trying to joke around with the players near her, but I could sense their unease. The perfect princess was starting to crack.

CHAPTER EIGHTEEN

Brit jerked her chin toward the door of her basement suite. "Open the door. My hands are full." I glanced down; Brit had only one small bag. "You know the code, don't you?"

A blanket of frost crept across my heart. "Um, sure." I punched in the numbers and swung open the door. Should I have pretended I didn't remember the pass code? I stepped into the room. I jumped when Brit jerked open the blinds on the small windows by the door.

"Do you want something to drink?" Brit asked. She bustled past me and dumped her bag on the sectional.

I hadn't been in the room since I'd broken in when she was gone. At that time it had seemed like one of those museum rooms set up to look like the people had just stepped out, but strangely empty. Today it looked like it always had when we hung out there. There was a pair of Pink sweatpants draped over the arm of the sofa and an empty yogurt cup sitting on the coffee table.

"Sure," I said. I relaxed my shoulders. Being here made me nervous. I sat down on the couch. Brit had been vague about what she wanted but had insisted we come back to her place after school. The thought that no one else knew I was here skittered across my mind. I felt trapped in Brit's personal clubhouse.

I heard the gasp of the seal on the large walk-in wine cooler as it opened, and I flinched. I couldn't look at the cooler without thinking of Beth's body being dragged inside. Her corpse propped up in a corner like she was trash. I picked up the magazine that was next to me and quickly flipped through the pages, trying to get interested in the photos of celebrities who had made a bunch of fashion don'ts. Brit was silent and I suddenly became convinced that she was creeping up behind me with a bat to kill me like she'd killed Beth. I spun around and Brit took a quick step back. Instead of a bat there were two cans of Diet Coke in her hands.

"Jesus, you freaked me out." Brit stepped around the sofa and passed me a can.

"Thanks." I popped the top and took a deep drink, glad that at least my hands weren't shaking. Once I was sure I was in control of my voice I spoke. "So what's up? You said you wanted to talk."

Brit sighed. She reached into her bag and pulled something out. She placed it in the center of the coffee table, turning it so it was facing me. She sat across from me and waited for my reaction.

It was the *Drink Me* bottle I'd taken from this room when she was missing. At the time I'd wanted it because I knew it was Beth's and it seemed wrong to leave it here. I'd been storing the anti-anxiety pills that I hadn't been taking inside. I had hidden the bottle on top shelf of my locker, in a shoe box where I kept a spare set of runners, a place where my parents wouldn't stumble across it, but it hadn't occurred to me that Brit would go through my space.

My mouth was dry. I kept blinking as if the bottle might disappear. "Um," I didn't even know what to say.

"I went into your locker to get some gum," Britney said.

I swallowed hard. No way had she gone into my locker because she wanted a piece of Dentyne. She'd suspected I'd been hiding things from her, and now she knew it.

"That bottle was my birthday gift to Beth," she said. "I never had a chance to give it to her. The last time I saw it, it was here." Brit pointed at the bookshelf, her lips pressed primly together. "You can imagine how surprised I was to find it in your locker."

"I came here when you gone," I admitted. There was no

point in denying it: the proof was sitting right between us.

"Why? What were you looking for?"

I felt pinned in place. I wondered if we were talking about the bottle that was between us or if she had finally discovered that the apron wasn't exactly where she'd left it. "I wasn't looking for anything."

"How do you think I feel knowing you stole from me?" Brit asked.

I sat up straighter. "I didn't *steal* from you. When I took the bottle I thought you were dead."

Brit sniffed. "And that makes it okay? Is that why you wanted to do the auction? You couldn't find enough good stuff down here, so you wanted an excuse to get into my room and go through the rest of my things?"

Anger stiffened my spine. "I missed you. And Beth. I wanted to be here where we used to hang out. I know it was wrong to break in, but you don't get it. Both of you were gone, and I was on my own." I poked my finger at her. "You can sit there and judge me now, but you have no idea what it was like."

"That doesn't make it right to take things," Brit said.

"I came here because I was alone. I took the bottle because it reminded me of Beth. That's all it was."

Brit leaned back in her seat. "You don't need to be so hostile. I brought it up because I'm worried."

I let out a slow breath. "I'm sorry," I said.

"And I'm sorry you had to handle all of this on your

own, but what I hate is that we have these secrets between us. That you didn't tell me."

"I don't know why I didn't tell you," I said. "I came here because I wanted to make sense of things." I kept my gaze steady.

Brit picked up the bottle and shook out one of my pills into her palm. "I looked up what these are," she said.

I wanted to snatch the pills out of her hand, but there was no point. The cat was out of the bag. "I don't take them because I don't like how they make me feel. My parents don't know."

"These are pretty serious," she said.

"I see Dr. Sherman too." I watched her expression to try and see if she was shocked or if she already knew. "She prescribed them."

"Because of how you felt when you thought I was dead?" Brit cocked one eyebrow.

Did she really think everything was about her, or had she done her research and knew that these kinds of meds aren't for getting through a short-term crisis? I'd be better off to tell her the truth. Use it as a way to build her confidence back in me. The fact that she knew I'd been in her space when she hadn't been here made her uneasy.

"Partly," I said. "When you and Beth were both gone I started having trouble with anxiety, but I've had problems before. There was sort of a situation at my last school."

I wiped my hands on my cropped jeans. I didn't want

to tell her, but I didn't know how to get out of it. She would find some way to dig up the information if I didn't tell her. I gave her a short summary of what had gone down with Madison. "So when I'd lost you and Beth, I fell apart a little."

Brit moved so she was sitting right next to me and threw her arm over my shoulder. "You didn't have to keep this a secret."

"I didn't want anyone to know."

"You told Beth," Brit said. I jolted in my seat. "She told me, you know." I swallowed hard. Had Beth told her or was she only saying that now to cover herself? "You didn't feel like you could tell me?" Brit asked.

"It wasn't that," I said.

Brit turned, pulling her legs up under her on the sofa. "Do you understand how that makes me feel? We're supposed to be best friends, but I can't trust you."

"You can trust me," I pleaded. "I didn't tell you because I didn't want you to think less of me."

Brit's face softened. "Kah-bear, I would never think less of you because you needed help." She cocked her head to the side. "Did you forget what my parents do for a living? Or the fact I'm seeing Dr. Sherman myself? If anyone was going to understand, it would be me." She made a waving motion with her hand. "I'm dealing with my own things, after all." Brit let out an exaggerated sigh. "Well, I'm glad we cleared the air. I hated that there was all this between us."

I bit my tongue. "I'm glad too," I said.

"No more secrets, okay?"

"No more secrets," I echoed.

"Anything else I should know?"

I worried she could hear my heart beating through my chest. Maybe she actually knew that I'd found the apron. Maybe she *had* been in East Lansing too. But why hadn't she said anything?

"Nope," I said. "Any deep dark secrets you've been keeping from me?" I held my breath in the pause, the silence around us felt almost electric. What would I do if she actually whispered quietly that she'd killed Beth?

Brit smiled after a beat. "Why would I keep anything from my best friend? We are besties, right?"

"Of course," I said.

Brit thrust out her hand, her pinky crooked. "Pinky swear." She shook her finger waiting for me. "C'mon, it's a vow. I used to do this with Beth all the time."

I linked fingers with her.

"Best friends forever," Brit said.

"Forever," I echoed.

CHAPTER NINETEEN

"What's on?" I flopped on the sofa.

"True crime," Dad said.

My dad loved these shows. The ones where bad actors reenacted various villainous acts interspersed with moody shots of the real crime scenes. I watched an expert explaining how the blood evidence told them who the killer was. Seeing the still photos of the blood smear made me vaguely nauseated. I wondered if every time I saw a TV crime scene or read a mystery novel, my first thought would be wondering how it compared to Beth's death. I knew there was still evidence in Brit's basement that could be found if people just looked for it. If these shows had taught me anything, it was that murder was messy. You might think you'd cleaned up, but there was always still something to be found. "I like that they always catch the bad guy," I said to my dad.

"Truth is most of the time it's not too much of a riddle. When in doubt, it's almost always the spouse. The only ones who are really hard to catch are the sociopaths."

I sat up straighter. "Why?"

"They don't care." Dad popped a handful of pretzels into his mouth. "It's usually guilt that trips people up: they act in passion or rage and then make mistakes."

I turned over what he said in my mind. I'd tossed the term *sociopath* around before, I'd even thought of Brit that way, but I didn't really understand what it meant. It was a real condition, not just an insult. "What do you know about sociopaths?"

Dad leaned back as if he were about to give a lecture. "I have the vast knowledge of two psychology classes when I was in college." He winked. "And a total obsession with mystery novels and these shows. Basically, sociopaths, or psychopaths, have no empathy. It's like other people only exist for their amusement. They could hurt someone and not feel a shred of guilt."

"So they don't feel any emotion," I said.

"Not exactly. They aren't robots. They still can get angry or hurt, but it's like they never got out of the stage of thinking the world revolves around them. They forget that the rest of us are people too." Dad popped another handful into his mouth, crumbs and loose salt sprinkling down on his shirt. "It doesn't mean they would kill someone, just that if they did, it wouldn't bother them much."

Brit.

As soon as I could I sprinted upstairs to my room and my laptop. A half hour later I had over ten pages of notes on sociopaths and a serious case of the heebie-jeebies. There was research showing that one out of twenty-five people met the definition of *sociopath*. That meant Britney likely wasn't even the only one we had in our school.

Brit ticked off all the warning signs: lack of feelings of shame when they do something wrong, constant lying, charming, intelligent, manipulative, capable of violence, and huge ego. She was basically a poster child for the disorder. It wasn't just a term, it was a real condition, and I was certain she had it.

I was no closer to proving Brit had murdered Beth, but I still felt like I'd taken a step closer. I knew my enemy better. I checked my email account again, but there was still no message from Nicole. I was still counting on the fact that she would have seen something when Brit lived with her. Nicole was apparently still wandering around Italy or something acting out her own vapid version of *Eat, Pray, Love*. I was going to have to do something else if I wanted to move this forward, and knowing this about Brit had given me an idea.

I sat across from Dr. Sherman. I tapped the side of my chair in beats of six to keep myself calm. I had to wait for just the right moment to put my plan into action. It had to seem natural.

"Have you ever heard the term 'confirmation bias' before?" Dr. Sherman asked.

I shook my head. "No."

"A British psychologist, Wason, came up with the theory. It's the idea that even though we tend to think of ourselves as open-minded, it's human tendency to seek out evidence that supports what we already believe and either ignore or downplay information that disagrees with our belief structure."

"You think that's what I do?" I asked. "Why I don't always see things clearly?"

"I think most people do it. This bias is especially strong when the topic is something that is highly emotional, things like politics, or abortion, or a memory of a traumatic event—"

"Like Beth dying," I finished for her.

"Exactly. What I want you to understand is that this is science, not conjecture. We can see this bias show up on MRIs. We know that for some people, even if they are faced with proof that what they believe is wrong, it won't change their opinion. I think it would be useful to look at how things went with Madison again to question if you always saw those interactions clearly, or through a filter."

I shifted in my seat. I wish I could believe she was right, that I'd simply gotten a wrong idea in my head and was unable to let it go, and maybe even with Madison I had, but that wasn't what was happening now.

Or was it? I bit down inside my lip. It wasn't the first time that this had occurred to me. I'd always pushed away the thought.

But this time there were clear signs. If Brit hadn't killed Beth, then why had she run? I knew Beth had been over at Brit's the night she disappeared and Brit lied about it. I'd found Beth's sweater there. Britney had stacks of lies. The skin on the back of my neck prickled.

I *guess* all of that could be explained away and I just couldn't see it. Had my love for Beth, and my inability to let go of thinking about her, built up everything in my mind until it formed a huge blind spot? Did I have this bias that Dr. Sherman was talking about and not even know it?

"Kalah?"

I looked up. I'd lost track of what she was saying. "Sorry." I could see she was waiting for me to say something. I had to act now. The only way I was going to find out the truth was if I found it for myself. I pretended to lean forward as if I were about to spill my guts and deliberately knocked over the coffee I'd asked for at the start of the session, watching the liquid splash onto her cream silk blouse. Dr. Sherman jolted back, pulling the fabric away from her skin.

"Oh my gosh! I'm so sorry." I leapt to my feet and grabbed a wad of Kleenex, passing them to her.

"It's okay, accidents happen," Dr. Sherman said with a wince, blotting at her shirt.

"You should rinse it out so it doesn't stain," I said. I had to clench my fists so I wouldn't start tapping. I could see her hesitate—I was entitled to my fifty-minute session—but the desire to save a designer blouse was strong.

"I'll be just a minute." Dr. Sherman headed to the waiting room and the washroom just beyond.

As soon as the door clicked I remembered something else. I wasn't the only one who knew Brit was a liar. The reporter's anonymous source had seen her in Ann Arbor. That had nothing to do with me and gave me the assurance I needed that I wasn't crazy.

I bolted over Dr. Sherman's desk and sat in her chair. I yanked open the file drawer in the credenza. My heart was beating so hard it felt as if it were able to rip free of the arteries that held it in place and fly out into the room like some kind of disgusting alien creature from a sci-fi movie.

My fingers flew over the file tabs, searching for Britney's patient file. I had to see what Dr. Sherman had in there. There was a chance she had a diagnosis written down so I could confirm my suspicions. It was also possible that Brit had let something else slip, something that Dr. Sherman might not realize was important. I might resent Dr. Sherman at times, but she was good at wheedling things out of a person.

There was no file. But that wasn't possible. There had to be a patient file. Brit told me herself that she had been coming here. My eyes shot around the room, looking for some other place Dr. Sherman might possibly keep it.

Why would Brit tell me that she was seeing Dr. Sherman if she wasn't?

An ugly idea, like a malformed creature, began to dawn on me. I slammed the cabinet drawer closed and looked down at my own file, which was still on the desk. I swallowed hard and then made myself start flipping through the sheets.

Anxiety

Delusional pattern

Passivity

Destructive Tendencies

That's when I saw that Brit's file was tucked into the back of mine. I pulled it out, skimming the pages. There was a lot about posttraumatic reactions, but then my name on the page popped out at me.

Patient expresses concern regarding her relationship with Kalah. When pressed to describe the emotion, she states she is frightened and feels Kalah may be obsessed with her. Is Kalah repeating behaviors?

What had that bitch told Dr. Sherman about me?

"Kalah?"

I jumped. Dr. Sherman was standing in the door, her shirt wet, looking at me horrified. I looked down at the file as if I had no idea how it had gotten there. My tongue was stuck to the roof of my mouth. I slowly shut the file, tucking the pages inside. *Busted.*

When I walked into the house my mouth started watering at the smell. My mom had made her famous green curry. I thought all the acid in my stomach still rolling around from the conflict with Dr. Sherman would ruin my appetite, but my body betrayed me. I followed my nose in the kitchen and lifted the pan lid to give the sauce a stir.

"I've got some oven-roasted veggies to mix in. Do you still hate eggplant?" Mom asked as she looked up from the book she was reading at the counter.

I nodded.

Mom shook her head. "You get that from your dad."

"That's my girl," Dad said, looking up from where he was setting the big wooden table. "'Never trust an eggplant lover' is one of my mottos."

Mom threw a towel at him and motioned for me to scoop up rice for our plates. I knew my parents were working up to something. They were both geniuses, but they would score a zero on hiding what they were thinking. All through dinner they kept shooting glances at each other and then filling any silence gap with a bursts of random small talk.

"How was school?" my mom asked.

I took another bite of the curry. "Okay. Busy."

The two of them did another round of meaningful eye

contact. "How was your appointment?" Dad asked.

Ah, now we were getting down to things. Dr. Sherman must have called them as soon as my appointment ended. She had been alarmed when she caught me—for obvious reasons—and I knew she would contact them. She couldn't legally tell them what happened, but she could tell my parents she was worried about me. I knew she was going to, but I hadn't expected her to do it so quickly. "Fine." I rested my fork on the plate.

Dad took a deep breath. "I know we agreed that we would allow you to discuss anything with Dr. Sherman and that we wouldn't pry," Dad said.

There was a screaming, unsaid *but* hanging over the table.

"Dr. Sherman is concerned that you seem to be stuck in a negative spiral that's getting worse," Dad said.

I wound the napkin around my fingers under the table. Had she told them she'd caught me going through my own file, or had she been more vague? I didn't know what I should admit to, so I stayed silent and stared down at my plate.

"We're wanting to know if it's a good idea for you to hang out with Britney," my mom blurted out.

"Dr. Sherman indicated that she seems to be a big source of your stress," Dad said. "Maybe creating a bit of distance would be a good thing."

"It's okay," I said. "I don't want to avoid her."

I couldn't be sure, but I suspected my mom was pressing

her hand on my dad's leg under the table. They weren't going to give up easily.

"If I pull away from Britney, then I'm giving in to all the stupid stuff running around in my head. I need to face up to things, not let them get the best of me the way they did at my last school." I crossed fingers, hoping my parents would bite. The idea that I was willing to face my delusions might seem like a sign of progress to them. "Besides, Brit's been through a lot. If I stop hanging out with her, that's not fair."

Mom's mouth was pinched. "I don't know, I still think for you the best thing might be to take some time."

"There are only a few weeks of school left. If I pull away from Brit now, everyone's going to wonder what's going on," I said.

"What everyone thinks isn't important," Mom said.

"But it is," I said. "I have to go back there next year. It's my senior year. I'm going to be captain of the field hockey team. I have *friends*." I held out both hands. "And before you say it, I know that doesn't seem important in the big picture. Look, Brit's not going to be there next year, so this will be over soon. But if I make a big deal out of things now and stop being Brit's friend, everyone's going to hate me."

I could tell my dad was wavering. He never said much, but I knew he'd been a bit of a geek in high school who'd liked chemistry class and playing Dungeons and Dragons. He hadn't been bullied exactly, but he hadn't had a lot of fun either. He liked the idea that I had a group of friends and was popular, or at least accepted.

"How about we compromise?" I suggested. "School's almost over. You let me do what I think is best for the next couple of weeks and then I'll contact the camp and tell them I would like to apply to be a counselor this summer after all. That will give me the distance from Brit."

Last summer I'd worked at Camp Cedars Ridge. I'd taught swimming. It had been fun, but I hadn't wanted to do it this year because I hadn't wanted to miss the summer with Beth and Brit before they went away to college.

"Working as a counselor does show leadership skills," Mom said. She looked at my dad to gauge his reaction. Dad nodded.

"Going back there would be fun," I said. "Besides, I could use a few hundred more floss bracelets." They smiled, and I could feel the tension in the room starting to loosen. "And since I'm going to be captain next year, doing all the swimming will help me keep in shape," I added.

I could see my mom starting to give in. Summer break was just a few weeks away; even she could live with Britney for that long. "I'll email Mr. Anthony right after dinner about putting in my application," I said.

My parents exchanged a silent communication, and then my dad smiled. "All right, you've got a deal."

"And Britney won't apply to the camp," Mom added.

My mom clearly didn't know Brit well. Her idea of roughing it was staying at a Marriott instead of her preferred

Four Seasons. No way was she going to spend the summer being followed around by a pack of preteen girls and sleeping in a cottage with a bathroom that always seemed to have spiders.

"Don't worry. Brit has a summer job lined up at her parents' office," I said.

"Okay." Dad lifted his glass of wine and indicated we should all toast. I raised my glass of milk to his. "Here's to getting through the rest of this school year and a successful summer."

"To summer," I repeated, and we all clinked.

CHAPTER TWENTY

Britney pulled me into the art room. She danced in a circle, humming a song that I couldn't quite place. She looked like she'd swallowed the bluebird of happiness. Maybe a flock of them. Brit grabbed my hand and waltzed me around the room.

"Are you going to tell me why you're in such a great mood?" I asked.

"Because I'm a genius," Brit bragged.

"Yeah, but we knew this," I said, making her laugh.

"Okay, check this out." Brit motioned for me to sit at one of the long art tables. She pulled her MacBook Air out of her bag and fired it up.

"Did you finish your final paper for government?" I asked.

"Even better." Brit pulled something up online and then spun it over for me to see. It was Sara's Facebook page. I stared at her and she motioned for me to look closer. It wasn't her page; someone had made up another for her—the title was *Slutty Sara* with her picture for the profile.

Why don't you fucking kill yourself?

I pulled back, shocked. It wasn't the only comment. The whole page was filled.

Whore

Do you realize stealing someone's boyfriend makes you shit?

Slut

How did someone so ugly get a guy anyway?

I bet it's not just your oboe that you blow.

I scrolled down; the messages just kept coming. A sour slick of bile bubbled up in my throat. I turned to Brit. "Did you do this?"

She smiled. "Not all of it. I more or less got the ball rolling."

"But people will know you set up the page," I said.

Britney rolled her eyes. "Please, give me some credit. I didn't use my own computer, and I sent the first few messages from a false account." The corner of her mouth turned up with a twitch. "It might amaze you what I know to do with computers."

My skin grew cold and clammy. Brit turned the computer so she could see the screen again. "I got things started with a few comments, but then people started to pile on. They're sheep—all you need to do is get the herd pointed in the right direction."

My mind was spinning. "Sara is going to be crushed," I said.

A giggle slipped out of Brit's mouth, and she made a big show of pinching her lips together. "Poor little lamb."

Jesus, she was cold. Did she want Sara to kill herself? The hair on the back of my neck stood attention as the truth of the statement hit me. She did. She'd get a thrill from it, impressed at what she'd accomplished without having to lift a finger.

"The school is going to nail everyone on here," I said, looking over the names. "You might have set up a fake account, but they didn't. The police might even get involved."

Brit sighed. "Yeah. They'll take the page down too as soon as some adult sees it. I figure sometime tonight, tomorrow at best." She jabbed me lightly in the ribs with her elbow. "That's why I had to show you now."

Did she expect me to thank her for making sure I got a peek? Or maybe she thought I would be impressed. And I couldn't escape the feeling she was telling me as a reminder of what she was capable of doing. Should I tell her I knew she'd talked to Dr. Sherman about me? Maybe I could impress her with what *I* was capable of for a change.

Brit shut her laptop with a click. "We should get going. They've got year in review happening in the café at lunch. I don't want to miss that."

I blinked, trying to get my brain to catch up with where she was going. Every spring the yearbook staff did a slide show of photos and gave out awards for the dorky poll they had—best dressed, cutest couple, best hair, the kind of thing you'd list on a résumé as a life achievement if you were a total loser.

"Yeah, sure, let's go," I said. I followed her down the hall. I was trying to act like everything was fine, but it felt like my feet weren't connected to the rest of me. Every step felt like a controlled fall.

Brit looked at me over her shoulder. "I heard the yearbook group came up with some kind of honorary award for Beth. I said we would collect it for her. I think that would be nice, don't you?"

I nodded. Beth's face flashed in front of me. Beth could be flighty and careless, she was woefully disorganized at times, but one thing she never was, was cruel. She never teased anyone who couldn't take it. She never hid a nasty comment by saying it was just a joke.

Beth would never do this to Sara. She wouldn't have allowed Brit to do it either. Beth would be disgusted by this plan, and by the fact I was just standing there letting it happen.

I couldn't do it.

I wouldn't do it.

I stopped short. "Hey, I forgot something in my locker. I'm going to run back and get it."

Brit's nose wrinkled up.

"It will take me just a second. You go ahead in case they get started. I'll meet you there."

"Fine, but hurry up or you'll miss the show."

I flew down the steps to the B wing. As I came around the corner I narrowly missed slamming into Chester, the school janitor, as she carried a stepladder.

"Whoa those horses," she said, putting her hand over her heart.

"Sorry, Ches," I called over my shoulder.

I skidded past Officer Siegel's office. She was standing there holding a Starbucks cup and a small paper bag. She watched me run past, and for a split second I thought she was going to call out and ask me to stop, but then the phone in her office rang and she turned and I was past her, rounding the corner.

I slid into the library, and when Ms. Hudson saw me she gave me a look and I slowed down. I skipped past the first few computer stations and took one on the end where no one could see over my shoulder. I couldn't take down the page or delete any of the comments, but I could tell someone. It didn't fix anything, but I might limit the damage by getting it down sooner. I pulled up the page and copied the address then opened another tab to log into my anonymous Gmail account and fired off a quick mail to Ms. Harding telling her about the page. I shut down the computer. I'd done all I could.

The hot lunch line wound its way out of the cafeteria; pizza Monday always drew a crowd. Brit must have been looking for me as she was at my side as soon as I walked in.

"You're late," she hissed. "They're going to start any minute." She yanked her head to the side where Jason sat at a table with a group of people. "Let's go."

That's when I saw Sara. She was at a table near the window. A group of her band friends were laughing and joking, but I could see she was watching Brit and Jason together. She didn't look angry, more hurt and confused, like she couldn't figure out what had happened. She had no idea the shit storm that was raining down on her as she sat there. She must not know about the page yet. I hoped Ms. Harding could get the page down before Sara saw it. Some things you were better off not knowing.

"You excited?"

I jumped and searched my memory for the guy who jostled me in the side. I'd had a class with him a year ago. Ethan? Erin? "Year in review is always good," I said. Evan!

That was it. He was on the yearbook committee.

"You know, you won for best female athlete for the junior class," Evan said, his voice lower. "I'm not supposed to tell anyone until it's official, but . . ." He gestured around us. "No point in keeping it a secret now. Act surprised when Vanderfeld calls your name. Congrats."

"I won?" I said.

Evan laughed. "Don't sound so shocked. You kicked ass on the field this year."

In that instant it was as if I could see through a portal to an alternate universe. When my name was called, Beth would have let out a loud whoop. She'd bend low and grab me around the thighs and heft me up into the air. I'd be whacking her on the back like I wanted her to put me down, but I would have felt like I was on top of the world. Winning was cool, but sharing it with Beth is what would have made it special.

"It's here, Northside! Your year in review!"

A bunch of people pounded on the table, like riffing on a drum. The slide show started. A shot from the first day as people walked in, the freshmen looking years younger instead of just a few months. The homecoming dance, football games. Shots from the school play, the jazz band looking serious. The photos slid past, set to music. My hands were shaking.

As the various titles were called out there was applause and cheers. When they called my name for junior female athlete I walked to the front. The flash from Mr. Vander-feld's camera blinded me. I suspected it would turn out like a mug shot. I walked back to join Brit's table.

"Put it on." Brit motioned for me to slide my arm into the beauty-pageant sash that declared *Best Athlete*. She was wearing three; they draped off her like she was a maypole: *Best Eyes, Hottest Senior, Cutest Couple*. She fingered her sashes like they were prayer beads. "It's the first time any senior has taken multiple titles. Mr. Vanderfeld told me they usually work the voting so the winners are spread around, but he thought there would be a student revolt if I didn't win in all the categories I was nominated in."

I sent up a mental prayer of thanks to Mr. Vanderfeld for bending the rules so she was in a good mood. "You are a bit of special case," I said.

"I guess not everyone comes back from the dead," Brit quipped.

"Just you and Jesus," I said.

Brit threw her head back and laughed. She seemed almost drunk. Then her mouth shut with a click. I noticed she was looking over my shoulder. Officer Siegel was walk-ing toward me. Brit's expression tightened.

"Uh-oh. The liaison officer is coming this way," Tyler said. "Someone's in trouble," he said in a singsong voice.

Siegel stopped at our table and looked down at me. "Kalah, can you come with me?"

Everyone at our table grew quiet and suddenly

developed a fierce interest in their lunch. "Sure, what's up?"

"Just come with me."

I got up slowly. Brit's jaw was tight, and she wouldn't meet my gaze. I followed Officer Siegel out in the hall. People were streaming past us on their way to classes. When we got to Officer Siegel's office, she shut the door behind me.

"Kalah, can you tell me anything about this Facebook page someone set up about Sara?"

I raised my shoulders as if the whole thing were a mystery to me. "Nothing."

"Don't lie to me." Officer Siegel's voice was sharp. "Your friend Zach told me about the page and that he was worried you might be involved. Minutes later I saw you running down the hall. I followed you to the library. After you left, the librarian told me which computer you'd been on. The page popped right up in the computer history."

Shit. "Why would Zach tell you I was involved?" I didn't expect her to answer, but the idea of it felt like a punch to the gut.

"It doesn't matter why he talked to me. That's not the issue. This is very serious, Kalah. Cyberbullying is a crime."

"I didn't have anything to do with it," I said. It was the truth, but the words tasted like lies in my mouth. "I heard about the page and I wanted to check it out."

"Who did you hear about it from?" Officer Siegel asked.

I shrugged again. "I don't remember, people were just

talking. I didn't leave any comments."

She stared at me across the desk. It was as if I could feel her crawling through my brain, looking in every nook and cranny for the truth.

"Did the page get taken down?" I put my hands under my thighs so I wouldn't start tapping.

"Concerned for Sara, are you?" She didn't wait for me to answer. "Ms. Harding has Sara in her office now. Her parents have been called. There's nothing you want to tell me?" Officer Siegel asked.

I wanted to tell her everything, but she wasn't going to believe me. It looked like I was the one who was hounding Sara. She would think I was just trying to stay out of trouble. "No, ma'am," I mumbled.

She shook her head disgusted. "Fine. Then I guess there's nothing left to say, but I'll be checking into this."

CHAPTER TWENTY-ONE

I tried to find Zach before first period. He hadn't answered any of my texts from the night before, and he owed me an explanation. I knew I was acting weird, but how could he start making accusations to the police when he had no proof? I knew he was mad about our breakup, but this made no sense. I couldn't find him, but I stopped looking when I heard the news. Officer Siegel had been suspended, but no one seemed to know why. I searched out Amy Chan after third period to get the dirt. Her dad was on the school board.

Amy slammed her locker. "I don't know why we even have to have a liaison officer." She pulled her long dark hair into a ponytail to get it up off her neck.

I cleared my throat. "I heard there was some kind of charge brought against Officer Siegel," I said. "Do you know anything?"

Amy hefted her bag over her shoulder. "You can't tell anyone," she said, looking at Kate and me. "I only know about it because I overheard my dad talking on the phone."

I crossed my finger over my chest.

"Brit's family filed a harassment case against her. They say she's been causing all kinds of trouble for Britney," Amy said.

Kate made a face. I had the sense she was getting sick of Brit's drama.

"What exactly did she do to Brit?" I asked.

Amy shrugged. "I don't know. You're her best friend; maybe you should ask her?"

I felt panicky. Had Siegel asked Brit if she thought I was guilty of putting up the page? Or maybe she asked her if we were both involved. Brit would be pissed if there was even a slim chance she could be caught. "Maybe I should," I said. "I've got a few questions for Brit."

"What kind of questions?" I whirled around. Brit was behind me.

"I heard about Officer Siegel," I said.

Brit mimed gagging. "I hate that woman." I searched her face, trying to figure out the cause of her dislike. Was it just that Officer Siegel wasn't in her thrall like most of the teachers, or did she worry that Siegel might suspect something?

The bell rang, and Brit groaned. "You guys want to skip? It's entirely too hot to be here. I can't face another class. It's like this year never ends."

It was one of the first really hot, sticky days of the year. Northside didn't have air-conditioning except for the computer labs, and whoever had designed the halls hadn't been too concerned about airflow. It was a cement block heat box. It wasn't even midmorning, and the building already felt like a sauna.

"No can do," Amy said.

"Me either," Kate added. "I've got Laurice this period, and knowing her she's got some evil pop quiz planned to prep us for exams next week."

"I'll go," I said impulsively. I could live with the heat, but I did want to hear what Brit had to say about Siegel.

Brit's eyes sparkled. "Let's do it." She turned and I followed her without another word.

Once we were out in the parking lot we debated where to go. Neither of us was hungry, and the idea of having coffee made me sick. I was jittery enough as it was.

Brit lightly slapped her steering wheel. "God, I hate this town. There's nothing to do."

"Should we go to your place?" I suggested. "We could watch a movie."

"We can't. My mom has some interior designer over taking measurements," Brit said. "She's on this kick where she wants to redo the basement so they can put the house on the market next fall. She figures with me going to college they could move into a condo by the water."

"Sounds nice."

Brit snorted. "What about the fact that it's my child-hood home? When I come back for summers I'll be stuck in some pokey spare room. I'm used to having my own room, plus the extra space so I can have people over."

I opened my mouth to say something when the impact of what she said hit me. If Brit's parents renovated the basement any evidence that was still there was going to be destroyed. I'd assumed that it didn't matter if Nicole was out of town for months, other than it was frustrating, but her testimony wasn't going to be enough. I'd counted on the idea that her statement would make the police check Brit's story more closely. Light up that basement with some lumi-nol like a fireworks show—but if all of that was gone, there wouldn't be enough to prove anything.

The pressure around my chest tightened another notch. I was running out of time.

I kept an eye on the front door of the school. It was just a matter of time until a teacher came out and realized we were just sitting there. "We should go somewhere," I said.

"Ooh, I know just the perfect thing." Brit fired up her car and we peeled out of the lot. When the radio came on, Brit whooped; it was one of her favorite songs. She jacked up the volume so loud that the seats throbbed with the bass.

When she pulled into the parking lot, I felt the blood drain out of my head. I stared ahead at the sign for the Point. Where Brit had supposedly leapt to her death and where she'd pushed Beth's body into the lake.

"I like being here," Brit said. "It reminds me of Beth." She unhooked her seat belt and jumped out of the SUV.

A million questions ran through my head. Did she think about dumping Beth's body? Planning her suicide, down to the tragic note left on the beach? Did she have even a sliver of regret when she realized Beth hadn't been sleeping with Jason?

"Are you coming?" Brit was already down the path leading to a rocky outcrop. She was whacking at the beach grass with a stick she'd picked up. I scrambled out of the car and followed her.

We came through the trees and out onto the bluff. A wooden guardrail ran across the bluff with a sign. *Danger. Sharp drop.* I took a step back so Brit wasn't behind me. Two accidents at the same location would be hard for her to explain away, but if anyone could find a way to do it, it would be her. She paused and smiled, and I had the sense she knew why I'd moved and that it amused her. Brit took a deep breath and closed her eyes to the sun. "This is so much better than being in school," she said. "Sometimes I feel like I can't really breathe in there."

"So what happened with Siegel?" I asked.

"What, no thank-you? I did it for you, after all." Brit

said. "Siegel was *not* your friend. She thought you were involved with Sara's page, you know." Brit took a seat on one of the larger rocks. "I had no idea they'd suspend Siegel. I thought they might make her leave the school, but she's off work completely."

"You did this for me?" I asked.

"I wasn't going to have her make it sound like you were responsible. I just don't get why you looked at the page at the library. You couldn't wait to get someplace more private?" Brit rolled her eyes. "And why was Siegel following you around anyway? Doesn't she have anything else to do?"

"I just wanted to see the page again," I said. "Siegel wouldn't have been able to prove anything."

"It made her suspicious." She fixed me with a stare, shading her face from the sun with her hand. "It made her suspect me."

I stood in front of her. "Are you in trouble?"

Brit shaded her eyes so she could look up at me. "She didn't say anything in particular. It wasn't a big deal."

I hadn't expected that answer. I dropped down so I was sitting next to her. "What do you mean?"

Brit was piling small stones on the rock next to her. "I mean she didn't *say* anything in particular, but I could tell she thinks I was involved. Every time she looked at me it was like she smelled something bad. It pissed me off."

Siegel had looked at her funny? "But your parents filed a harassment case." There must be more to it. Did Brit suspect that Siegel was checking into her amnesia story?

Brit laughed. "Well, they weren't going to cause trouble for her just because I didn't like her. I had to have a better story than that." She shook her head ruefully, like she couldn't get over how naïve I was. "I told my parents that she was hounding me." Brit made her voice waver as if she was about to cry. "It's like I can't even walk down the hall without her following me and whispering all this horrible stuff." A sob escaped from her throat. "I tried to talk to her, but she told me she doesn't want to listen. I'm afraid of what she might do." Then she stopped and beamed. "Not bad, huh?"

Her ability to turn her emotions on and off was unnerving. "She could lose her job, Brit. This is serious."

"Then she shouldn't have been such a fucking bitch to me all the time."

"You can't get someone fired because you don't like them," I said.

Brit stood and brushed the sand off her butt. "Apparently I can." Her voice was casual, as if we were talking about something like what to have for dinner.

I pressed my fingers into my temples. I couldn't believe the stuff that came out of her mouth. "You have to drop this case. She never harassed you."

Britney shrugged. "It really comes down to what I say versus what she says. Besides, I said you were around for some of it, so you can back up my story."

I was mad at myself for being shocked. I should have known she'd drag me into this mess. "I don't know," I hedged. "This is the *police*, Brit. Why did you go after Siegel in the first place?"

Brit suddenly chucked a large stone into the air over the cliff's edge. "I had to do something. I'm so fucking bored, I feel like I'm going to explode," she yelled.

I stared at her in shock. "Bored?"

Brit paced back and forth in front of me. "I had this horrible thing happen to me, and I had to fight, freaking crawl and scratch my memories back so I could return. And I finally get here and this is it. People don't even care anymore."

"What do you mean?"

"It's all the same. I've got Jason back, and sure, he's good-looking and smart, but he's still this high school guy. He's actually happy with how things are. He doesn't want to run off together or do something huge. He's happy to rent a bunch of lame action movies and have a barbeque on the beach. I'm stuck in the same classes, reading the same stupid textbooks, taking the same tests. The hot lunch menu is the same, week after week. Everyone tells the same jokes, they watch the same shows, they listen to the same music. It drives me insane." Her pacing picked up speed, the sand grinding under her feet. "If I have to act like I give a shit one more time when someone whines about how stressed they are over exams, or how it's a national tragedy that their hairstylist cut off an extra quarter of an inch, or because their mommy makes their curfew too early, I'm going to start screaming and I don't think I'm going to be able to stop. Oh, and speaking of parents, guess what mine are all lathered up about?" She stopped and put her hands on her hips.

"I don't know," I said softly.

"They aren't happy with my grades. They think I should be doing better. They are already riding my ass about Cornell and how I have to up my game if I expect to do well. Up my game," she said, spittle flying from her mouth. "I came back from the dead and they still want me to up my goddamn game." Her face was bright red and I could see the vein in her forehead throbbing. "I came back and I still have to deal with all this bullshit."

"Your parents worry about you," I said. "They went after Officer Siegel for upsetting you. Doesn't that prove that they care?"

"What they care about is making sure they look like the best parents in the world." She ran her hands through her hair. "My dad went after Officer Siegel because she pissed him off. He told me how when I was missing she rubbed him the wrong way, making it sound like maybe they had something to do with why I might want to kill myself. Trust me, there's nothing my dad hates more than someone blaming him. I just gave him an excuse to go after Officer Siegel. He didn't do it for me."

She looked ready to fly into a million pieces, hard

shrapnel spraying out, causing collateral damage all around her. "Listen, Brit, it's going to be okay," I said, trying to defuse the situation. It scared me that she was out of control.

Her head dropped back, and she slumped as if she'd crossed a marathon finish line, spent and exhausted. "But that's the problem. It's all . . . okay. Is there anything more boring than just okay?"

I sat there staring at her. I didn't know what to say; she'd told me more than she'd expected to. She'd shown me more. A tiny flicker of clarity sprung up in my chest. She needed a fix, like a junkie. The truth was Brit had enjoyed all of this. Maybe what had happened with Beth had been an accident, or a crime of passion, as they say, but once it was done, she'd liked the challenge. She'd had to figure out how to get rid of Beth's body, how to get away with it. She had to come up with a way to escape, to disappear, and then once she was gone she'd had to engineer a way to return. It must have been scary, but it had also been an adrenaline rush. Now she was back and everyday life wasn't enough anymore. Prom had been a letdown, Jason wasn't living up to expectations, and baiting Sara was all she had left, and it wasn't cutting it.

I rubbed my face. Every nerve in my body was tingling as the insight into Brit's mind was laid open to me. All of this: posting the photo of Sara, feeding lies about me to Dr. Sherman, setting up the slut page for Sara, trying to get

Officer Siegel fired, was her trying to re-create that thrill. She'd likely always needed some kind of excitement, a problem to solve. I would almost feel sorry for her if she weren't willing to hurt others to get what she wanted.

"Look, none of this matters. You have to back me up with Officer Siegel. If the school board wants to hear from you, you need to tell them that she harassed me."

"Brit, I can't lie to the cops."

She rolled her eyes. "C'mon, you owe me. Your stupid stunt with going to the library almost sank us both into hot water. You can say you don't remember any specifics, just that she said a bunch of stuff and it made me cry. Besides, I got rid of Siegel for you. Did you really want her prying into your history?"

"Maybe you can say it was someone else who was there," I suggested.

Brit's nose twitched in irritation, and she cocked one eyebrow. "Maybe you can find another way back to your car."

"What?"

Her earlier emotional outburst had cleared, like a storm that raged in and then blew itself out. She seemed perfectly calm. "I forgot I have a dentist appointment. I have to go." Brit started walking down the path. I scrambled after her.

"You're leaving me here?" I tripped over a root as we walked through the trees and stumbled. "Just because I won't back up your story?"

"Don't be a drama queen. I told you. I have to be somewhere, and it's the opposite direction of school. Just call your mom. I'm sure she'll pick you up."

"I can't call my mom. She's going to want to know what I'm doing out here in the middle of the school day," I said.

Brit already had her SUV open. "Jeez, sounds like a problem. If you can't get a ride, let me know and I'll pick you up later." She climbed into her car and slammed the door. She waved at me through the windshield and then pulled out without looking back.

Once she pulled out it was totally silent. Just the sound of the distant waves hitting the rocks. Brit was teaching me a lesson.

Now I had to figure out how to teach her one.

CHAPTER TWENTY-TWO

I had to jog from the Point back to school to get my car, and I was exhausted with a headache beating behind my eyes by the time I made it home. I came into the house, the air-conditioning instantly cooling the layer of sweat on my skin.

I dropped my school bag on the floor by the door and rolled my neck. On the way home, as cars had whizzed past, I kept thinking about the fact that Brit's parents were planning to renovate. All the evidence would be wiped away for good. I had to move things forward quickly, but I wasn't sure how to do it. I couldn't shake the feeling that I was missing something—some key piece of information that would make things fall into place. It made sense to start with things that were out of place and Zach talking to Siegel about me didn't fit. He was ticked at me, and he had reason to be, but making accusations wasn't his style.

I picked up our home phone and dialed Zach using *67 so our number wouldn't show and he might pick it up.

"Hello," Zach said.

"It's me," I said. He was silent. "You weren't answering my texts."

"Because I didn't want to talk to you."

I flinched at his honesty. "I just need to ask you one thing, and then I'll leave you alone." When he didn't hang up I pushed forward. "Why were you so sure I had something to do with Sara's photo leak and her online page?"

"Are you still denying it?"

"I just need to know why you think I could do that."

Zach sighed. "Brit talked to me."

I sucked in a breath. "She told you I did it?"

"She didn't say that," Zach said. "She was worried. She thought you might have done it to try to get on her good side because you knew she was mad at Sara. And she was mad, but she said she would never want Sara to be hurt. It was always so important to you that you be in good with Brit and Beth, I thought it was possible."

I bet she said that. I bet she said all sorts of things. That bitch was setting me up. "Zach, I didn't do this," I insisted.

"That's not up to me to figure out," Zach said, hanging up the phone.

I stared at the receiver. He thought I was guilty. I felt a ripple of panic. I was ending up isolated, just like when everything went bad with Madison. I had to get someone to see my side. I'd talk to Nadir.

It's not that I think it is my older brother's job to fix my problems; it's just that he's pretty good at it. When I was little and Vince from down the street used to pop the heads off my Barbie dolls and hide them, it was Nadir who went over and told him if he didn't leave me alone he would fight him. When I accidentally broke the ballerina figurine my mom liked by hitting it with a ball in the house, it was my brother who stuck her arm back on with superglue and promised Mom would never find out. He coached me through algebra my first year of high school and was always available for advice. It might be that he's older, or maybe he's just better at staying calm and figuring out what to do, but he's always been someone I knew had my back. And I needed to count on someone because I'd suddenly realized I was running out of options.

As soon as we got through the usual checking in on our parents, I jumped right in. "I want to talk to you about something, and I need you to listen," I said.

"I always listen," Nadir said.

I sighed. "With an open mind," I stressed. "You know how everyone thinks Beth's death was an accident? It wasn't."

"Okay," Nadir said doubtfully.

"When all this went down, Brit believed Beth was fooling around with her boyfriend, Jason. I found a note. I know Beth was over at Brit's the night she disappeared. I think Brit confronted Beth and things went badly."

There was a long beat of silence of the phone. "So you think Britney did something to Beth," Nadir said.

"Not *something*. I think she killed her." I made sure my voice stayed calm and rational. I knew this was a big leap for someone else to make, but if anyone would hear me out it would be my brother.

"But weren't they friends forever?" Nadir sounded confused.

I wanted to throw something at the wall in frustration. "Yes. But that's the point. Britney believed her best friend betrayed her by sleeping with her boyfriend. She confronted Beth and then maybe Beth laughed it off, or denied it, and then Brit snapped."

"Kay-Kay, people can have fights without it turning to murder."

"I'm not saying she set out to kill her, it might have been an accident," I said.

Nadir gave a strangled laugh. "Well, that's a relief. Then it's only manslaughter."

My jaw tightened. "I'm not joking."

There was a pause. "I know, and that's what has me worried," Nadir said.

"Beth is dead. You're acting like this is all in my head.

Remember when I asked you about records of online chats? Those were from Brit. She was pretending to be Beth, but it was her the whole time. She was checking out her options, figuring out if she could come back. And I have some other stuff too that pokes holes in her story, and now I think she's setting it up so people won't believe me."

"If something happened, and that's a big *if*, you should leave it to the cops."

I rubbed my temple with one hand and made myself loosen the grip I had on the phone with the other. "But that's the whole point. The police aren't investigating." I didn't mention that they were more likely to think I was guilty of cyberbullying than they were that Brit was guilty of murder. "That's why I called you, to see if you could help me think of some way to get in touch with this girl Nicole Bradon. She lived over on Charles in this big white house. Brit was down there in East Lansing when she was supposedly amnesic. Nicole was her roommate. She might be able to fill in the missing information."

"Is that why you came to see me?" Nadir asked.

"Partly. Listen, I can't get back down there because of exams, but could you go back to her place? Someone must have some kind of emergency number for her, or know her parents, or when she will be in some particular location, and then I can call any hostels in the area. She's in Europe, after all; it's not like she's on the moon." Nadir was totally silent. "I'm not asking you to agree with me—maybe I'm wrong, but help me find out for sure." I knew I wasn't mistaken about this, but as much as I wanted Nadir to see things the way I did, what I needed most of all was some help. "The police aren't going to look into it until I give them a reason."

"Maybe they're not looking into it because there's nothing to see."

I jumped off my bed and paced around my room. "Never mind. It was a mistake for me to call you."

"Kalah, you don't even know for sure that this Nicole knows anything about Brit. You're just guessing. You can always call me, but you can't be pissed if I tell you something you don't want to hear."

"I'm not pissed," I yelled. We were both silent for a beat, letting my obvious lie wash over the both of us. "Okay, I'm ticked, but it's because I really believe Brit did something to Beth. All I'm asking you is to help me investigate it further so I can find out for certain. She and I keep dancing around the subject. I don't know how to explain it, but it's like she's daring me to confront her."

Nadir sighed. "All I'm saying is that you always liked drama. Remember when Grandpa convinced you he'd trapped the tooth fairy in a box and you got all excited because you were going to take it to show-and-tell and then you lost your shit when he told you he was just kidding?"

"What's your point?" I asked.

"My point is you love drama. You want the world to be more exciting than it is."

Each one of his words felt like it was covered in spikes as it bounced off of me. "That's not what this is about," I said. My eyes stung, and I used the back of my hand to wipe away a tear.

"You need to drop this," Nadir said.

"You're not my parent; you don't get to tell me what to do," I said.

Nadir sighed. "Kay-Kay, you know I love you, but you're sensitive. You feel things more than other people. Sometimes that's awesome. When you're happy you're like a million watts. When you care about someone you do it with every atom of your being, but there are downsides. When you're hurt, you don't bounce back easily. You feel slighted by things that other people wouldn't even notice. You read meanings and subtext into all sorts of stuff that isn't there."

There was a dull ache in my chest. "You don't believe me."

"I don't believe you're in a place to look at this situation objectively," Nadir said. "You need to share all of this with your psychologist."

"I'll think about it," I lied. If no one would help me, then I'd figure it out on my own. Talking to Dr. Sherman wasn't going to do anything other than be a distraction.

"I'm going to talk to Mom and Dad," Nadir said.

Traitor. "Why on earth would you do that?" I asked. "You know how they can be. They'll freak out."

"They *should* freak out. Kalah, you're talking about one

of your friends killing the other. Look at it this way: if you're right, then this is a serious situation, not something you can deal with on your own."

"If I'm right." I snorted. "Don't make this sound like you're now trying to do me a favor."

"You may not believe me, but I'm doing this because I want to help."

"If you want to help me, then don't talk to Mom and Dad." My heart was speeding up. I could already picture my parents sitting across from me at the dining room table, both of them making their serious conversation faces. They'd try to sound calm and relaxed, but their eyes would show the panic they'd be feeling.

"Mom and Dad aren't the bad guys," Nadir said.

"I know, but they're going to blow it into something it isn't. I'll drop it, okay? Don't drag them into this."

"You're not going to drop it." Nadir sounded exhausted.

"I will. I promise." I crossed my fingers behind my back. I felt bad lying to my brother, but the last thing I needed was my parents dragged in this. "I talked the situation through with you, which is what I wanted to do. If I decide to do anything else, I'll tell you first." I held my breath, hoping.

"I don't know. . . ."

"All I'm saying is that if I drop it, then there's nothing to tell them. If I go further, you'll know and you can decide if you want to tell them then."

Nadir was silent. "I won't talk to them," he said, "but I

think you should. And I'm reserving the right to change my mind depending on the circumstances."

The tight band around my chest disappeared and I could finally take a deep breath. "Thanks," I mumbled. "I'll think about it."

"Don't make me regret it," he said. "I'm just trying to take care of my baby sister."

"I know. You're the best brother ever."

"I'm your only brother," he said.

I smiled at our ongoing family joke. "Then you're lucky; there's no chance you'll lose your title."

We talked for a couple more minutes about Nadir's final exams before hanging up. As soon as I clicked off with him I flopped back down on my bed. I could feel sweat prickling under my arms. The silence in the house felt like a balm. My parents were going on a date night after work. Dad had scored tickets to a play, and they were going to dinner too. It felt good to be alone.

I got up and wandered around the house. I couldn't focus on anything. I could hear a giant clock ticking down to Brit's renovations, as if a bulldozer were outside my window, ready to take me out. I clicked on the TV and then realized I'd been staring at it for twenty minutes with zero idea of what was on. I clicked it off. I picked up a book and then put it back down. If TV was too complicated, reading *A Tale of Two Cities* for my English exam wasn't going to go any better. I flipped through one of my mom's magazines and dropped it too.

It felt like I had ants crawling around just inside my skin. I couldn't get comfortable. I went out into the kitchen and opened the fridge. I pushed aside the leftover quinoa salad my mom had left for me. I didn't want it. I ran my hand over the items on the shelves as if perhaps by Braille I could figure out what I was in the mood to eat. Nothing looked good. I shut the fridge and tried the pantry. I ate a handful of salty cashews from a bag, but that wasn't what I wanted either.

Then I noticed my parents' bar shelf. They liked to make cocktails: old-fashioneds, martinis, negronis, and whiskey sours. They had everything, rum, mescal, Scotch, Grand Marnier, Campari, and a whole row of tiny bottles that held bitters. I held up a bottle of Bombay Sapphire gin. I liked how the glass was bright blue, the color of Beth's eyes trapped in a genie bottle. I picked up the squat bottle of bourbon at the back. It made me think of the first time I kissed Beth out at the Point. She'd brought her dad's bottle for us to share. It was the only time I'd ever tried it. I unscrewed the cap and sniffed. The smoky smell reminded me of Beth. Maybe I would have a small drink. It might calm me down.

My parents had special cups just for cocktails. Their highball glasses had thick glass bottoms. They looked like they were off the set of *Mad Men*. Beth would have loved the heft of them, how substantial they felt. These weren't glasses that you would use to serve anything frothy and pink. They were for serious drinking. The ice I put in mine clinked importantly at the bottom, and when I added the whiskey it looked like it was meant to be in my hand. I felt more competent just holding it.

I wandered into the living room and took a sip. I coughed. I'd forgotten how strong it was. It was liquid fire, burning heat as it slid down my throat and into my stomach. The warmth spread through my gut. I turned on the stereo and sank into the leather sofa. I swirled the ice with my index finger.

"Here Comes the Sun" by the Beatles came on. I closed my eyes and sighed. Beth had loved this song. She'd loved the whole *Abbey Road* album. I got up and put it on repeat letting the songs play over and over. I belted out "Maxwell's Silver Hammer" at the top of my lungs, picturing Beth singing into her hairbrush as we got ready to go out.

The happy image of Beth faded away, replaced by Britney's smug face. There was no way around it. Brit was winning. Her life was charmed. She got away with everything. She'd also managed to turn Zach against me. I had no doubts that she'd left me at the Point to remind me that she could destroy me. She couldn't have picked a more meaningful place.

Then there was the situation with Officer Siegel and Sara. I took a long sip of my drink, hoping the burn would obliterate the wave of shame I felt. The situation was spinning out of control. If Sara killed herself over all of this, I was going to be partly to blame. I'd found ways to justify not telling anyone of Brit's involvement, convincing myself that I had to keep Brit close. But maybe the truth was that I was the kind of person who did whatever they had to in order to get what they want. Look at how I'd lied to Zach. I'd come up with excuses then too, that there was no point in telling him because Beth was gone, but the truth was I hadn't told him because I was scared. I was acting just like Brit.

I leaned back and let the music wash over me, hypnotizing me. The bourbon was working; I could feel the tension in my body leaking out, melting into the leather seat beneath me. I still didn't have any answers, but the problem felt more distant. I curled into the cushions my mom had made from old printed sari fabric, the bright colors slightly faded.

I refilled my drink a couple of times, maybe three or four. As the album cycled over and over, I lost track of time. I had long, imagined conversations with Britney that ended with her breaking into tears and confessing everything. I could almost feel the thrill of victory when everyone realized what she was capable of doing. I replayed the scene in my head, giving myself a chance to try out different lines, honing my accusations.

I heard the rumble of the garage door and sat straight up. *Oh, shit.* Had I drifted off? The bourbon bottle was still sitting on the kitchen counter. I'd planned to mix in a bit of water before my parents came home and then crawl into bed to avoid any chance they'd notice I'd been drinking.

My mind was racing around, trying to figure out what to do first. Dump the glass in my hand? Go up to my room? Should I pretend to be asleep? I hadn't even sorted out all the options when my mom was standing right in front of me. She clicked off the stereo. I hadn't even realized it had been up that high. John Lennon and the rest of the band abandoned me to face this by myself. The silence felt thick. My mom took the glass from my hand and sniffed it before putting it down on the coffee table.

"I can explain," I said. My voice was slurred.

"Really?" Mom put her hands on her hips. "I rather doubt that."

I opened my mouth, but whatever lame excuse I'd been considering vaporized from my brain. "Um."

"What were you thinking?" Mom didn't even pause, so I knew it wasn't the kind of question I was supposed to answer. "Your dad and I have always trusted you and your brother. Do you want to live in a home where we have to lock things away? Where we have to come home and do an inspection?"

"No," I mumbled.

"I don't understand what is going on with you. We're trying to be very supportive of what we know is a difficult time for you, but you seem to insist on making things more complicated. Do you know who left a message on my phone this afternoon?"

I shook my head, but moving made the room tilt, so I stopped.

"The school. They said you weren't in any of your afternoon classes, so in addition to this, we can add truancy to your list of things you need to explain."

My stomach did a slow rollover. I was regretting not having eaten anything all evening.

My dad touched my mom's shoulder lightly. "I don't think we're going to get anywhere discussing this tonight. Kalah's in no shape."

I swayed slightly on my feet. I'd never loved my dad more than I did in that moment.

"You should go up to your room. We'll clean up down here," Dad said.

"I'm sorry," I said. I was saying that a lot lately. I should just get a tattoo across my forehead and save myself the trouble.

Mom sighed. "Go to bed."

I slipped past them and up the stairs, passing the wall of photos. It seemed like every family member we had, including younger versions of myself, was watching my walk of shame. My vision had black spots in the corner, threatening to take me under. The list of people who were disappointed in me was growing longer every day. I took a cold shower, trying to sober up. My head was already thumping. I stood over the toilet, hoping to puke it up, but despite the fact that my stomach was clearly unhappy with the current state of events, it wasn't going to give up the bourbon easily. I couldn't bring myself to stick my finger down my throat. I eventually gave up and just crawled into bed.

I'd almost fallen asleep when there was a light tap. My dad cracked the door and peeked in.

I pulled myself up. "Hey."

"Hey," he said. He came in and handled me a bottle of Tylenol and put a glass of water on my bedside table. "You'll want to do yourself a favor and take a couple of those and drink the water."

I tossed the pills back and took a sip of water. "Thanks."

Dad sat on the edge of my bed. "I'd like to say I've never been in your shoes, but I have." He looked over. "Not that I think what you did was a good idea."

"Mom's really pissed," I said. Something about being in the dark made it easier to talk. "I ruined your night out."

"Your mom is worried." Dad sighed. "I am too."

"Does it make it better or worse that I'm also worried?" My voice sounded small in the dim light.

"It shows some insight; that's never a bad thing. What happened, Kalah?"

"I don't know what I was thinking," I said.

"You know we caught your brother drinking a couple of times."

"Really?" *Nadir? Perfect Nadir?* I felt a tiny flicker of hope. If Nadir could screw up too and still turn out okay, it meant there might be hope for me.

"We didn't tell you at the time because it wasn't your problem. The usual stuff. Out with friends. Beer. Bad decisions," Dad said. He looked around the room at the various posters and ads I'd taped to the walls in tidy, precise rows. "The thing was, we never came home and found him drinking by himself. That's what really has me concerned. This wasn't you at a party getting carried away. Can you tell me what happened today that made you come home and decide you needed to have a drink?"

"It was a bad decision," I said.

"Well, we can agree on that."

I surprised myself by laughing. "Yeah." I played with Roogs's worn ear, amazed that an ancient stuffed dog could still make me feel better. "I was just mad and sad about all these things, and I thought that having a drink would make it all disappear. I know it was a stupid thing to do."

Dad patted my hands. "Growing up isn't ever easy, but it's that much harder when you've been through the things you've had to deal with this year," he said. "I'm not saying that your problems are because you're young, I'm just acknowledging that when you get older it gets a bit easier to handle heartache and pain. Maybe because you've had some experience. You know you'll survive. When it's the first time you lose someone you love, you honestly don't know if you'll make it." Dad smiled. "That's my way of saying you will survive. A little older and a little wiser."

"Sometimes it doesn't feel like I'm getting any wiser," I

admitted. "I know I keep screwing up. I just wish I could go back in time and do things differently."

"Ah. The immortal quest for a time machine. If I ever make one in my robot lab, I'll let you know, but until then you're going to have to do the best you can."

I closed my eyes. I'd been afraid that was the answer.

"Hang in there, kiddo." Dad leaned over and kissed my forehead. "We love you and we always will." He tapped me on the nose. "Doesn't mean you're not still in trouble."

I smiled. "I love you guys too. You're the best parents I've got."

"We're the only parents you've got," Dad said, and then slipped the door shut.

CHAPTER TWENTY-THREE

However it might look, don't be fooled: bourbon is not your friend. When my alarm went off in the morning I whacked it off my bedside table sending it flying into the pile of dirty clothes I'd been wearing yesterday. There was a low drumbeat behind my eyes, and my skull felt too small to contain my brain. My tongue was stuck to the roof of my mouth with some kid of sour smoky paste. My stomach lurched and gurgled, making noises best suited to a horror movie sound track.

I dragged myself into the shower. The sound of the water hitting the tile hurt. As much as I wanted to crawl back into bed under my big blue duvet, there was no way I was getting out of going to school. I was lucky my mom hadn't woken me up by blowing a whistle and making a giant vat of smelly fish curry downstairs.

My parents didn't say much. I almost wished we could have it out first thing, but my mom had to work the early shift at the hospital, so our "big talk" was going to have to wait until dinner. Instead they both bustled around the kitchen like they were really focused on making their coffee. I couldn't tell if they were deliberately being loud with clanking dishes on the marble counter or if it was just my hangover. Their disappointment in me hung over the room like a fog.

I pulled into the student lot and parked in the back. Despite the fact that I'd brushed my teeth three times already, my mouth still tasted sour. Like I'd gargled with salad dressing, a nasty mix of acid and oil. I opened the door and spit.

"Gross." A couple of sophomore girls were standing by my car; their noses wrinkled up.

"Sorry," I mumbled. I pulled myself out of the car. They didn't have to act so grossed out; it was just spit.

The two of them whispered together and giggled. My eyes narrowed. "Something funny?" I asked them.

They shook their heads quickly as if caught doing something they shouldn't and then skirted around my car and hustled toward the school. I watched them go. I had the sense that I was missing something, some vital piece of information, but I was running at half speed compared to the rest of the world.

"Kalah!"

I clenched my eyes shut as the sound of my name being yelled seared through my brain. When I opened them I spotted Officer Siegel standing across the street. She waved me over. I wanted to turn away and ignore her, but I couldn't do it. I walked over, my feet dragging on the asphalt. She looked me up and down, and I had the sense she knew I was hungover. Between this and prom, she most likely thought I belonged in rehab.

"Sorry to ambush you in the parking lot, but I'm not allowed to be on school grounds," she said.

"Oh." I didn't know how else to respond. I fidgeted with the strap of my bag.

"I had a meeting this morning with the school administrators. I stuck around because I wanted to find you. Come sit with me." She motioned for me to get into her car.

I sank into the passenger seat and tried not to stare. It was weird to see her in jeans and a crisp white shirt. It was like seeing her naked without her uniform.

"I'm really sorry about what happened with your job," I mumbled. I crossed my fingers that she didn't know Brit was counting on me to be her witness.

Siegel took a sip of the coffee she had stashed in the cup holder, and the bitter smell of it made my stomach clench.

"I'm pretty sure the whole thing will blow over. My record is clean and my performance reviews are all pretty solid. They're going to keep me out of the school for this year, but I suspect that will be it. Do you know why Britney's making up this story and siccing her parents on me?"

I shrugged. "I don't know. I don't think she likes you very much."

Officer Siegel snorted. "Well, it's mutual."

"Brit's the kind of person people have strong feelings about," I said. "And her parents don't do anything halfway."

Officer Siegel's hand clenched the steering wheel as if she were guiding us through a minefield. "I didn't come here today to talk to you about Brit's complaint. I wanted to tell you something I heard from the administrators this morning. I thought you should know Brit's parents have been hounding that reporter about his source."

The saliva in my mouth dried up. Whoever it was had no idea how much danger they were in. If Brit found out who they were, she would find a way to silence them.

"The reporter confessed it was you," Office Siegel said.

My mouth fell open in shock. "But—I didn't—"

"Look, I've known you think Brit is somehow involved in Beth's death, but you're going too far. Making up stories to get her in trouble is going to backfire on you. We checked out the Ann Arbor lead after the article came out, and there was nothing there. Nothing. Now with the news that you were behind the story the school administration is keeping an even closer eye on you."

"Me?" I squeaked. "Why?"

"There's some concern about what happened at your other school and if it's happening again." My headache tightened, my skull shrinking around my brain, trying to put all the pieces of the puzzle together. There was no point in asking how people had found out. Brit had told them.

"I never talked to that reporter," I said firmly.

Siegel raised an eyebrow. "I'm not debating this with you. I came to tell you because I felt you deserved a heads-up. All I'm going to say is that the issue isn't unclear; we know you did it." There wasn't an ounce of doubt in her voice.

I had a flash of sitting in Ms. Harding's office when Brit had made it look like Sara was to blame for the top-less photo. Brit had set me up. When Derek started asking her family questions about the police investigation she saw the opportunity. She must have sent the false lead to Derek, knowing no one would ever believe me about her being in East Lansing if they thought I'd cried wolf and sent them chasing their tails in Ann Arbor first. The realization of how carefully she'd put everything in place to protect her-self, and for how long, made me want to bend over and catch my breath.

"There have been some discussions about what you might do and what the school's responsibility is if something happens. I know the police are going to talk to your parents about the newspaper story. A couple of students have complained about you, saying that your behavior makes them uncomfortable."

"Who?" My brain tried to run through the Northside student body.

Officer Siegel cocked her head at me. "I'm not going to tell you that. That's not the point. There's an implication that you caused problems for Beth."

At first I wasn't even sure I understood her. "What?"

"That you liked Beth, but that her feelings weren't the same. That the reason she left town initially was in part to get away from you."

It felt like she'd kicked me in the chest. "That's not true."

"The problem is there really isn't anyone to back up your story, except for Brit," she pointed out. I closed my eyes, telling myself it didn't matter, that I knew the truth. "There are hints that you may also be stalking . . ." She stopped herself. "That's too strong of a word. It has been suggested that you might be putting some pressure on Brit. That you're the one pushing the friendship."

"Did she say that?" I asked. I thought of the lies she'd told Zach. How many other people had she talked to? I could picture her dripping poisoned lies into the ears of all my classmates, the police, Derek, my psychologist, my parents. Whispering about my unstable past and how she hoped I wouldn't do anything to her. Telling people she was just the tiniest bit afraid of me. Making certain no one would ever believe me. And I'd been right there by her side, acting like I was her best friend. I'd never even suspected.

"No. It was something that Ms. Harding raised. She's concerned that if you were pressuring Beth for more than she was ready to give, it stands to reason there may be some stress on Britney now," Officer Siegel said.

"Are they going to kick me out of school?" I asked. If they did, everything was lost. I'd already agreed to let my parents send me away for the summer. Brit's parents were going to start renovations on the basement any day. If I didn't figure out a way to get Brit to fall apart in the next week then I was going to fail. If they suspended me, there was no way my parents would let me hang out with Brit, and with the lie that I had been talking to reporters I'd likely be grounded. They'd come up with lists of chores for me to do or ship me off to my grandparents' until camp started.

"The decision isn't up to me, and given my current status around here it's not like they're going to include me in the discussion. I doubt they'll kick you out with exams starting next week, but I thought you should understand the situation."

I reached for the door handle. "Okay. Thanks."

"Kalah," she started. I paused, one foot out of the car. "There's nothing shameful about making mistakes. We all do. Maybe we trust someone we shouldn't, maybe we get involved in something we wish we hadn't. The problem is when we keep repeating mistakes."

I scrambled out of the car, glad to get away. When I first met Officer Siegel, right after Beth disappeared, I hadn't liked her, but over time she'd grown on me. She was cynical and distrustful, but she was honest. I knew she wanted to help me, and I appreciated that, but even she couldn't believe me when Brit was playing her awful games with her too. She wasn't prepared to make that final leap, especially now that the rumors of what had happened at my last school had spread to here. I'd been certain the situation with Madison was behind me when I changed schools, but my past had come back to haunt me. It was like a dark shadow following me everywhere, coloring how other people saw me. A deep, dark shadow dragging me back down. "I really hope things work out for you with your job," I said.

"I hope things work out for you too," she said.

I could feel her eyes drilling through my back as I went back across the street and into the school. As soon as I was in the front door my phone buzzed. My heart raced when I saw the name on my text screen, but then came crashing down as I read the message.

Hey Nicole here. Your brother found me through my art teacher. Happy to talk to you, but don't know what I can tell you. I only talked to Beth a few times, I spent most the time at my boyfriend's place.

I clicked off the phone and slumped against the wall. Everything was falling apart. I'd been stupid to think that Nicole was going to solve everything, but I'd wanted to believe she would know *something*. Now I was even further behind than I'd thought. Brit had known all along not to trust me, and now I didn't have a single thing to back up my story.

CHAPTER TWENTY-FOUR

As I walked into the school people turned to stare. I told myself I was being paranoid and, combined with a hangover, imagining things that weren't there, but there was no denying it was happening. My headache ratcheted up another level. I'd never noticed before how often people slammed their locker doors or insisted on yelling at top volume to their friends.

"Hi-ya!" Brit said.

I winced at her voice, which sounded to my throbbing head like a drill going through a block of ice. "Hey," I said. Brit was staring at me like she was waiting for something. "What?"

"Did you get me a coffee?"

I shut my locker softly and hefted up my bag. "Sorry, I forgot." Brit blinked. "I'm not feeling that good," I explained.

"Oh, no." Brit enveloped me in a hug. The smell of her perfume made me want to heave. "Did you stay up too late studying?" The corner of her mouth twitched. She knew exactly what she was doing.

"I think I'm just coming down with something," I mumbled.

"Spring colds are the worst." Brit fell in step beside me.

"Yep."

"I thought maybe you were upset because I left you up at the Point yesterday. I swear I really did have an appointment."

"No problem," I said. If she was going to play the game that everything was fine, I wasn't going to give her the satisfaction of knowing she was getting to me.

"Listen, I hate to dump this on you first thing, but some people . . . well, there are some rumors going around." Brit bit her bottom lip.

"I heard," I said. I had to hand it to Brit, however she had spread the news, it had set a new speed record.

"Look, I told my parents that I know you weren't the one who sent those messages to the reporter. I'll make sure they don't press charges or anything. Someone must have used your email account to send the message to him as some kind of sick joke. All it takes is someone watching over your shoulder as you log in and then they have your password."

She smiled. "I've got your back."

I nodded. "Thanks."

Brit hugged me. "I want you to know that I'm here for you. I know you wouldn't betray me. If anyone causes you any problems, you let me know. You can count on me." She gave me another squeeze. I heard the threat in her words. If we weren't friends, I was vulnerable. She'd thrown me into the lion pit and then made sure she was the only one who could pull me back out. She jogged off toward her class.

I made sure my head was high as I walked down the hall. No one spoke directly to me. It was like I'd contracted Ebola: everyone left a pocket of space around me, careful not to touch. No one wanted to be contaminated by whatever was wrong with me.

I overheard snippets of conversations as I walked.

"My cousin said she went crazy at her last school and had to be locked up."

"The police think she did something to Beth. She sent a whole bunch of lies to that reporter about Brit too."

"Poor Brit. Kalah's basically stalking her."

"I heard the police might arrest her."

I wanted to spin and respond, but I knew it wouldn't make a difference. What hurt the most was the idea that I'd done something to Beth. When I walked into history I expected Melissa to be cackling about the news with her friends. She'd never liked me and instead of being nice to her after Brit had come back I'd been bitchy. I was now paying for that. Zach wouldn't even look at me.

By lunch I knew there was no way I could face walking into the cafeteria; not only did I still feel sick, but also the idea of everyone not even bothering to pretend that they weren't staring was more than I could face. I ducked into the bathroom instead. I was in the stall when a group of people came in and gathered around the sinks. When I heard Melissa's voice I pulled my feet up so they couldn't be seen under the stall door. It was a bunch of girls from the team.

"I didn't think reporters ever gave up their sources," Karen said.

"Brit's parents suspected her, so they went to him with the details of Kalah's old school and a note from some psychologist and basically threatened him that if it was Kalah and he didn't admit it and print a retraction based on what they told him they would sue his ass," Melissa added.

"My brother's girlfriend goes to Windsor Prep," Karen said. "She said Kalah had some kind of breakdown there."

"The whole thing is freaky," Amy said.

"I feel so bad for Brit," Melissa said. "I talked to her this morning, and it's clear she's really upset. Can you imagine finding out that one of your best friends is mental? She couldn't even talk about it. She's sticking by Kalah's side, but that's just because she's so loyal."

"No one knows what's really going on," Amy said. "At the end of the day Kalah's still a part of our team."

Someone pushed on my stall door and, finding it locked, assumed it was out of order and moved to the next one. "I can't believe she was allowed to come to this school given what happened at her last one, though," Melissa said. "You'd think there would be some kind of rule."

"What exactly did happen?" Karen asked.

"Kalah attacked this girl because the girl didn't want to be her friend. I heard Kalah clawed her in the face. Apparently she'll be scarred for life," Melissa said in a hushed voice as if she were telling ghost stories around a campfire while grilling weenies on a stick. "Kalah would have gone to jail except she was too young to be criminally charged."

I wanted to unlock the door and tell them this story was total bullshit. I never once hit Madison, or scratched her, or even spit on her. The way the story was growing, by the end of the day Madison would be in a wheelchair because I'd dragged her behind my car.

"Do you know if that's true?" Amy asked over a rush of water in the sink. I felt a wave of affection for her. "I'm not saying it's not, but unless you know for certain I'm not sure it's fair to talk about it."

"But someone has to talk about it. I mean, if nothing else then as a warning. You know Brit and Beth wouldn't have hung out with her if they'd known she was capable of something like that." Melissa sniffed. "I always thought she was odd."

"So were Kalah and Beth having a thing or what?" Karen asked.

"You know how Beth was: she flirted with everyone. I'm betting she kissed Kalah once and then she blew it into some big love affair," Melissa said. "I just hope Kalah didn't have anything to do with Beth's death."

"But that doesn't make any sense. I thought Beth saved Brit from throwing herself off the Point. Was Kalah even there?" Amy asked.

"I'm not saying I know exactly what happened, all I'm saying is that there's something really weird with Kalah," Melissa said. The door swished shut behind them, cutting off anything else someone might say.

I couldn't tell if I was glad I'd heard what they had to say or not. Other than Amy, who seemed to be the only one who was convinced I wasn't likely to turn into some kind of unhinged serial killer, everyone was already certain I was guilty. They didn't even know what exactly I was guilty of, but they were sure it was something.

There would be almost no way to change people's minds. What was the term Dr. Sherman had tried to teach me? Confirmation bias. Everyone had decided I was crazy, so anything I did or said would be seen through that lens. I was going to have to do something radical, something that would be irrefutable, if I wanted to make a difference.

My eyes skimmed over the graffiti scratched and written on the stall wall. There wasn't going to be any wisdom to be found in here. I yanked a Sharpie marker out of my bag and wrote in giant letters down the door, *We're all mad here.*

I stared at the words. It was a quote from Beth's copy of *Alice in Wonderland*. And somewhere along the way it had become my life.

Bean Around the World used to be Brit and Beth's favorite coffee destination. It's near the community college, and it smells like a mix of coffee and weed, and the windows are perpetually steamed up.

It was strangely quiet today. The college had exams a week earlier, and summer classes hadn't started yet. I grabbed my tea and, after some debate, a chocolate croissant. Beth was the one who'd gotten me hooked on them. Bread and chocolate together seemed like a bad combo, but the buttery, flaky pastry with the melty strip of dark chocolate down the center was sublime. I grabbed a seat by the front window and tore chunks off the croissant and dropped them in my mouth. This way I'd be able to see Brit as soon as she arrived.

I was lucky to be out this afternoon. Once I talked to my parents tonight about the bourbon incident combined with the police showing up to tell them I'd been sending fake stories to the press I'd likely be grounded for life. They weren't going to believe that I hadn't sent the email. Brit had made sure it was from my account, and my brother would tell them I thought Brit was guilty. If it weren't for

Brit sticking up for me with her parents, I would likely have some kind of criminal charges. I could just picture my next appointment with Dr. Sherman.

I took a sip of tea and then put it right back down. It was nuclear hot. I'd been somewhat surprised to get the text from Brit inviting me to meet her here after school. It made me unsettled that I didn't know what she wanted to discuss.

I watched out the large front window. Summer had arrived, and we were just waiting for the calendar to catch up. Everyone was out in shorts and barely there skirts. Then I saw her. Brit was standing outside with Melissa. I sat up straighter. I hadn't known Britney had invited her to join us. The two of them stood outside talking. Then Melissa saw me. She nudged Brit, and they both turned to stare. There was a pause. I felt almost like a creature in the zoo. I made a goofy face, hoping to make them laugh, but Melissa stepped back quickly. She acted as if I'd lunged at the glass and started beating on it.

Brit gave Melissa a hug and then came in. She waved at me and then went to the counter to get her drink. Melissa stood watching for a second and then hustled off. I started to feel uneasy again. What had Brit told her?

Brit slopped a bit of her latte into the saucer and then onto the table when she put it down. "Shit. Hang on." She returned a second later with a wad of napkins and mopped it up. No wonder she'd made such a crap waitress—she couldn't even carry one cup of coffee without spilling.

Brit sighed dramatically as she dropped into her seat. "I keep reminding myself we have only one week of classes left. Five days. I can make it that long."

"Five days, one hundred twenty hours," I said. I had my own countdown going. I was well aware of how much time was left.

"Feels like a lifetime." Brit stirred her latte, the spoon clanking on the side of the cup. "I can't wait for school to be over." She picked up her cup and blew across the top. "How did things go today?"

"Not great." *Understatement of the year.* "I just can't figure out how people found out what happened at my last school," I said.

Brit's eyes widened. "You're not hinting that I told people, are you? You know how seriously I take keeping secrets."

We stared across the table at each other, the air crackling with tension. She knew I knew she was lying, and she was waiting for me to call her on it.

Brit looked away first. "I suspect it was Ms. Harding who spilled the beans. Trust me, I see my parents chatting with other people in the field all the time. There's nothing they like more than spreading stories about the patients they're working with. Most likely she struck up a conversation with the school counselor over there."

"Maybe," I said.

Brit put her cup down in the saucer with a clink. "Listen,

this will all blow over. With me as your best friend people will eventually realize that there's nothing to the story."

I felt the implied threat—if she wasn't by my side then people would believe it. I'd better come to heel or she'd make me sorry. I'd end up with comments on my Facebook page that made the stuff on Sara's look tame.

"I wanted to meet to talk to you today about the team and plans since you'll be captain," Britney said.

I blew on my tea. Part of me wanted to remind her that we were done for the year and next season she wasn't involved. She'd be at Cornell. It had nothing to do with her anymore. "What about them?"

Brit ripped off a corner of my croissant and popped it into her mouth. A tiny flake of pastry stuck to her lip. "It's been a hard year for the team. Coming in second, losing Beth."

"Thinking they'd lost you," I added.

Brit smiled. "True." She sipped her coffee. "It's going to be important to start the year off right. Get some new blood on the team."

I nodded. "Sure. I think overall we're in pretty good shape. The freshmen that came on this year are strong. Assuming we work on getting some good defense players at tryouts, we're going to kick some ass." I expected Brit to agree, but instead she sighed.

"See, that's the thing," Brit said. "I think you need to be careful of expectations. If you set up everyone to think you guys will go all the way, and then things don't come together, you can take down a team's spirit for a few years."

I could feel my eyebrows draw together. "You don't think we'll do well next year?" I didn't get what she was playing at. Was she trying to chip away at my confidence? After everything that had happened, did she really think my big worry was the field hockey team?

"It's not that I think you guys won't work hard, but I've been looking over the competition. It's a brutal season."

"This year was pretty harsh, and we held our own," I countered.

"The thing is, sometimes you're outmatched. You can't win. It's not a matter of effort or heart; it's just the facts. You're outgunned." Brit's face was calm. "You've lost some good people on the team. Your guys aren't as solid as you think."

"But you still try your best," I said. The milk in my tea started to taste sour, and I put down the cup.

"If you come up against an opponent that has you beat, you have to know it. If you try to take them down, you could get hurt." Brit stared across the table at me, and I realized we weren't talking about field hockey. "No one wants anyone to get hurt."

The sounds of the coffee shop drifted into the background, and I felt almost as if she were hypnotizing me. "What do you mean?"

"I mean there are games you won't win. The sooner you

know that, the better off you'll be. If you insist on trying to take out someone who is better than you, you'll lose."

I knew it was only my imagination, but it felt like the temperature around us had dropped. "I don't give up," I said.

Brit made a tsk-ing sound. "That's where you're making a mistake."

My breath was getting shallow. "Maybe a team that thinks it is unbeatable only comes across that way because no one ever really challenged it before."

Brit shrugged. "Maybe. Maybe not. I just thought I should warn you."

"I'm not scared of you," I said softly. My voice shook, making a liar out of me.

Brit's lips twitched as if her smile wanted to poke out, jack-in-the-box style. "Kalah, what are you talking about?"

"You know," I said.

"I didn't mean to make you upset," Brit said. "It's this intensity that made me bring it up at all. You don't want to push the team past what they're capable of. It's not always about winning. If you push some of those girls too hard they'll break."

"I know," I whispered.

"You need some perspective, Kalah. It's high school field hockey. It's not an Olympic medal, or war—it's a game." Britney pulled her bag out from under her chair and began to fuss with the things inside. "Look, I'm your best friend, so I have to tell you, even if you don't want to hear it. You're not doing well. Everyone is talking about it. You have huge black circles under your eyes, you need a haircut, and your nails look like shit." I glanced down at my hands. She was right. "You're also acting weird, and with everything going around school, you're not helping yourself. I want to believe you had nothing to do with that reporter, that you would never do anything to hurt me, but you're making it hard. I can protect you this year, but next year you'll be on your own."

"I know you told Dr. Sherman that you're afraid of me."

Her lips twitched again. "What I tell her is supposed to be confidential. I only talked to her about you because I'm worried."

"Uh-huh." I thought I had been so clever, sneaking around trying to prove Brit had done something, and the whole time she'd been playing me. Setting me up. Nicole wasn't going to help me, and I didn't have proof of anything. Based on all Brit had done, not a soul was going to believe any accusations I made against her.

"I'm trying to be patient because I know how much Beth meant to you and how hard her loss hit you, but you aren't the center of the universe." Brit dabbed her napkin at the corner of her mouth, wiping away a tiny smear of chocolate.

"I know." My voice came out small and weak.

"I've been through my own trauma, I'm dealing with Jason, trying to take exams, graduate, and then figure out what the hell I'm going to do next year. I could use some support from my best friend. In case you forgot, Beth had been my friend long before you were in the picture. I've had a loss. I'm struggling too."

I suddenly felt like crying. "Brit," I said.

"You said your parents are worried about you." Brit stood. "It seems to me maybe you need to worry about yourself."

CHAPTER TWENTY-FIVE

Beth and I were at the park. It was early spring, just a week or so before she would vanish. She was sitting on the metal merry-go-round and my arms ached from spinning her. Her head was back and she was laughing.

"Can you picture it?" Dr. Sherman asked.

I nodded, keeping my eyes closed. I could almost feel the moment. The cold spring air felt like it was burning my cheeks. My hands stung as I slapped the rusted metal bars coated in thick paint as they whipped past, trying to make her go faster. Beth's laughter gave me a feeling like champagne, bubbles of happiness shooting up through my chest. I wanted to crawl inside the memory and never leave.

It was as if I could see the past like an observer. My

eyes were sparkling, and I was almost bent over from my own laughter. I looked good. I scrambled to figure out what it was exactly, but the best I could come up with was that I was happy. The sense of being content seemed to light something up inside me, changing the structure of my features, how my body moved, my gestures—everything.

"What are you feeling?" Dr. Sherman asked. I opened my eyes to see her across the desk from me. The time at the park with Beth wasn't that long ago, but it felt like a different lifetime. As if it were an impossibly long journey from that point and I'd lost my way. I had no idea how to get back to that version of myself. I wasn't even sure it was possible. I caught a glance of my reflection in the window behind her. My hair looked lank and there were dark circles under my eyes. I looked nothing like the girl in the memory. No wonder my parents had encouraged me to leave school early for today's appointment. They were willing to do anything, squeeze me into any open slot with Dr. Sherman, to keep me from falling further apart. I could tell they thought I had sent the note to the reporter and they were afraid to dig too deep to find out for sure. That's why they had Dr. Sherman. They were counting on her to hold me together until they could bustle me off to camp.

"I was really happy with Beth," I said. "I know everyone thinks it was just in my head, but it wasn't."

Dr. Sherman's mouth pressed into a line. "Kalah, I don't think you should assume from a few comments that everyone thinks your relationship with Beth was imaginary."

"Really? Because if you were to take a poll at my school I think you'd discover otherwise. At first people made what we felt for each other into just some physical thing, but now they've decided it's something else, that I stalked her. Hounded her. Just like I supposedly did to Madison." I realized that I had peeled another sliver of skin away around my nail. I stuck my thumb in my mouth to suck away the blood.

Walking through the halls at school felt like running a gauntlet, the whispers hitting me like punches on my already bruised flesh. When Brit was around me things quieted down, but when she wasn't it was worse. "No one believes me," I mumbled.

"Your brother helped you, didn't he?"

I sighed and nodded. Nadir had found a way to chase down Nicole, but he'd done it because he wanted me to face the truth, not because he thought Nicole would reveal a big secret. On the phone he'd kept telling me that now that I'd talked to Nicole I could move on.

"I don't know if Beth would like me anymore," I said softly, putting into words one of my biggest fears. "I'm nothing like the person I used to be." My breath caught in my chest, if I let it go I knew I'd start crying.

"What do you want to happen?" Dr. Sherman asked. "If you could wave a wand and fast-forward time, what is the outcome you'd like to see?"

"I want my life back. I want everyone to stop whispering about me, twisting everything I say or do into something else. I want everyone to forget what happened at my old school and stop using it as an excuse to ignore what I'm saying now." The wants spilled out of my mouth faster and faster, an avalanche. "I want to stop feeling bad for disappointing my parents and Zach. I want to think about Beth without it hurting so much. And I really want Brit to be held accountable for what she did." The last words out of my mouth were almost shouting, and I shut my mouth with a click, surprised at how angry I sounded.

Dr. Sherman didn't seem shocked at my outburst. She put down her pen. "Kalah, be honest with me. Are you taking your medication?"

My arms were wrapped around my chest, as if I could hold myself together. "No. But a bunch of pills aren't going to help." As soon as the words were out of my mouth I closed my eyes. I hadn't meant to tell her, but there was no point in keeping it a secret. No doubt Brit had already shared that little detail with her during one of their little chats.

Dr. Sherman stepped around her desk and sat in the seat next to mine. "Kalah, I believe this is real for you. And I want you to know that there are many of us—me, your mom and dad, your brother—who want to help you get through this. I can tell you feel alone, but you're not."

I felt exhausted. She could dress it up any way she wanted; what she was saying was that she didn't believe me.

"I'm concerned that you've been lying about your medication."

I shifted in the seat. *Lying* made it sound shifty and wrong. "I don't feel right when I take the medication."

"Part of what we're trying to do is to take the edge off of your emotions. Think of it as turning down the volume in the room so that you can focus on one particular thing."

"I can't do that. I can't afford to miss a single thing."

Dr. Sherman leaned forward. "Even if it comes at the cost of your health?"

"What about Beth's health? She's dead," I fired back. "Do you realize that could be my fault? Beth was the only one who was Brit's equal. If Beth hadn't been distracted with what was happening between the two of us, then she might have realized how on edge Britney was. She might never have died." I sat back. I felt light-headed, like I might pass out.

My fault. This was my fault. That was the thing I hadn't been willing to face. I'd distracted Beth, and that was why she was dead.

"I'm going to talk to your parents. Perhaps it's not a great idea for you to head off to camp."

A ripple of excitement ran down my spine. If I didn't have to go away to camp, I might have a few more weeks before renos started in Brit's basement—time to find some other angle that might offer proof. Brit was sure she'd won; it might mean that her guard was lowered. There still had to be a way to make this work. I wasn't going to give up. I wasn't a quitter.

I forced myself to focus on Dr. Sherman. I had to get her to fully embrace her idea that going away for the summer was a bad plan. "I guess going to camp might not be best," I said. "If I stayed here, we could maybe see each other more frequently." I hoped she wouldn't hear the excitement in my voice. It would be better if she and my parents thought I was a bit reluctant.

"I'm thinking of a residential program."

Her words slammed into me like a semitruck. "A what?"

"A residential program would give you the chance to do some in-depth work on your mental health with a counselor while also trying a medication regime." She gave me a look. "This way you could be monitored for compliance."

"I don't need to be on drugs." I had the sudden urge to check the door to the office to make sure it wasn't locked or someone wasn't waiting for me in the lobby with a straitjacket.

"There's nothing wrong with medication; often people find the right mix of medicine can clear the fog, make it easier to see what the problems are and how to best tackle them. The program I'm thinking of is in upper Michigan. It's designed for teens and young adults. You may find it comforting to talk to other people struggling with some of the same issues. It has a lot of outdoor activities, a nice mix of group sessions as well as one-on-one. I believe you'd really benefit from a dual-diagnosis approach."

I couldn't believe this was happening. "You want to lock me in some psych hospital for mentally ill teens?"

"I believe you need to focus on your mental health free of any distractions. Getting away from here to go to a summer job may reduce your stress because it's removing the triggers, but it isn't addressing the underlying issues. You need to face those straight on."

"I'm not going to some camp for psychos," I said. "I won't do it." Instead of coming out stern and serious, my voice shook.

"I understand this isn't what you want, but I need you to answer a question for me." She paused and waited until I reluctantly nodded. "How is your current approach working for you?"

I welled up with tears and hated myself for having that reaction to some stupid Dr. Phil tagline. "I don't want to go away," I said.

"I think you are seeing this as a step back, when in reality this can be a very positive step forward for you. This is a chance for you to take control of your health."

Dr. Sherman stood and went over to the credenza on the far wall. She pulled out a brochure from the drawer and brought it over to me. She sat in the chair next to mine as if she was going to read it to me like a bedtime story.

I flipped through the glossy pages. It looked like one of the college brochures that were coming in the mail now that

I was almost a senior. People, one of each race to feel inclusive, were all airbrushed perfect and posed sitting in front of a huge stone fireplace, with another shot of a girl smiling as she paddled a canoe, and another of a group sitting in a circle, their faces all serious as they reached new levels of mental wellness. The ink on the back of the slick brochure was sticking to my fingers. I wanted to wipe it off on my jeans.

"I don't know what my parents will think of this," I said. "It looks expensive."

"They want what's best for you," she said.

"I don't think I need to do something this extreme," I said, trying to pass her the brochure back. "I'll see you more often and I promise I'll take the medication—my mom can watch me if she needs to—but I don't want to go away. It's not going to help me."

Dr. Sherman leaned toward me. "Kalah, I want you to try and see this from an outsider's perspective. You're having the same problem you had at your previous school, only this time the outcome has been more serious. There's what happened to your classmate Sara, and with this reporter. . . ." She held up a hand to stop me from interrupting her. "I'm not going to argue those things with you, all I'm saying is that if this situation continues unaddressed it could become even more dire."

"Brit is going away to college in the fall," I said. "There isn't going to be a problem."

"I know you don't want to find yourself in this same situation a year from now only with different people. You want to tackle this so you can have it behind you once and for all."

I was willing to bet there would be no way I'd find myself facing the same problem ever again in my life. What are the odds that one of your best friends would murder the other and then find a way to manipulate the whole thing? The absurd urge to laugh started to burble up inside me. I bit the inside of my lip to make it stop, but it was too late and the desire was too strong.

Dr. Sherman pulled back when I started to laugh. I slapped my hand over my mouth and tried to make it sound like I'd been coughing, but there was no way she was going to fall for that.

"I'm nervous," I said. "I wasn't expecting this."

Dr. Sherman went to sit behind her desk. The session had to be almost over. I'd been trapped in here forever.

"I'll take this and think about it," I said. I made a big production of tucking the brochure into my bag. "My parents and I can talk about it at home. I don't want to make any decisions right away because I need to focus on exams." I made a show of looking at her clock. "In fact, I should get back to school. I can catch final period."

Dr. Sherman smiled. "You should know me better by now, or maybe it's that I know you."

"What?"

"I know a delay tactic when I see one."

"I really do need to study," I protested.

Dr. Sherman leaned back in her chair. "That's fine. And you're welcome to take the brochure and talk about it to your parents."

"Okay," I stood. I wanted to bolt for the door, but I knew that wouldn't look good.

"What you need to understand, Kalah, is that regardless of how long you would like to think on the issue, I'm going to recommend this course of action to your family. I strongly believe that you need a residential program. I understand that you don't feel it is the right decision for you, but I don't believe you're in a place to make a good choice at this time."

I felt myself go cold. "So you're saying everything has already been decided."

"I know when you look back on this you're going to agree this was the best choice."

I didn't even bother to answer her and instead pulled the brochure out of my bag, dropped it on the floor, and walked out.

CHAPTER TWENTY-SIX

My skin felt like it had been stung all over by a million microscopic bees. It was as if I were hyperaware, each nerve at full attention. The smell of oil paint and the spongy wet rot smell of papier-mâché hung in the air. I could hear people outside the window yelling and calling out to each other. School had been out for almost an hour, but there were still people hanging around the halls.

I'd called Brit as soon as I left Dr. Sherman's office. The idea had come to me perfectly formed. It was time for me to confront Brit with what I knew. I had nothing to lose. She had to be dying to tell someone. This was the biggest thing that had ever happened to her, that she'd ever done. I know Brit. She wanted to brag. She'd been dancing around it, so now was the time to give her a chance to gloat. Besides, she already knew I suspected what happened. All the games she was playing were to keep me in my place and let me know how much I had to lose if I caused her trouble. Britney would think it was safe to tell me. Everyone already thinks I'm crazy. Who would believe me? Only she wouldn't know I wasn't counting on anyone believing me. I was going to bring them proof.

My eyes kept darting around the art room. If this worked, she'd be here in seconds. I knew I should leave it alone, but I couldn't resist touching my phone. I'd tucked it directly behind a few bottles of poster paint on the bookshelf. The record function was still on.

"Testing," I said softly. The line on the bottom of the screen wriggled, letting me know it was recording. I wanted to turn it off and double-check that it was picking up enough sound, but I didn't have time. I'd already tested it at least a dozen times. I briefly debated setting it to video record, but I worried I didn't have enough battery life left. Audio recording would require less juice, and I needed to make sure I got as much taped as possible. I put the phone back down and shifted the paint bottle just a few millimeters to the left.

This had to work. My hands shook. Once I confronted Brit there would be no going back, no pretending. Maybe I should take off before she got there and take more time to make sure I had a foolproof plan. This was the only thing

I could think of that stood any chance at all. School would be over in days and then I'd be shipped off to a residential program. The evidence would be gone from her basement, and there would be no way to pin it on her. I had to come up with something that would be beyond doubt. It wasn't just about Beth anymore. Now I had to protect myself. Even if I wanted to walk away I couldn't. I tapped my foot in beats of six to try to calm myself.

"What's all the cloak-and-dagger?" Brit leaned on the doorjamb. She held up her phone, showing the text I'd sent her.

"I have to talk to you. Just us," I said. "I knew we could be alone here."

Brit came in the room. She wandered slowly past the bookshelf, and I tried not to stare at where the phone was hidden. Her finger trailed along the table. She looked over the final art projects as if she were a curator from the Louvre. She seemed completely unruffled.

I took a deep breath when I realized she'd come alone. I'd been half convinced she'd have a posse trailing in her wake under the guise that they were looking out for her. "Thanks for coming," I said.

She looked up from the art on the table. "What do you want?"

"I want to talk about what happened. About the truth." The anxiety I'd been feeling all day flowed out of me, and in its place there was sudden anger. It felt good to confront her, like a huge release of this toxic thing I'd kept inside. "If we're going to be friends, real friends, we can't have any secrets."

The corner of Brit's mouth lifted. "Of course. After all, what are friends for if you can't tell them the absolute truth? Are you saying you did tell that reporter Derek those lies about me?"

"Don't bother playing games. I know what you did." I pronounced each word loud and clear as if I were reading out a sentence from the court.

Brit placed a hand over her heart in fake shock. "What I did?"

"Was it an accident? I really want to believe that it was. That you didn't plan any of this." My throat grew tight. "I know you loved Beth."

"Yes," Brit said. Her head tilted down and her hair swung to cover her face. Did she finally feel some shame?

"Brit, we can still make this right. If it was an accident, you must have been scared. I know how it is: you tell one lie and then you have to tell another to cover for the first. You got in over your head. Maybe you want to believe your own story, but the fact is I know the truth. I know you killed Beth."

I half expected her to break down in tears or maybe to throw something at me, but she didn't seem to react at all. She just stood there with a tiny smile on her face. She began to stroll around the room. I had to keep turning to face her.

I didn't want her behind me.

"Why would I kill Beth? Are you listening to yourself right now?"

"You were mad because you thought she was with Jason. You guys were always competing, and you couldn't stand the idea that you were losing." She didn't respond. I had to make her angrier, get her to react. "You hated whenever someone picked Beth over you. Colleges did. Guys did. The truth was that Beth was the one people really liked, not you. I think we all knew you really were nothing more than a shallow bitch who would peak in high school."

Brit paused and leaned against the bookcase. She seemed to evaluate what I'd been saying, but instead of lashing out at me she seemed almost pleased. Proud. "Beth was worried about you. I told her that she shouldn't have kissed you. You know how she was; everything was just a game to her. I think she wondered how quiet little Kalah would react, but I don't think she ever expected your response. I tried to tell her you couldn't take teasing like that."

"You're lying," I said.

Brit sighed. "She thought you were too into her. I told her you can't expect to play with people's feelings and not get burned. She left to get away from you."

"That's not true," I said. "She never left. You killed her in your basement. She came over to talk to you about Jason the night of her birthday, and you killed her."

"Does it make it easier for you if you think I'm to blame?"

"You're lying," I said. "Maybe you're the one who can't accept what you've done. You killed your best friend over something that wasn't even true."

Brit shook her head sadly. "What did you do to Beth, Kalah?"

"What?"

"My mom asked me if it was possible that the reason I blocked out what happened at the Point was because maybe I saw something. Something I didn't want to face. Did you know Beth was coming to stop me and try to use that as an opportunity to talk to her? Did she tell you to go away? Did you snap?" She smiled again. "Maybe you pushed her."

I could feel all the energy I'd built up start to melt away. She wasn't going to admit to anything. I'd been so sure if I confronted her she would say something, admit her role. I'd already pictured myself clutching my phone as if it were buried treasure and hustling the recording directly to Officer Siegel.

The entire police department would gather around to listen to the confession. My parents would be standing there relieved, realizing that it was over, that I had been right all along. Then they would bring Brit in. She would try to lie her way out of it again, but when she was confronted with the tape she would break down. I'd come back to school and instead of people talking about me in hushed tones dripping with fake sympathy they would be in awe. They'd wonder how they missed everything.

"Kalah, stop it. You're scaring me," Brit said. "Stay over there."

I looked up confused. I hadn't moved.

"I shouldn't have come," Brit said. "I didn't want to believe what everyone was saying about what happened at your old school."

Before I could respond, Britney grabbed a corner of the bookcase and pulled sending the art on the shelves flying to the floor. The sound was like an explosion. The pottery shattered and one of the paint bottles broke, splashing bright turquoise spatters everywhere.

"Kalah, don't!" Brit yelled. "Please don't hurt me."

I stared at her with my mouth hanging open. What the hell was she doing?

Brit made sure I was watching her and then she slapped herself hard in the face. She let out a cry and the bent down, picking up a piece of broken pottery. She tossed the pottery up as if it were a baseball and then, before I could respond, smashed the pottery into the side of her face.

"Oh, Kalah, please stop." Brit stepped gingerly through the mess on the floor, making sure to keep her feet clear of the paint. She pointed down at the phone lying in the middle of the mess and waggled her finger silently in my face. She'd seen it all along. Or maybe she'd just guessed. Known that was something she would have done if the situation were reversed.

There was a slam of a door down the hall and the sound

of footsteps. Brit blew me a kiss. There was a trickle of blood running from a cut just above her mouth. Then she ran from the room, calling for help.

I hadn't stood a chance. Brit had always been one step ahead of me. All I'd done was put my head in the noose I thought I'd made for her.

CHAPTER TWENTY-SEVEN

Watching the science show *Nova* with my dad I'd learned about dark matter. This invisible mass neither emits nor absorbs light. You only know it is there because of its gravitational pull on everything around it. That's what I felt like I'd become. This thing in the room that everyone pretended they couldn't see, but I was sucking in all the energy, growing heavier and denser. My own mini–black hole.

We were all crammed into Principal Hamstead's office, Brit sandwiched between her two parents like they were her personal bodyguards. There was a hint of a bruise near her eye, and the cut above her lip was covered with a small bandage that she was sporting like a badge of honor.

Principal Hamstead looked at me as if I were something

he'd scraped off his shoe. His neck jutted out from his shoulders, with his head looking unnaturally large at the end of it. It gave him the appearance of a vulture. "You must understand that we have zero tolerance for physical violence here at Northside."

"Of course," my dad said. He'd worn a tie for the meeting. He looked as uncomfortable and as out of place as I felt. Having Nadir as their first kid hadn't prepared my parents for this kind of trouble.

"I want to thank everyone for making time for this meeting. I know things are busy with the end of the school year and graduation around the corner," Hamstead said.

"We also have home renovations starting in a week," Brit's dad said with a scowl on his face.

"I know how stressful home projects can be," Principal Hamstead said. "However, we need to discuss how to best handle this situation."

"This was an assault. You're lucky we don't file criminal charges," Dr. Reyerson spit. She'd done nothing but shoot daggers at me since they'd arrived. If she could have reached over with her perfectly French-tipped manicure and slapped me for daring to harm her precious Brit, she would have done it. "I knew we should have done something when we heard she was the source to the paper, but I let Brit convince me to let it go, and now this."

"We appreciate you not making this a criminal matter." Dad shifted in his chair.

"I think we all understand that Kalah isn't well," Ms. Harding said. She was the only one who looked happy to be in this meeting—hell, she looked practically gleeful. This had to be a school counselor's wet dream situation. Drama. Mental health. High emotions. A chance for her to sound like an expert. She could sit between our warring families like she was a hostage negotiator.

"We've come together because it's important we're all on the same page and create a plan to finish out this school year," Mr. Hamstead said. "Our number one priority is that Britney feel safe."

Everyone in the room nodded. Poor, poor Brit. I bit the inside of my cheek until I tasted blood.

"I don't want her to have any access to Britney," Dr. Ryerson said. "We're considering a restraining order."

"Mom, don't. I know Kalah didn't mean it," Britney said. Everyone's face softened when they looked at her, like they could hardly believe how kind she was to forgive me. "I don't want what happened to cause her any more problems."

I clenched my hands into fists and stared down at the floor.

"We're going to need assurances that Kalah is going to get some help before the start of school next year. You understand that other parents are going to hold the school accountable to ensuring there is no repeat of this behavior," Mr. Hamstead said.

"We've arranged for Kalah to have additional treatment,

but I'm sure her doctor can provide some kind of note before the start of school next year," my mom said.

Dr. Ryerson sniffed. It was clear what she thought of the treatment I might get. Most likely she would advocate that I get some kind electric shock therapy. Maybe waterboarding.

"One of the reasons that we wanted to get everyone together is also to clear the air. I know that Britney and Kalah have been friends. This is a wonderful opportunity for Kalah to apologize." Ms. Harding smiled. "I often find that a sincere sorry is one of the most valuable steps toward healing."

I took a deep breath. My fingernails were digging into the palms of my hands as I tried to keep my hands still. My parents had warned me I'd be expected to apologize. There hadn't been any discussion about what if I didn't want to. Or the truth that I hadn't done a damn thing to her. This was a command performance.

I closed my eyes for a second and pictured Beth. How her front tooth was a bit crooked and how she smiled when she was planning to cause some trouble in the best way possible. I imagined I was talking to her instead of Brit. "I want to say how really sorry I am. I let you down, but more than that, I let myself down." When I opened my eyes Brit was staring directly at me.

"Thank you, Kalah," Ms. Harding said. "I imagine you already feel better with that off your chest."

"Loads," I said flatly. My mom squeezed my knee.

"Any kind of physical violence or fighting is normally an automatic suspension. However, Britney has requested that not happen, both because it is so close to the end of the year and given the extraordinary . . . um, circumstances." Hamstead fiddled with his tie. Extraordinary circumstances—that was an interesting spin on the situation.

"Kalah, I want you to know I'm not mad at you at all," Brit said. Her dad patted her back.

"Thanks," I managed to push out.

"I know you're not in a good place," Britney added. I nodded. She was at least right about that. I *was* in a shitty place. And she'd put me there.

"I just hope that you get the help you need and that you can come back next year and start fresh. I really hope someday we can reach out to each other and if not be friends, still be friendly." The sun was streaming in the window turning Brit's light blond hair into a golden halo around her face.

Everyone smiled at Brit, like she was some kind of saint or martyr who had come down from on high to share her benevolence. She was a regular Gandhi, turning the other cheek.

"That is remarkably mature of you, Britney," Ms. Harding said.

Brit's parents sat up straight as if they were about to receive an award for raising such a fine upstanding citizen. None of them seemed to realize that Brit was turning the knife by bringing up next year. She was making sure I knew that there would be no way that I would escape this stain. Everyone at school was certain I was some kind of psycho. At best they thought I was some kind of stalker who had an obsession with Brit. At worst they thought I was somehow involved in what had happened to Beth. Everyone would know I'd spent the summer in a psych program.

Brit was trying to look brave and noble, but I could see just a tiny hint of satisfaction on her face. She was enjoying this. She turned to the window and tilted her chin up slightly.

"I think this has been a positive meeting," Ms. Harding said. Everyone mumbled agreement and started to collect their things.

Mr. Hamstead shook Brit's parents' hands. "I'll look forward to seeing you both at graduation."

"We wanted to ask you about getting some seats reserved near the front," Dr. Ryerson said. "Britney's grandparents are coming, and her grandfather doesn't have very good mobility."

"He was in the military," Dr. Matson said. "Physician in the medical corps." I managed to avoid rolling my eyes. Brit's dad always made it sound like his father was some World War II vet who had been wounded while single-handedly taking out Hitler and saving the lives of other less brave soldiers. Brit told me he'd never even been in any kind of combat. He'd been stationed in Hawaii long after the war and spent most of his time treating VD and sunburns. The reason he couldn't walk well now was arthritis.

"We don't have any reserved seating," Mr. Hamstead said. "We've always done a first come, first served with the seating for graduation."

Brit's parents stood there silently. They didn't have to say anything.

"I'm sure we could make an exception, given this particular situation."

Her parents smiled. It must be nice to live in a world where things always worked out in your favor. I was surprised the leaves from the trees in their yard didn't fall in tidy piles. Or maybe just blow over onto the neighbor's lawn.

My dad stood, but Brit's parents made it clear they weren't going to shake his hand. Maybe they thought our entire family was contaminated.

"We wish you the best," Dr. Ryerson said, her nose slightly in the air. Then their whole family swept out.

My parents thanked Ms. Harding and Mr. Hamstead for their time. They muttered platitudes about how much they appreciated the sensitive way things had been handled. I stood by the door with my arms crossed over my chest.

"Kalah, I hope you make the best of this fresh start," Mr. Hamstead said.

I nodded. He didn't want to hear that there was no such thing as a fresh start. What had happened would be with me forever. Brit was pretending to be bruised from our encounter, but I was the one who was scarred.

Brit was waiting for me by my locker after the meeting. I stopped short when I saw her leaning there putting on another coat of lip gloss. Her lips were so shiny that they looked wet. She pushed off and took a few steps toward me.

"Aren't you afraid?" I asked. "What if I attack you again?"

She pursed her lips into a big fake pout. "Don't be like that. You know I had to do that."

"Lie?"

She shook her head, the same expression my mom would make when I'd done something that disappointed her. "It doesn't have to be like this, but it's up to you. You're the one who keeps turning on me."

My head felt ready to explode. "Me?"

Her voice turned sharp. "Yes, you. Making those accusations. Snooping in my room. *Sneaking off* to East Lansing. Plotting. Saying those nasty things. I know you're not well. You had to know no one would believe you. Not Zach. Not your parents."

"*I'm* not well," I said. A wave of exhaustion threatened to take me under. I stepped past her and went to my locker. "Fine. You're right. I'm sorry. I shouldn't have said those things to you."

"And you shouldn't have hit me," Brit added.

I looked at the small bandage above her lip. I could see a small dark shadow of blood coming through. Did she really expect me to apologize for that? It was possible that she'd convinced herself it really did go down that way. I turned back and threw some books in my bag.

Brit touched my elbow. "I said, you shouldn't have hit me." Her eyes were ice-cold. When I didn't say anything she sighed. "We can get past this. I'm not someone who holds a grudge. We're best friends, and that's not something I take lightly. I didn't think it was something you took lightly either."

"What do you want from me?"

"After I heard what happened at your last school, I felt bad for you, but I also thought it meant you would get this situation more than other people. That what happened with this Madison bitch might have taught you a lesson. That friendship is supposed to be forever. It's supposed to be about loyalty, about having that person's back. I *am* your friend, but you're making it hard."

Brit stopped and took a deep breath as if collecting herself. "Together there's nothing we can't do. Mark my words: I'm going to do great things. I'm going to be somebody, but I need to know I can count on you. I need to know my best friend is with me. I want you by my side, but only if I know I can trust you," she said. "But to do that, we have to move forward together. What happened to Beth was horrible."

She shifted her eyes away from me. "It shouldn't have happened."

My breath caught in my throat.

"But it happened. Beth's gone. She's dead. Nothing you or I do is going to bring her back. No story you tell is going to change that."

"I know."

"Do you? Because you seem to think that telling stories is going to make a difference. But the only thing it does is hurt you. People think you're unstable." Brit smiled. "Heck, you *have* been a little unstable." She rubbed my upper arm. "But what I'm saying is that doesn't have to be a problem. My parents don't want me to have anything to do with you, but I'm not like that. I'm not someone who abandons a best friend just because she's down. Now I need to know that you are the kind of person who understands the importance of loyalty." Her voice was calm, but her eyelid was twitching.

Even if I had thought to tape the conversation, there wasn't anything she'd said that couldn't be explained away. I heard her loud and clear. If I crossed her, if I betrayed her, she would destroy me. If I walked away from getting justice for Beth, then we could go back to the way it was before. She'd be my best friend. She'd protect me from the worst of the rumors. She's stand up for me, make sure that I didn't get eaten alive by my past. She needed me at her side to help reinforce her own distorted image—that she wasn't a really bad person. That she'd only done what she had to. She'd built up so many lies that she needed me to help support them.

"I worry about you, Kah-bear," Brit said. "With the way things are going, people think it wouldn't be unexpected if you killed yourself. And I wouldn't want that." Her lips pressed together in a thin tight line.

Her words surrounded my heart like a thousand frozen vines, tightening, making it impossible for me to take a breath. I was afraid to look away from her gaze.

She leaned closer and closer. I kept waiting for her to strike, but instead she leaned even closer, pausing for a beat, and then pressed her mouth down on mine. It wasn't remotely sexual; it was as if she was marking me. Letting me know that she could and that there was nothing I could do. Her lips were sticky from the gloss, and when she stopped I could still feel their oil slick on my mouth.

Brit stepped back. "Think about it."

Then, as if nothing had happened, she swung her bag over she shoulder and headed down the hall. "Have a good weekend. Don't study too hard," she called over her shoulder.

I broke into a cold sweat after she was gone. My legs felt weak, and I slid down the wall to the floor. Years ago I'd been in a car accident with my parents and Nadir. We'd been headed to my grandparents' for Christmas. A truck in the opposite lane had lost control and slid into ours. My dad slammed on the brakes and yanked the wheel. We missed the truck, but we hit a patch of ice and our car spun, like a top, in dizzying circles.

Nadir's phone flew out of his hand. My mom screamed. Her arms up in front of her face, waiting for the windshield to explode. It seemed to be happening so fast and so slow all at the same time. I was oddly calm, as if I were watching it happen to someone else. Out the window I heard horns and saw the flash of headlights as we spun. There was a loud crash and crunch as other cars careened into each other. We hit the ditch at the side of the road and for a sickening second the car tilted on its side—we were going to flip, but the force was just shy of what was needed and the car thumped back down on all four tires.

The four of us had sat there silently for a second, before my dad called out to make sure everyone was okay then squeezed my mom's hand before he unclicked his seat belt to get out and make sure no one in the other cars was hurt.

We were fine. The risk was over, but it was only after the car was stopped that I got scared. I realized only then how much danger I had been in. That it had been possible, likely even, that we could have been badly injured, or killed. In that second everything in our lives could have turned out completely different. I hadn't felt that kind of fear again until this moment.

Once again everything in my life was spinning out of control, and this time I didn't think I'd avoid the crash.

CHAPTER TWENTY-EIGHT

I was supposed to be spending the weekend studying for finals. My parents pretty much left me alone. I sensed Dr. Sherman had advised them to give me some space, to let me focus on my upcoming exams. My parents didn't mention the residential program, but I'd seen the brochure on the kitchen counter. In the morning it was gone, tucked away somewhere. I could practically hear the clock ticking down, getting me closer to when they would ship me off. I'd find myself compulsively rubbing Beth's pocket watch pendant as if I could slow time down through sheer will.

I couldn't even imagine what would happen if I went to the program. Would they pump me with more medication when I didn't give up my "delusion" about Britney? Or would I learn to lie? Tell people what they wanted to hear: that poor, kind Britney had never done a thing and that it was all in my head. Pretend to be riveted by what my fellow inmates said during group counseling. Make dream catchers out of Popsicle sticks and yarn, or some other kind of dorky craft that was supposed to relax me? Maybe take up knitting? Nah, they probably didn't let crazy people have sharp, pointed sticks.

I stared down at my chemistry textbook, trying to learn formulas, but the only thing spinning through my head was Brit and what would happen next. I'd been focused on how I was going to prove what she'd done, get justice, but it was more than that now. Britney wasn't going to let me go. It wasn't enough for me to just drop it—she wanted us to be friends. She wanted me to be Robin to her Batman. And if I didn't want to stick with her, it was going to be a problem. A big problem.

I got up, antsy. I couldn't sit at my desk anymore. I went out and grabbed my bike out of the garage and sped down to Lighthouse Park before my parents could ask where I was going. Once I was there I took off my shoes. The sand was searing hot on top, but as my feet slid deeper the temperature dropped. I had the place to myself.

I went to the edge of the Point. I could hear the waves crashing into the rocks and beach below. As the waves went back out they let out a hissing sound. I gave one more look around to make sure I was alone and then screamed into the wind.

I started with yelling out obscenities. I called Brit every foul name I could think of, and when I ran out of names I knew, I made up new ones. In the end I wasn't even yelling words, just howling into the void.

I only stopped when I ran out of energy and my throat was raw. I walked back down the trail to the beach and plopped down on a log. Other people must have built a fire in the same pit that Beth and I had used. There were charred pieces of wood in the center.

The wind felt good on my skin. I picked a piece of beach grass and held it between my cupped hands the way Nadir had taught me. I blew hard and got a shrill whistle for my efforts.

I scooped a handful of sand and let it trickle out of my palms like an hourglass. I saw a burned match lying there. I knew it wasn't likely, but I wanted to believe it was the same one from when Beth and I had been out here. I went to pick it up, but the burned end crushed between my fingers, leaving only a black smear.

I could still remember our first kiss. Once Beth kissed me it seemed like the world was irrevocably different. Now it was different again, but in a very dark way.

Britney was unbeatable. She'd convinced everyone of every single lie that flew out of her mouth. I'd never believed it would be easy to prove what she'd done, but it wasn't just difficult, it was impossible. Every time I tried I slid further back, lost more ground, and became more and more isolated. My teammates, my brother, my teachers, my family—none of them could help me. Nadir had tried: he'd found Nicole for me, but all that turned out to be was another dead end.

Brit had been smart. She'd killed Beth first, the one person who knew her best. The only one who would believe me because she knew what Brit was capable of doing. Most likely the only person who could have beaten Brit at this game. Those of us who were left didn't stand a chance.

Beth was the one who really knew her. Years of whispered secrets in the dark at slumber parties. Truth or Dare confessions. Shared experiences where when they were over you would make the other promise to never tell. I knew Brit, but nowhere near as well as Beth had.

Beth would have known how to beat Brit, but I didn't. We hadn't been friends long enough. We hadn't been close enough to share real confidences. I chuckled. The odd thing was I was closer to Brit after she killed Beth. At least I'd really known her then. Finally we had a secret together.

Britney needed me. She'd reached out to me to hear what she was missing while she was gone. She'd used me to figure out how she might be able to come back. I think she kept me close afterward because she still wanted that connection to Beth, to who she had been before all of this happened. If she could get me to believe her lie, she could maybe convince herself of it too. She still wanted me around. She needed me as the one person who knew what she did, someone who could appreciate her true capabilities and could keep up her vision of who she wanted to be.

I dug my feet into the cool sand. I didn't know if Britney was smarter than me, but there was no doubt in my mind she was way more skilled at this game then I was. She was varsity in manipulation; I was barely a scratch player. She had a bigger, better team.

A better team.

Unbeatable.

The words bounced around in my head. *Unbeatable. A better team.* Knocking. Reminding me. I did have the answer. Beth had even told it to me.

"I am so sick of hearing how we don't stand a chance," I huffed. *I was out of breath as I jogged on the treadmill in the gym. Beth was next to me, somehow managing to look good even while she sweated. "Our team is in the best shape ever."*

"Yeah, but the Spartans are better."

I was so shocked at her answer I missed a step and almost face-planted. Beth's laugh bounced off the mirrors in the fitness room.

"You can't think they're better than us." I turned off my machine. *"We've won five straight games. Our score average is up from last year, people are running faster, and our defense is way better since we started those drills."*

Beth jumped off the belt and motioned for me to follow her over to the bikes. "Don't get me wrong, we're kicking ass this year, but the Spartans are better. They've got a killer offense. Did you see the videos of their past games? And they're solid; at least two-thirds of their team is seniors, so they're more experienced. They don't get thrown easily. And their goalkeeper—that girl is a freaking tank. She practically fills the entire net, and she can move. Shit, she's like on speed."

My enthusiasm drained. "So you think we're going to lose?"

Beth snorted and punched me in the shoulder. "I didn't say that. I said they're the better team." She jumped up on one of the bikes. "Are you going to just stand there?"

I got on and started pedaling, my quads protesting. "I don't get it. If they're better, how are we going to beat them?"

Beth held up a finger. "Pay attention, future captain: I'm about to teach you a few things. You'll need this wisdom for when you're the leader."

"There's no way to be sure I'll be captain next year," I said.

"Of course you will, but that's not the point; this advice is good for life in general."

I slowed down and took a drink from my water bottle. "Okay, teach me."

"There are almost always going to be teams that are better than you. Or people that are better than you—after all, there can only be one person on top at any one time, so that means the rest of the time you're in second place at best."

I nodded. "Fair enough."

"So the secret is to figure out how to play the game."

I screwed up my face. "I don't get it."

"Here's the thing: if someone is better than you at defense, attacking it directly means you're going to lose. If you go head-to-head on a skill where you are lacking, ninety-nine times out of a hundred it will be a huge mistake."

"So you attack where they're weaker," I said.

Beth smiled, her eyebrows bopping up and down. "That's part of it. Look to chip away at their advantages. If they play a better fast game, you've got to look at how to slow it down, get them to play your kind of ball."

I chewed on my lip, thinking it over. "And what if they don't have any weaknesses?"

She held up a finger. "Excellent question. I'll show you. Push my hand." She held up her palm like she was stopping traffic, the whole time keeping up her speed on the stationary bike.

I pressed my palm against hers, enjoying the zing I felt when our skin touched. Beth pushed against my hand, thrusting mine back. "Is that the best ya got?"

I pushed back. The two of us swayed a bit on our bikes, our strength evenly matched. Then Beth stopped, her arm going slack. I was still pushing, so I fell forward, catching myself with one hand on the floor just before I completely stumbled off the bike.

Beth laughed. She reached down to help me get my balance. "That's the secret right there."

"What, trick the other team so they fall?" I asked.

"If you can't win a straight battle, stop trying. Be willing to let yourself go. Let that person beat themselves."

"But what if they don't fall like I did?"

Brit smiled. "Then you have to pull out the big guns and sacrifice yourself." She saw my raised eyebrow. "Take a hit, burn yourself out doing a full-on run, take a penalty if you need to, but your sacrifice will inspire others to step up. Do something unexpected and get them off their game—if they're off their game they might make a mistake. And you never know what might happen then." Beth winked and then leaned over and kissed me.

Beth's advice ran around in my head. Was it that simple? Maybe the way to beat Brit was by giving up. I thought about what Dr. Sherman had pointed out to me: that what I had been doing wasn't working.

In English class last year we'd read Shakespeare's *Romeo and Juliet*. One of the girls in the class had gotten frustrated and wanted to know why the two families couldn't get along. Our teacher had told us, Capulets have to be Capulets; Montagues have to be Montagues.

Brit had to be Brit, but I didn't have to stay the same. If I kept pushing back I would never win, but there was the chance that if I gave up Brit just might beat herself. But it might call for sacrifice. An inkling of an idea began to grow in my mind. I almost rejected it entirely. It was crazy. Insane. Dangerous.

I held up a fist of sand and let the wind blow it out of my hand. It was time to do this differently.

* * *

I opened the stall door and jumped back when I saw Brit leaning against the sink. I'd managed to dodge her all morning and hadn't answered a single one of the texts that she'd sent over the weekend. But even while taking my exam I hadn't been able to forget her, and now it was as if by thinking about her I'd summoned her like an evil demon.

"I haven't heard from you," she said. "I don't appreciate you making me hunt you down."

I walked past her to the sink and washed my hands.

"I can't believe you want things this way." Brit shook her head. "It breaks my heart. I've lost Beth, and I feel like I'm losing you too."

I knew she was trying to needle me, get me to say something, but I wasn't going to bite. I hadn't texted her or reached out all weekend. I knew she found my silence annoying. More than annoying . . . disturbing. She needed me to push back to hold her up.

"My parents said you'll be going to a mental health program as soon as school gets out," she said. "The downside is they tell me problems like yours rarely get better. I told them I'm not willing to give up on you." She turned away from me and primped in the mirror. "Have you thought about what I said on Friday?"

"That's all I've done, think about it and what you did to Beth."

Brit looked disappointed. "It breaks my heart that you think so little of me."

"Spare me," I said cutting her off. "I'm not taping this, so you don't need to keep up the act. I don't even have my phone on me. It's in my locker because of exams." I turned my pockets out. I raised my shirt so she could see my bare chest. "No wire." I could see the wheels in Brit's mind turning. "No one is ever going to know we had this talk, so don't bother to tell your story all over again—I don't want to hear it."

"Do you think if we really had a private discussion I'd admit something?"

I shook my head. "You don't get it. I don't need you to admit anything. I was taping you in the art room because I wanted to show it to other people. I don't need proof. I *know* the truth. You killed Beth, and you're going to get away with it."

"I'm not getting away with anything," Brit said.

I cocked my head as if I were able to read her mind. "I bet you're not. You might lie to everyone else, but I have to believe if there is a shred of humanity inside of you, even the smallest bit, you know what you did. Even if no one else ever knows, you know the truth. You killed your best friend and you covered it up. You're a shitty excuse for a human."

"You're never going to prove any of that," Brit said. Her voice was calm, but her left eyelid twitched with a tic.

"I know. Took me a while to figure it out, but you're right. I give."

"So you're going to let me win?" Brit's voice dripped with sarcasm.

"No one in this situation wins. I'm just not going to play your game anymore. I think messing with me keeps your mind occupied, keeps you from spending too much time with your own thoughts. So I'm out. You don't need to worry about me trying to catch you in a lie. Now you can just live with it."

"That's it, you're just going to give up?" Brit leaned against the pink tile wall, trying to look casual, but I could tell there was something off about how she held herself. As if all of her muscles were tensed.

"Yep. I don't want anything to do with you anymore. I'm talking to my parents; I'm going to see if they'll homeschool me next year. There's no point in me coming back."

Brit smirked. "But if you drop out, you won't be captain of the team anymore. Beth had been so proud of you too."

I raised my chin in defiance. "Yeah, she had been, and she'd be proud of me now. What was it you told me? Field hockey is just a game. I'm moving on. I may not be able to do anything about what you did, but I don't have to stand by you."

"You can't just move on," Brit spit. The tic above her eye kept firing. She seemed offended by my calm.

I laughed at her. "But I can. Don't you get it? It's all moving on. You may be queen of Northside, but it's already fading. You graduate in a week. Do you really think people are going to be talking about you next year? Whatever popularity you spent all these years building up doesn't matter

—294—

once school ends. The real world doesn't care that you were a big deal in high school. The media doesn't care about your back-from-the-dead story anymore; there's new stuff, more interesting than you. Your book deal fell through, and you couldn't get a reporter to follow you around now if you tried. In your heart you know you aren't going to matter at Cornell either, and you can't stand it. Your big dream of doing something great is just that—a dream."

"I will too."

"No, you won't. Ivy League schools are full of people who were the top of their class, captains of different teams, who volunteered in some remote African village, or otherwise impressed the hell out of the admissions staff. Your miracle recovery isn't going to set you apart. It's not even anything you did; it's something that happened to you. You won't be special, Brit; you're going to be one of many people who used to be a big deal. Welcome to the bigger pond. You didn't even get in on your own merits."

"I know what you're trying to do," Brit said. "You think you can upset me and get me to say something." She sighed. "You're so transparent it's pathetic."

"But you are upset. Maybe not as much as a normal person, but it bothers you."

"What bothers me is how you're acting," Brit said.

I grabbed a wad of brown paper towels from the dispenser. "What is it you told me that one time? You like to choose your own reality, but whatever you want to believe doesn't change the facts. Cornell only took you because of your connections. You aren't exactly a rare breed. You're pretty, but not an outstanding beauty. You're smart, but you're no genius. You're good at sports, but you're not some Olympic athlete. The only thing that made you stick out was what happened to you. Whatever claim to fame you made by coming back from the dead is already fading, and you know the reason you haven't been able to stay in the limelight?" She stared at me, breathing heavy. The vein above her eye throbbed. "You won't stay in the limelight because the truth is you're boring." I dragged out the word *boring*, giving it extra emphasis, and enjoying how she flinched from the term.

"Shut up."

"You know the real benefit of a good friend? They push you to be a better person. Beth made you a better person. You killed the one thing that made you interesting." I shook my head. "She believed in you, that you could be someone. She actually liked you, and you wiped that goodness from this earth."

"I said shut up," Brit repeated.

I carefully dried my hands as if I were a surgeon. I tossed the wad of paper towels toward the trash, and they went in with a swoosh. Ten points. "Fine. I'll shut up, but when you lie in bed at night, I hope you think about all of this."

She crossed her arms over her chest, trying to look like

she didn't care, but I could tell I'd gotten to her. I'd pierced that armor shell.

I stepped past her and pushed the door. The tension that had been wound around me like some kind of evil poison ivy from a fairy tale disappeared. I felt as if I could take a deep breath for the first time in forever. I paused and turned back to Brit. "You'd better hope nine hundred fifty million Hindus are wrong."

"Why?"

"Because karma can be a bitch," I said, and then walked out.

I don't believe in ghosts, but I knew if Beth were watching me from the beyond she would be cheering for me.

I felt good for the first time in forever. I practically skipped down the hall and then I saw Sara standing by her locker. I stopped short. She saw my gaze, but then looked away.

I didn't let myself hesitate in case I lost my nerve. I crossed the hall, and Sara flinched away from me. I could tell it was taking everything she had not to run.

"What do you want?" she asked with her chin thrust up in the air.

"I wanted to say I'm sorry," I said.

Her eyebrows drew together in confusion. She looked over my shoulder and I could tell she didn't trust me, thought I was up to something.

"I wanted to say I'm sorry about everything that happened. I wasn't directly responsible, but I didn't do anything to stop it either. I thought I had good reasons, but I'm not so sure anymore," I admitted.

Sara swallowed hard and I could tell she wanted to cry. Her eyes were already red and swollen. She'd been crying a lot lately. "Do you think saying sorry makes what happened okay?"

"I know it doesn't, but I promise you I am going to try to fix it."

"What are you talking about?" Sara asked.

I didn't answer and instead just walked away. I couldn't tell her, but she'd find out soon enough. Everyone would. The next step I had to take scared me, but I was now more certain than ever that it was the right thing to do.

CHAPTER TWENTY-NINE

I brought the dark lavender lilacs to Beth's grave. The bouquet, along with the thick glass vase they came in, had cost almost fifty bucks, but I wanted to do this right. Besides, I wasn't likely to need a lot of cash where I was going, so I might as well splurge. Once I'd put down the flowers I traced Beth's name carved in the granite with my index finger. The stone felt hot from the late-afternoon sun.

The confrontation with Brit seemed to have banished the fog that had taken up permanent residence in my head. Or maybe it was the apology to Sara, but either way, it felt like I was thinking clearly for the first time in a long time.

I'd avoided talking to anyone the rest of the day. Not that people were exactly beating a path to my door to hang out. I could still hear whispers as I walked past, like the quiet rustle of mice in the walls. At lunch I'd snagged a table in the far corner of the library where the bookcases hid me from sight. I could hear groups of people drilling one another or whispering horror stories of exams that were already over, but I had the corner all to myself. All the windows in the library were thrown open, and there was the smallest hint of a breeze. I lifted my hair off my neck and let the wind cool me. I'd brought my books, but I didn't bother to study. After tomorrow none of it would matter. I was fairly certain I wouldn't be allowed to finish the rest of my exams.

"I wanted to come and see you one more time." I sat on the ground next to Beth's grave, the grass tickling the back of my legs. I hadn't been there since the day I'd come with Brit and she'd taken a photo of the two of us. It seemed like something that had happened years in the past instead of just weeks ago. I plucked at the thick lawn, inhaling the fresh, clean smell.

The cemetery was abandoned; I was the only person there. A few of the graves were covered with some fading plastic floral arrangements, but Beth's would be the only one with fresh flowers that I could see. There was a grave a few rows over that had two plastic geese figures that were dressed up in pastel Easter-themed dresses, complete with frilly mobcaps on their heads. I suspected there was an entire wardrobe of geese outfits, and in just a month or so it would be time to Velcro on their Fourth of July wear.

There didn't seem to be any of Beth's spirit in this place—it was too quiet. Even the rush of cars on the road beyond the wall was muffled by the row of pine trees. Beth had always been in motion; she seemed to travel with her own sound track, the kind of music where it was impossible to stand still. She was always laughing or singing or calling out encouragement on the field. Whatever had made Beth who she was, it wasn't here, and yet I still felt it was important to come one more time. I wasn't sure when I would be able to come again.

I'd set things in motion today by pulling away from Brit, but it wouldn't be enough. Sacrifice was required.

I was going to confess to killing Beth.

Even though everyone was sure I was crazy, a confession of murder wasn't the kind of thing the police could ignore. If anything, the fact that I was mentally unhinged should give them all the more reason to make sure I wasn't telling the truth. They wouldn't know what I might be capable of doing. They'd have to check it out.

I'd tell them I'd killed her, but not alone. I'd tell them Brit was involved. We'd done the deed in Britney's basement and then covered it up together. Now I could no longer keep the secret. The guilt was eating me alive.

I watched enough CSI to know there were all sorts of tests they would run. I was certain Britney had killed Beth in that space, and if there was even a drop of blood they would find it. I'd tell them how we hid her body in the wine cooler until we could get rid of it. They would check there too, spray chemicals, use blue lights, and peer in every corner. They'd sniff out the truth. I had to stop waiting for everyone else to fix my problems and do it myself.

I'd tell them the entire time Britney had been "dead" we'd been in touch. Plotting together. Seeing if we could get away with it. Maybe they could find a way to get our chats back or find something else in the computers that was unexplained. I'd tell them how I knew she'd been hiding in East Lansing. And even if she and Nicole hadn't been close, Brit must have made a mistake somewhere with someone. Even she couldn't be that good. There would be a conversation she had that didn't add up. A time she'd used her real name. They'd check out Nicole's room in Lizard's house too. Who knows what other evidence she might have left behind?

They would do all the things they should have done when Brit first came back but never did. They might even want her to take a lie detector test. Oh, how much would I pay to be in the room for that? Watching the detectives hook her up to the machine, the delicate dials and sensors swinging wildly, broadcasting that she was nothing more than a huge liar.

Brit was good, but she wasn't perfect. She will have messed up, slipped up, made a mistake. I just needed someone to find it.

Would it be enough to convict her? I wasn't sure. She'd deny the whole thing, and if I'd learned anything from the situation so far, it was that people wanted to believe Brit. Brit wanted to believe it so much she had practically convinced herself.

Brit might not do jail time, but people would wonder about her. There would be sidelong glances. Questions. The hint of scandal. People would always wonder. She would be smeared with a taint. Like a bad taste in your mouth that you can't shake. The fact she'd been accused of murder would follow her.

Of course, confessing to murder wasn't going to do me any favors. I was frightened of what would happen, but not as scared as I was of the idea of doing nothing and living with the knowledge that Brit was out there enjoying her life without having to pay any price at all.

I'd made a list during lunch of all the things I needed to do before tomorrow. Unlike when I confronted Brit in the art room, this time I would take the time to prepare. Make sure I had everything ready to go. Some things were obvious and others were a bit odd. I wanted to clean my room. I suspected after I confessed the police would search it. It seemed absurd that I was willing to let people think I'd kill someone, but I didn't want them to think I was a slob. I knew people would look through my shelves and rummage through my drawers, and I wanted them to find them in order. To make sure there wasn't anything I would be embarrassed for them to find: underwear with broken elastic, pages folded over on the steamy parts of various romance novels, or notes from Beth that belonged to me alone.

I fished my phone out of my bag and sent a text to Zach.

I wanted to say I'm sorry again. It's important to me that you know that hurting you was one of the biggest regrets I have. I know I let you down and for what it's worth I hope that one of these days I live up to the person you thought I was.

I hit SEND and shoved the phone into my pocket. I had to go. There was still so much to do and not enough time. I didn't expect to hear back from Zach. There was the chance that he would just skim the message and delete it, but I hoped once everything came to light he would realize that I meant it.

When my alarm went off in the morning I rolled over fully awake in an instant, as if I hadn't been sleeping but instead recharging for the day ahead. I rubbed the sand out of my eyes and looked around my room. I'd spent hours cleaning last night. There was a small trash bag behind the door. I planned to smuggle it out of the house this morning and drop it in the Dumpster behind Starbucks on the way to school. There wasn't much that I didn't want anyone to find, but there was enough, and I couldn't trust that the cops wouldn't go through the trash here at the house.

In the end I hadn't been able to throw away the few notes I had from Beth. I had so little from our time together. Her skin had touched the paper; the handwriting was hers. I'd taken them downstairs and slipped them inside the giant dictionary that sat on the shelf in the living room. No one would find them there, and someday I might need them. I knew I would want them.

I'd done almost everything on my list, except for the last item, which had to wait until this morning. My room was ready. Being compulsive had its benefits: things were already pretty organized. My eyes skipped over the dresser top, everything lined up the way I liked it. My clothes for today were laid out and hung over the back of my desk chair. I'd chosen them carefully. I wondered if I would see my room again. It was likely that they'd send me to jail, although I supposed it was possible they might send me to a mental hospital instead. It was likely I would be gone a long time.

A quick tap on the door made me jump. My dad popped his head in my room. "Good luck."

I inhaled quickly—did he know something? "With what?"

His regrown eyebrows, still scraggly and uneven from when he'd burned them off in his robot lab, rose into his hairline. "With your exams."

I made a show of shaking myself awake. "Of course. Although what is it you say, genius doesn't need luck?"

He chuckled. "Knock 'em dead. Your mom and I are

making lasagna tonight, so that should give you something to look forward to." He stepped back into the hall.

I scrambled out of bed. "Wait a minute." When I reached him, I patted a hank of his hair that was sticking up in the back and then hugged him. I wanted to hold on to him, but I knew I couldn't. He would know something was off. "Hug for luck," I said.

Dad tapped me on the nose. "Always." He squeezed me again and then headed downstairs. "Your mom made up some granola; it's in the tub on the counter. Be sure to eat some breakfast. Energy food."

"I will," I said, but I wasn't sure he heard me. I hoped after everything happened he'd remember the hug and know that I loved him and if I could do this without hurting him and my mom I would. I hated the idea that people would make judgments about them, implying that they must have screwed up as parents.

As I was getting out of the shower I heard my mom call out her good-byes and the rumble of the garage door. A part of me wanted to change my mind. I hadn't taken the final step yet, but there was another part that wanted to race to school and get it over with. It didn't take long to get dressed. I took a bit of extra time on my hair and makeup. It was vain, but there might be press, and if they took photos I wanted to look good.

When I went downstairs I couldn't eat anything; my stomach was too tight. I picked up the phone in the kitchen and looked at the clock. This was the last thing on my list.

"Hey, sis. What's up?"

Nadir's voice felt like liquid Valium. "I called so you could wish me good luck on my exams and I'll do the same for you," I said.

He laughed. "I'm done. I took my last test yesterday and I turn in my final paper today. I'll be spending the rest of the week eating Mexican food, drinking beer, and sleeping late."

"Sure, rub it in." I was glad his exams were over; at least he wouldn't have to cope with those when this went public.

"Hello?" Nadir said, jolting me back to our conversation.

"What?" I said. "Sorry, I got distracted."

"You call me and then you don't even listen. Way to make a guy feel boring."

"I'm sorry." My voice cracked.

"Easy. I'm just teasing you. I was just asking what exams you've got today."

My mind was completely blank. "I can't remember," I confessed.

Nadir was quiet. "You don't remember?"

I realized how bizarre that must sound. "I called because I wanted to make sure you know who I am—I mean, no matter what else anyone might say."

"Is this about the stuff from Windsor Prep? Mom told me people at school were talking about it."

"No," I said. "I mean, yes, in part. It's just that people

say all kinds of stuff—you know how it is. They get ideas in their heads because they've heard part of a story, or because they make assumptions and that doesn't tell the whole story."

"Yeah, sure," Nadir said.

"I want you to know that I'm still your sister, that you know me, that the stuff they say isn't necessarily the whole truth." I scrambled to try to explain without tipping my hand.

"Listen, Kay-Kay, is everything okay?"

A harsh laugh, shrill, escaped my throat. Things were so far from okay I couldn't even see it from here. "There are things I need to do, things that are important, and I want you to know that while it might not look like it, the reason I'm doing it is because it is the right thing to do." I shut my mouth. I was babbling. I'd been so sure of what I'd wanted to say, but now it was coming out all garbled and wrong.

"What are you talking about, Kalah?" I could hear Nadir's confusion through the phone and also his increasing unease.

"I don't care what other people think of me, but your opinion matters." I swallowed hard. "It matters a lot." That was the most important thing I'd wanted him to know. Nadir and I had always teased each other, and there were times I hated how he seemed to do everything first and better, but he was my older brother. I needed him to look past what I was going to tell everyone. I needed him to believe in his heart, to know, that I wasn't capable of anything like that.

"Are you upset that Nicole didn't know anything about Brit?"

"Not really. Not anymore," I said.

"Kay-Kay, are Mom and Dad around?"

I wiped my nose. I had to pull myself together. If I couldn't get through this conversation with Nadir, how was I going to handle the rest of the day? "They've gone to work," I said.

"I'm worried about you," Nadir said. There was no joking in his voice.

I closed my eyes and just let myself feel the love he had for me. Someday I hoped he would understand. "I'll be okay," I said. "Look, I have to go. I've got to get to school."

"No, wait. Listen, let's talk a bit longer—"

"Don't be silly. You've got to drop off that paper, and I've got exams. You've got beer to drink, enchiladas to eat. We'll talk later."

I knew he was about to say something else. Maybe tell me to wait on the line while he used another phone to call one of our parents, but I didn't give him the chance. "Love you," I said and hung up the phone. I grabbed my stuff and looked around the kitchen.

I ran my hand over the porcelain chicken and rooster my mom had inherited from her grandparents. She and my dad had declared them to be the ugliest things on the planet, but they said this with affection, and they'd had a place of honor in our kitchen as long as I could remember. There was a cooking magazine on the island with a Post-it note marking something they planned to make later in the week. The table was a mess: my mom's book club book, Donna Tartt's *The Secret History*, my dad's *Servo* magazine, and even one of my textbooks mixed up with parts of the newspaper, granola crumbs, and a stack of bills from the mail. My parents had left their coffee cups out and I took them from the table, rinsed them, and placed them in the dishwasher. I put the mail on the desk and stacked the books and magazine. Finally I wiped the table down. There was nothing left to do. I shut the door quietly and locked it behind me. Even if Nadir called my parents they wouldn't be able to stop me now.

It was time to end this.

CHAPTER THIRTY

I half expected the school to look different when I arrived. Like the building itself should recognize what a monumental event was about to occur. I stood in the parking lot and looked up at Northside, its yellow brick exterior nearly gleaming in the bright sun. I'd considered going directly to the police station, but it seemed somehow fitting to do it here. Where I met Brit and Beth. Where all of it started. Besides, this was scary enough without having to face down the front door of the police station.

It was funny that school now felt safe. The first day of my sophomore year I'd been terrified to go inside. Northside was easily three or four times the size of Windsor Prep. A sprawling two-story building connected by a covered overhang to an annex that had been built years later when the student population kept growing. I'd never gone to school anywhere that big. However, by the end of the first day I'd fallen in love with the place. Unlike Windsor I could blend into the crowds and disappear if I wanted. I loved the bright-colored posters all over the walls encouraging people to cheer for the football team or come to the next volleyball game. There was blue and gold everywhere—the place practically dripped school spirit. There were notices about debate matches, glee clubs, play try-outs, study groups, and even a group that got together to watch sci-fi movies—SpaceGeeks. I'd seen right away that at Northside I could be anyone I wanted to be. By the end of that first week I'd spotted the notice about field hockey and known I was going to give it a try.

Once Brit and Beth had taken me into their circle, Northside had gotten even better. I'd liked how other people looked at me in the halls, like I was someone. I enjoyed coming around a corner and seeing people look at me and smile. Friends calling out greetings, saving me a seat at lunch and assemblies. I'd fit in. I'd liked it here.

I wove my way through the crowds in the hall. I saw Brit surrounded by a group of our teammates. As soon as she spotted me she poked Melissa in the ribs and said something to her. Melissa and a few others laughed. Kate looked uncomfortable. She crossed her arms over her chest and looked away.

I took a few more steps and then realized what the latest round of whispers was about. Someone had scribbled *Crazy Bitch* in black Sharpie across the front of my locker. I stared at the words. They looked almost carved into the gray paint.

There were a few more snickers. I turned; Brit was watching me with a huge smile on her face. I smiled back. She didn't look good. I couldn't put my finger on what was wrong; her hair was still perfect and there were no dark circles under her eyes, but she looked strained. As if any moment she would fly apart into a million pieces.

Talking to Nadir had reminded me of something: I'd survived before. I could survive now. What most people thought of me didn't matter. When things had blown up with Madison at my last school I'd been so certain my world was ending, but it hadn't. I'd started over. Somehow, someway I'd start over again. Brit was tight perfection; she had no flex. She would break. I would bend and give.

Sara was on the far side of the hall. I could tell she'd seen the locker and Brit and her posse laughing. I couldn't tell if she felt sorry for me, or maybe she thought I'd gotten what I deserved for being friends with Britney.

Maybe it was as simple as she was glad someone else had Brit's attention. Soon, like everyone else, she'd assume I was guilty, but maybe some small part of her would get it. Put together my confession with my apology. Or at least know that if I could have changed things I would have. She was one of the few totally innocent people in this whole mess. I tossed a few things into my locker and slammed it shut, putting the past behind me.

The bell rang and a shot of adrenaline shot through my system. This was it. Brit watched me walk down the hall. I could tell she wanted to know where I was going. She knew my schedule. She knew I was supposed to be going down B wing, but instead I was headed in the opposite direction. I wondered if she would follow me all the way to the office, if she had any idea what I was about to do. I was tempted to start skipping, but instead I kept my pace slow and steady. Almost regal.

Brit turned to watch my progress, and I could feel her unease coming off her, as if it were a smell. I lifted my chin a bit higher.

I might be a crazy bitch, but she was about to discover just how much of a bitch I was capable of being.

CHAPTER THIRTY-ONE

I had assumed once I confessed to murder I'd have everyone's full attention, but I was stuck sitting alone in the office lobby while Ms. Harding and Mr. Hamstead argued in his office. The school secretary was charged with keeping an eye on me, and she jumped anytime I shifted in the chair. Maybe she thought I was going to chase her down and club her with a stapler.

When I'd first come into the office the secretary had told me in a snooty voice that I couldn't see Mr. Hamstead without an appointment. Like he was the president of the country, instead of a principal. It hadn't occurred to me that I might get sent away from the office before I even had a chance to get things started. I had to make this happen now. Brit's family was starting renovations any day. It was now or never. I had a flash of panic, but then realized I didn't have to do what she said. If I was about to be branded as a homicidal maniac, I could handle being thought of as noncompliant with some puffed-up-with-her-own-self-importance school secretary. I insisted I wasn't going to leave the office. The end of her nose twitched; she looked like an angry rabbit. It was setting up to be a standoff when Ms. Harding came in and asked what the problem was.

"I want to talk to Mr. Hamstead," I said.

"And I've clarified that Miss Richards needs to make an appointment; this isn't a drop-in center." The secretary sniffed.

"Is there something I can help with?" Ms. Harding offered.

"I've come to confess that I murdered Beth Taylor."

That got the smug, pinched look off the secretary's face, and suddenly it seemed perhaps Mr. Hamstead could fit me into his busy schedule.

Mr. Hamstead and Ms. Harding stood in front of me while I repeated my claim. "I killed Beth, but I didn't do it alone."

"You mean you feel guilty about her death, not that you did anything," Ms. Harding tried to clarify. The blood drained out of her head and her mouth, coated in lipstick, looked unnaturally bright, like a slash across her face.

"No, I mean we murdered her. There's another killer in this school: Britney. I'm here to confess to you. And Officer Siegel too. I want her to be here."

Mr. Hamstead started to fire off questions, but Ms. Harding cut him off. She'd dragged him into his office. I could hear her telling him that I was mentally unwell and that they needed to be careful about what I was asked. She was worried about how vulnerable I might be. Ms. Harding insisted they should call the police and my parents before asking me anything else.

I suspected Hamstead was far less sympathetic about my vulnerability but did worry that if I was asked something without a lawyer or my parents, the school might somehow be found responsible for shirking their duty. He had to know this was going to be a big deal, an our-school-in-the-media kind of deal, and he wanted to make sure everything was done correctly so he couldn't be blamed. The secretary had been summoned to get my parents' work numbers from the system.

I felt bad for my parents. I imagined both of them scrambling to get out of work, asking other people to cover for them, calling each other on their cells trying to figure out what the hell was going on. I didn't think our family had a lawyer, and it didn't seem like the kind of thing you could just Google and expect to get anyone decent and available on a moment's notice. I thought about texting them, but I had no idea what I would even say.

But there was someone I wanted to text. Let her sweat for a change.

Your secret is out.

Brit texted back almost immediately.

What r u talking about?

I confessed, I typed. **Told them we did it together.**

Brit didn't respond. She must be freaking out. It never occurred to her that I was capable of this kind of sacrifice. She'd put together what this confession would mean. She'd mentally race through everything, trying to figure out what people would think, what might trip her up. Relief flooded through my system; whatever happened, at least it was underway. I smiled and then caught the secretary staring at me, her eyes wide. She looked ready to fend me off armed only with her keyboard.

Someone slapped the glass behind me and I jolted in my seat. Brit was standing outside the office looking in. Her neck was mottled and blotchy. She was breathing hard, like she had run down to the office. She jerked her head to the side, indicating that she wanted me to join her in the hall.

I turned away like I hadn't seen her. I wasn't doing what she told me to anymore.

She stood out in the hallway for what felt like forever, but she must have realized I wasn't going to give in. Brit yanked the heavy glass office door open. The secretary stood. "Britney, now isn't a good time for you to be here."

Brit ignored her, barreling her way over to me. "What are you doing?"

"I told you. I'm confessing." I smiled up at her. "I can't live with the guilt anymore."

"You can't do this," she hissed. She was almost vibrating with energy, twitching with anger.

"But I already have."

The secretary touched Britney's elbow. "Sweetie, you need to go back to your class."

Brit yanked her arm back. "Don't touch me!"

The secretary jerked back as if Brit had spit in her face. She looked back and forth between the two of us and hustled off to get Mr. Hamstead.

"I don't know what the hell you think you're doing, but they'll send you to jail," Brit said.

I nodded. "Maybe. Of course, I'm only seventeen, so there's a chance I'll go to juvie." I tapped my chin as if I'd just recalled something. "You're eighteen, though, right? Legally an adult."

Brit grabbed me by the shoulders. I could feel her shaking. "You're crazy."

I nodded. "Probably."

Brit seemed offended by my calm. "Do you have any idea what you've done?"

"I think so." I smiled. "I'm guessing the media is going to be pretty interested in this story again. Maybe more interested than they were when you came back. Murder is way more fascinating than an accident. Guess who's going to get a book deal now?"

"What's going on here?" Officer Siegel and another officer were standing in the doorway. Hamstead had called them when he'd called my parents.

"I came to confess, I guess for both of us." I winked at Brit. "We did it together. Besties."

"Did what?" Officer Siegel said.

"Murdered Beth," I said as if it were the most obvious thing in the world.

Brit shook her head, like a dog shaking off water. "She's really sick. Everyone knows this. People shouldn't be listening to her."

I ignored Brit. "We thought she was messing around with Britney's boyfriend, Jason," I explained. "It turns out it was Sara, but we didn't know that then. We thought Beth betrayed her."

"Kalah, you shouldn't say anything else until your parents get here," Ms. Harding said. Her hands twisted together.

I pressed on. This was it. I had to get it out now, before anyone tried to silence me. I needed everyone to hear me. To hear Brit was involved so they would have to take action. "We didn't mean to kill her. We just wanted to teach her a lesson. Beth was the leader of our group, but that didn't mean she could walk over us—"

"Beth was not the leader," Brit said.

"We told Beth to come to Brit's house—"

"Shut your mouth," Brit said.

"Brit confronted her, but it turned into a fight," I continued. I had everyone's rapt attention now. "Beth fell and hit her head. She was dead." I looked down and shook my head like I still couldn't believe how quickly it had gone wrong. "That's when we came up with the idea. We'd get rid of her body and convince everyone that Beth had just taken off. She always talked about it, so people wouldn't be that surprised. We had her phone, so we could send some messages, make our story seem real."

"Oh my god." The secretary covered her mouth with her hands.

"Which one of you came up with this plan?" Officer Siegel said. Everyone was staring at me, and I could feel the power shift in the room. Adults are always a bit frightened of teens. That's why they put in so many rules; they want to control us, to feel as if they're in charge. They were repulsed, but there was also something like admiration in their eyes. Brit saw it too, and she resented that they were looking at me that way.

"I did," I said.

Brit's eyelid twitched. "You can't possibly think she's telling the truth."

"I'm Brit's best friend. I didn't want her to go to jail."

Brit's skin was blotchy. "I can explain everything." She opened her mouth, but nothing came out. Her ability to spin lie after lie seemed to have dried up.

"There's no point in keeping it a secret. They're going to find everything, you know. Once they search the basement," I said.

Ms. Harding sucked in her breath, horrified. "What did you girls do to that sweet angel?"

"Beth wasn't an angel," Brit snapped. Her hands ran down her side as if tucking everything into place, but her hands were shaking. "Kalah's confused."

"Not anymore," I said, cutting her off.

"Oh, Kalah, what have you done?" Ms. Harding said.

"Please. Kalah doesn't have what it takes to pull something like this off," Brit said.

"Once the press hears about this—" Mr. Hamstead said, shaking his head slowly.

Brit's eyelid began twitching again.

"I'm guessing it will make what happened earlier seem like no big deal." I tried to make my voice sound resigned, but enjoyed digging at Brit. Not only would I try and take her down with me, but I planned to take the attention away from her. I wasn't sure what she would hate more.

Siegel snorted. "That's an understatement."

I shrugged. "I did what I had to do."

"You can't believe she did this," Brit said. "She can't even lead the freaking field hockey team without me to hold her hand. Do you have any idea what was involved? In making all of you think I was dead? In coming up with a plan to come back? That takes fucking genius. That's not Kalah— I'm the only one who could pull this off." Brit looked around the room as if she expected people to applaud and then a split second later realized what she'd said.

A jolt of excitement ran down my spine. Brit had screwed up. I glanced around the room to make sure they'd all understood what she said. What it meant.

"You didn't have anything to do with this, did you?" Officer Siegel said to me.

"Then why did she confess?" The secretary was looking back and forth between Britney and me, her nose twitching double time.

"You hoped to get her to take credit." Officer Siegel was looking at me with a mix of respect and surprise.

My legs felt shaky, as if I'd just gotten out of bed after having had the flu for weeks. "I didn't expect her to con-fess," I admitted. "I just wanted her to be in trouble too. I wanted to piss her off."

"I didn't know what you were talking about," Brit said, her voice rising. "I didn't mean anything I said."

"Let's go down to the police station and talk about it," Officer Siegel said. "It should be simple enough to check out both of your stories."

"Whatever that bitch tells you is a lie." Brit pointed at me. "She's obsessed with me. My parents wanted to file a restraining order. She attacked me just last week!"

"We'll evaluate what Kalah tells us and the evidence," Officer Siegel said.

"She did it!" Brit yelled out, pointing at me. Her finger was shaking. "She killed Beth the night of her birthday because Beth didn't want to date her." She was practically panting. "I was scared of her. I didn't know what to do. Ask my psychologist: she'll tell you."

"Scared?" Ms. Harding said.

"Yes. I thought if I didn't support her she might hurt me too." Brit's words were picking up speed as she spun her story.

"But Kalah spent the night of Beth's birthday at her boyfriend, Zach's, house," Mr. Hamstead said. "You both came to my office after Beth disappeared and told me that."

Brit blinked. Her story was unraveling. Too many loose ends. "Kalah lied," she said.

"We'll check everything out," Siegel said. "Kalah's alibi for that night and yours. Should be easy enough to clear up. Now let's get going."

When Officer Siegel reached for her, Brit skittered back. "I'm not going anywhere with you. This is some kind of mistake." She patted her hair into place, but I could see her hands were shaking even harder now.

There was a hum of whispering from up and down the hall. Class had ended and the news of cops and yelling in the office was too irresistible to ignore. Ms. Eisberg, the

English teacher, was trying to herd people down the hall, but no one was moving.

"You need to come with us, Miss Matson," the other officer said. "We can talk about this down at the station. If there's nothing to her story, then you'll be on your way."

Brit looked down her nose like he was some kind of simpleton. "Are you deaf? I told you I'm not going anywhere." It was over. She was caught and she knew it.

Officer Siegel spun Brit around by her shoulder so they were facing. "Then we'll do this the hard way. Britney Matson, you are under arrest for the murder of Beth Taylor. You have a right to remain—"

Officer Siegel's voice kept going, but I couldn't hear it over the keening noise Brit made. It was like a howl. Officer Siegel clicked the handcuffs over Britney's wrists. She sank to the floor like every bone in her body had liquefied. The buzz in the hall increased.

Under arrest.

Under arrest.

Under arrest.

I stood straighter, like a sentinel or honor guard. I didn't want to miss a second of this. People's voices were speeding up as news of what was happening spread down the hall. This was an exam week that no one would ever forget.

"Let's go," Officer Siegel said. Mr. Hamstead was standing in the hall, wringing his hands. I could see panic in Ms. Harding's face. "Kalah, you aren't free to go. I can't take you together, but you'll need to make a statement too. I'll send another car to bring you and your parents."

I nodded to show I understood.

Officer Siegel pulled Britney up from the floor; her hands were locked in front of her as if she were praying. Brit was crying. There was a thick smear of snot under her nose.

"You did this," she spit at me. "You cannot ruin my life. I won't let you."

The other officer walked in front and Officer Siegel with Brit behind him. It was like a military formation, except that Britney kept dragging her feet and had to be pulled along. The people in the hall backed up to let them pass. A few whipped out their phones to get a picture.

"I wish we'd never become friends." Spit was flying from Brit's mouth, and her entire body shook as if she were falling apart.

Officer Siegel yanked on her arm to move her forward. I wanted to speak. I'd imagined this moment for so long, but I couldn't think of a thing to say.

Brit reached up with her handcuffed hands and pulled something from her neck, hurling it at my face. I flinched as it struck my cheek with a sharp sting. I looked down and saw Beth's blue enamel teacup spinning in a circle on the floor.

"Okay, that's enough. We're out of here." Officer Siegel said grabbing Brit around the waist and bodily dragging her down the hall.

"I'll get you for this, Kalah Richards. If you think what happened to Beth was bad, you have no idea what I'm capable of doing," Brit screamed over her shoulder. The door clanged shut behind them, and it was suddenly totally silent in the hall.

The people outside the classrooms stood there with their mouths hanging open. Brit's final performance at Northside had been a showstopper. My breath came slow and shallow. I felt sick, as if I'd swallowed a gallon of acid.

Mr. Hamstead seemed to suddenly come to and remember he was in charge. "Okay, people, let's move along."

"Holy shit," someone said, putting into words what everyone was thinking.

Teachers began to direct people back into rooms as they stared at me in disbelief. Sara stepped out from the crowd. She and I stood a few feet apart. It seemed to me she was standing straighter. We locked eyes and after a moment she nodded, as if she understood what I wanted to say. She bent down and scooped up Beth's pendant, handing it to me. My hand closed around it.

"Thank you," she said softly, and then moved off, her friends rushing to her side.

Ms. Harding approached. "Are you okay?"

I nodded. I looked down at the tiny enamel teacup. I blinked and pictured Beth lifting her hair from her neck so I could slip the two pendants onto the chain. I knew it was impossible, but for a split second I could smell Beth's rosemary-and-mint shampoo. It filled my senses.

Ms. Harding patted my arm. "Your parents should be here any minute."

"They arrested Brit," I said. I let the words roll around in my mouth as if I was trying to taste them.

"Yes, it appears so." Ms. Harding stared at the closed front door as if she was trying to catch up to reality.

"I didn't know how else to prove it," I said. "I had to confess so people would investigate. I never would have hurt Beth."

Her eyes filled with tears. "Maybe you shouldn't say anything else, honey." Her hands kept fluttering around as if she were going to knit a new reality out of the air around us. I let her lead me back down toward her office. I felt dizzy, as if I needed to touch the wall to keep from falling over.

"We'll update your parents on what just happened as soon as they get here," Ms. Harding said. She squeezed my hand.

"Okay," I mumbled. My voice sounded faraway, as if someone else were speaking.

I tuned out Ms. Harding. It had finally happened. They'd arrested Brit. They knew she murdered Beth. I kept waiting for this wave of relief, but it didn't happen. All I heard was the echo of Brit's voice.

I'll get you.

I whipped around, half expecting to see Brit lunging for

me, her hands out like claws, her lips pulled up in a snarl, but the hall was empty.

Things went quickly after my parents arrived. I couldn't stop shaking. A rushed consultation between Mr. Hamstead, Ms. Harding, and a few of my teachers resulted in the plan that my grades would be based on what I had achieved already in the semester. The same for Brit. Our school year was over.

My mom had ahold of my hand and wouldn't let go. I could tell she and my dad had a thousand questions for me but didn't want to ask them now. We had to go directly to the police station from there. There was no point in telling the whole story twice. I wasn't under arrest, at least not yet. My parents had arrived at the school just as Brit was being dragged out. For a second before they saw her clearly, they thought that it might be me. Now they knew Brit had confessed, and they were reeling from the change in events. My dad kept shooting glances at me as if he wasn't sure he recognized me anymore.

While everyone was still in class they sent me to get my things from my locker. I knew Mr. Hamstead and Ms. Harding wanted to talk to my parents without me around. I peeled the pictures off the inside walls. I threw most things away. I felt light-headed thinking about how I'd done this for Brit's locker just weeks ago.

I jumped up to make sure there was nothing left inside.

It seemed weird to see my locker stripped of everything that had made it mine. Next year it would be assigned to someone else. Maybe it would develop into an urban legend. The locker that used to belong to someone crazy. The best friend of the murderer. The girlfriend of the dead girl. The story would be if you hung a mirror inside and said my name three times in a row you would see something that drove you mad too. The idea made me smile. It was the kind of story Beth would have told and petrified a group of freshmen.

It was weird to think next year none of us would be here. I'd never come back. It had seemed like the school belonged to us, but the truth was we'd just been borrowing it. In a few more years there wouldn't be anyone who even remembered us. Our names would still be engraved on various trophies in the case outside the gym, our yearbooks would be dusty on some shelf, but no one would even give us the tiniest thought. Just in the same way that I never paused to think about what had happened to the people in the black-and-white photos that lined some of the halls. They were just ghosts. Dead and gone. I couldn't decide if that made me feel better or worse.

CHAPTER THIRTY-TWO

It was late by the time we left the police station, but still earlier than I'd suspected. I'd lost track of time in the interrogation room. There had been endless questions. Why did I confess if I hadn't done it? What did I know? When did I suspect Britney? They asked the same questions in different ways, hoping to trip me up. There are some advantages of finally telling the truth—it's easy to remember. They weren't a hundred percent certain, but I could tell they believed me.

Brit hadn't stayed as long at the station. Apparently she'd become hysterical and had been taken to the hospital. The police wouldn't tell me any specifics, but it was clear she'd spun out a thousand different stories, as if hoping if she came up with enough lies one of them would be good enough to convince everyone around her. Instead the multitude of stories was burying her. And they'd be checking into them now. She'd been hooked and the more she thrashed and tried to get away, the deeper the hook sank.

I'd beat her.

As my parents pulled into our driveway I could barely make out someone sitting on our front stoop. Then I realized who it was and warmth spread through my stomach. I opened the door as soon as the car came to a stop.

"Zach, I'm not sure Kalah is up to seeing anyone tonight," my mom said.

"It's okay," I said, cutting her off. I turned to him. "Take a walk?" He nodded.

My dad sighed. "Don't be long." He and my mom leaned against each other as if they each needed the support and went into the house.

Zach and I walked silently through my neighborhood. The lights were on in other houses. It was as if real life was happening in there, and Zach and I were in some alternate universe. Separate.

I smiled when I saw the Thompson house up ahead. I'd babysat for them for years. All of their lights were out. I held my finger to my lips to indicate Zach should be quiet, and I led him around to their huge backyard. At the far end, butting up against the woods was a tree house. Calling it a tree house almost wasn't fair. Mr. Thompson was a carpenter and he'd created a tree McMansion. I climbed up the ladder and Zach followed. Stacks of patio cushions were on the floor, and I passed him one. I sat and leaned against the wall, letting the smell of cedar relax me.

"I don't know what to say," Zach said finally. "Is it true?"

"Which part?" I asked.

Zach fidgeted on his cushion. "People are saying Brit killed Beth."

I nodded.

He let out a long breath. "Whoa."

"I knew, but I didn't know how to prove it," I said. "She was going to get away with it. I had to keep her close until I could find a way to make sure she was caught. In the end I had to confess so that someone would listen to me, but then she snapped."

"She told me you did that stuff to Sara so I wouldn't trust you, didn't she?" Zach asked.

My throat tightened and my eyes burned. I nodded.

"I had no idea," Zach said. "I'm sorry. You know, for all the stuff I said." He picked at the seam of the cushion. "I should have known you weren't like that."

"It's okay," I said.

"It's not okay." Zach rubbed his face. "Look, I know you and I weren't dating anymore, but we were friends. I knew something was wrong. I should have had faith in you."

The idea that things between us might be okay again felt like slipping into a warm bath, letting each muscle in my body loosen. There wasn't anything romantic there, but Zach was one of the best people I knew. Knowing he wanted to be my friend made me want to forgive myself too. "I'm still sorry for what I did to you," I said. "None of this shit with Brit makes it right."

He reached over and took my hand. "Then we're both sorry, so we'll call it even. Deal?"

"Deal," I echoed. We sat in comfortable silence for a few minutes. "What are people at school saying?"

Zach whistled. "People are pretty freaked out. Now everyone's rushing to say they knew there was something weird about Britney and her story the whole time. I heard on the radio on the way over here that they've got cops at Brit's place. Apparently they're carrying out paper bags of stuff."

The crime forensics people. They'd found something. I felt yet another band of tension disappear.

"Damn, girl, I knew you were a field hockey goddess, brilliant at chem, and able to quote *Star Wars* movies with the best of them, but I had no idea you were also a crime fighter."

I giggled. "I don't think I have to worry about getting fitted for a Wonder Woman outfit quite yet."

"Shame, because you could rock that look."

I punched him in the arm.

Zach rubbed his arm. "Seriously, though, what you did

was brave. Stupid and insane, but brave." He paused. "Beth would have been proud of you."

A flicker of pride smoldered in my stomach and spread through my body. "I did do it, didn't I?"

"You sure did."

I was filled with a rush of energy, and I jumped up. "Get some ice cream with me? The DQ should be open for another half hour or so."

Zach looked at his phone to check the time. "We'll have to hustle. You up for running?"

I kicked his foot lightly. "You worry about keeping up with me."

He smiled. "We all have to worry about that—you're a force to be reckoned with, and if chocolate is on the line, let alone sprinkles . . ."

I didn't wait for him to finish. I dropped to the ground from the tree house, filled my lungs with a deep breath, and started to run. I wasn't running away from anything anymore. I was running forward.

The air-conditioning in Dr. Sherman's office was turned too high, and I shivered. My parents had offered to set me up with another psychologist. They worried I might not want to work with her since she hadn't believed me. I couldn't really blame Dr. Sherman. I wouldn't have believed me either. On our first appointment back, she'd fallen all over herself to apologize for letting one patient influence her view of another. I think she felt ashamed that she'd been caught swallowing every lie that Brit fed her, but she wasn't the only one. No one could sugarcoat a lie quite like Britney.

"Is Brit going to go to jail?" There was a part of me that wanted to see her in an orange jumpsuit, stuck behind bars for life. I wanted her to pay for what she'd done to Beth and to me. To raise my hands in victory as I stood over her crushed form. Then there was the part of me that couldn't forget that Brit had once been my friend. There would be moments when I would remember her telling a joke, or how when Brit laughed really hard she would get the hiccups. That part of me didn't want her to rot in jail. Spinning back and forth between the two perspectives was enough to keep me up at night.

"There hasn't even been a trial yet. Britney is still under observation, but given the evidence the police have collected and her various confessions I wouldn't be surprised if she took some kind of plea deal."

I shifted in my seat. It made me uneasy that Brit was locked up in a psychiatric facility. It was like she was living out the future that had been destined for me. It felt as if I'd ducked out of something and left her holding the bag. She was under a suicide watch after she'd broken a glass and tried to cut her wrists. I'd been told they were very superficial cuts. I didn't believe Brit really wanted to die, but it scared me that she'd gone to that extreme.

"I just want everything to be over," I said.

Dr. Sherman nodded. "Unfortunately these things take a long time. You have to be patient and to know that the real justice is that this ugly thing has come to light. Britney isn't going to be free for a long time. She may not be in jail, but she'll be in care. You don't need to worry about her. Your focus needs to be on moving forward in a positive way."

I took a deep breath, letting myself imagine a future. A good one. One without Brit. "My parents and I are talking about some options for next year," I said.

"A fresh start might be good for you," Dr. Sherman said.

I smiled. "It's not fresh. This time I'm taking what I learned with me." Brit was to blame for what happened, but I'd been passive for too long. I'd whined about how unfair all of it was instead of doing something. I wouldn't make that mistake again.

At the end of the day, Beth was still gone. Proving Brit had done it didn't bring Beth back. Now, with the truth out, it was all the more clear that there was a huge hole in my life and no one would replace Beth. I'd move on. I'd be okay, but I would always miss her.

"How are you coping with the police interviews?" Dr. Sherman asked.

I sighed. I'd been in and out of the police station so often in the past three weeks that I half expected them to issue me my own laminated ID card. They went over and over what I knew about Beth and Brit's friendship and every detail I could remember from the day Beth disappeared. It felt like I was talking in circles, but they insisted it was important. "The police are okay," I said.

Dr. Sherman cocked her head to the side as if she were trying to read my mind. "I know you've been through a very difficult time, but I get the sense you haven't given yourself permission to let go of that pain yet, to let yourself be happy again." She leaned forward as if she was going to share the secret of life with me. "This horrible situation is over, and you survived. It's okay to enjoy that."

Of course I was happy Brit had been arrested. But Dr. Sherman was wrong if she thought it was over. I want to believe Brit's time had run out, but that would be the worst thing I could do. Underestimating Britney can be lethal. "It's hard," I mumbled.

"What would Beth tell you?" Dr. Sherman cocked her head to the side as if she could almost hear Beth's whispered advice.

I sat silently for a moment. I pictured Beth sitting on the log at the beach, her hair blowing around, and how she would tip her face up to the sun.

"Don't worry, Kalah—you win some, you lose some, but what really matters is that you keep getting back up and into the game. You never know what might happen, but if you quit, nothing happens."

I swallowed hard. Beth wouldn't want me to be afraid. Or at the very least she wouldn't want that fear to stop me from living my life. I closed my eyes and let myself think of her again and then opened them, ready to face whatever came next.

ACKNOWLEDGMENTS

Thanks to Anica Rissi for suggesting this adventure, and Melissa Miller for ensuring that I completed it. Without Melissa's cheerleading and willingness to brainstorm, this book wouldn't exist. I can't express how much I appreciate her support. The entire crew of Katherine Tegen Books is also to be thanked and is deserving of cupcakes, but Alex Arnold, Kelsey Horton, and Joel Tippie in particular deserve seconds.

I'd also like to do a special shout-out to librarians and booksellers who do such an amazing job of connecting readers to books. Special thanks to Taylor, Levi, and Brett at my local North Vancouver Chapters and to Helen and Susan and Kidsbooks for introducing me, and my books, to so many.

I could not do any of this without the support of so many friends and family. For all the good wishes, chocolate sent, listening ears as needed, and butt kicking as required—I owe you all.

Lastly, to readers far and wide who reached out on social media or by email to let me know you enjoyed the book—thank you. Writing is a solitary venture, but knowing there are readers at the end of the journey makes every word worth it.